We Live Dying

Tyler J. Klumpenhower

Black Rose Writing

www.blackrosewriting.com

ISBN: 978-1-61296-254-2

PUBLISHED BY BLACK ROSE WRITING

www.blackrosewriting.com

Printed in the United States of America

We Live Dying is printed in Perpetua
Edited by Judy Serrano

Dedicated to Devan G.

"When you see those scars, Tyler, remember me."

"And you will know the truth, and the truth will set you free." - John 8:32

"Sanctify them in the truth; your word is truth." - John 17:17

We Live Dying

Introduction

Life is like a cute cottage nestled in the midst of giant coniferous trees standing nearby a beautiful placid lake. The undergrowth of the forest is thick with sprouting trees, unkempt grass, and scraggly bushes. Robins dance on the trees as their beautiful melodies float through the air, adding a calming tune to the serene atmosphere. Caressing the branches of the trees, the gentle breeze shakes the leaves, which wave goodbye to the traveling wind. A wooden dock protrudes from the marshy shore and provides a perfect place for a person to cast his hook into the water. With the fiery sunset on the horizon, the dock is the perfect place to take a significant other and enjoy each other's company, while holding hands and whispering quietly into each other's ears. The peace is so precious one wishes it would never be broken.

We all have our own realities. Each eye perceives something different about a situation, circumstance, person, or idea. This is then sent through a sieve of experiences, personal philosophy, and theology. Skewed relationships are an inevitable result, for no one can understand why there is no mutual agreement on a particular piece of information. Despite all the disagreement, there are usually universal objects, which speak the same message to the array of realities. Take, for example, the cute cottage nestled in the midst of coniferous trees with a beautiful placid lake a few steps away from the front door. People see such a place and wish they were privileged enough to spend a couple days escaping the chaos of their falling worlds. They see the beauty, the peace, and the radiance of the cottage, and become envious of what they do not have. The physical manifestation of the cottage feeds the lusts of the eye and people drool over how beautiful they perceive it to be.

However, I know the inside of the cottage is not as beautiful as the naive and ignorant admit. The cute exterior is merely a wall protecting the fallen interior. I know, for I lived in the cottage and my experience tells this type of tale. This tale is one of horror and disgust; a frightening sequence of the reality of what the cottage really holds. It is not as beautiful as the outside world perceives. What the world perceives is a lie, which is carefully constructed to protect the envy and jealousy from disappearing. Seeing drool drip from the mouth used to bring me great pleasure. The world has been deceived by outward appearance and it is not aware of the wretchedness, which dwells on the inside. When one sees the ugliness he can respond in three different ways:

hide, ignore, or embrace. My choice has been made and I have chosen to embrace the ugliness with arms wide open. Embracing is the first step to confessing, which then leads to healing and forgiveness.

As twisted as the story may seem, I am the cottage and I am here to tell my story.

Tucker Wilson
Spring-Summer 20--

The Key

"Warning! Warning!" cried the wise man as he ran through the streets, "Not everything is as it seems!"

I Was... I Think... I Don't Know...

My name is Brian Cruse and I am a very confused man. I am a psychologist in the psychiatric ward at Bermingham Penitentiary where I deal with society's craziest, most frightening, creepy characters who go for a psychological assessment. Their lawyers are filing for mental insanity, which would result in leniency in jail time. Actually, the criminal wouldn't even go to jail. Instead, he would go to a mental institution where he would be treated like a guest rather than a dangerous criminal. It is not the most pleasant job but it provides quite a bit of excitement, and confusion. Oh, did I mention I was a very confused man? I am married to a beautiful woman named Adelaide, who has been my sweetheart for the past five years, dating for two and married for three. A little house on the corner of Venture Street and 15th Street is where we reside in the city of Bermingham. Like I said, I work at the Bermingham Penitentiary while Adelaide works as a waitress at the 50's Family Diner. Both of us enjoy our jobs immensely and love the neighborhood where we live.

Oh, wait. I forgot. Actually, I was a psychologist in the psychiatric ward in Bermingham and was in love with my sweetheart Adelaide for the past five years, dating for two and married for three. On the corner of Venture Street and 15th Avenue was where we resided but I have not been there for a couple of weeks; I have now sought refuge in this shack. The scary thing is I am not exactly sure what happened. Wait! Yes I do. It was Tucker Wilson, or maybe it was me. I don't know, I don't remember. Shoot! The battery in my flashlight is running low, which means I only have limited time to tell my story. Hopefully I'll finish before the beam flickers its last or before they come and kick down the door.

You see, as a clinical psychologist, my job mainly consisted of having inmates come to my office where I would ask them a series of questions, which would reveal what type, if any, mental disorder they had. Most of them came into my office either in straightjackets or with their murderous, evil hands twisted behind their backs and latched together by a set of handcuffs. Serial killers, murderers, and rapists - these were the type of people I spent the majority of my day with. They were devious, dangerous delinquents whose minds had snapped and society was the recipient of the disastrous reaction.

The human mind subconsciously stereotypes people based on skin color, their past, their present, and simply on appearance. It is a terrible misfortune. Society stereotypes men and women like Tucker Wilson as the epitome of evil which most, especially the one doing the judging, will never achieve. However, as I have spent years studying the human mind, I have come to believe that each of us is on the brink of mental insanity. It is lurking, searching, begging for an opportunity for the mind to snap and completely consume it. A month ago I would have never believed this, but after having the horrifying privilege of assessing a man by the name of Tucker Wilson, a crazy schizophrenic who was charged with two accounts of first-degree murder and one attempted murder, I believe it with my whole heart. Actually, truth be told, he only really murdered one "person." It was a complicated case to say the least.

Right now, none of that matters. All that matters at the moment is where I currently am. I have been hiding out in this shack for the last twenty-four hours and I think they know where I am. It is just a matter of hours before they come and kick in the door, handcuff me, and bring me to the very place where I once worked, or thought I worked. I would have never guessed I would be capable of doing such horrible and wretched things. But, now I know I did. If it was all a dream, I would not be running. The too real, too vivid, too tangible look of her frightened eyes, the blinding, flashing lights, the sound of horrific screaming, and the sight of fresh blood – none of this would be embedded in my mind. I always told myself it was all just a dream, but if that were true, then why am I hiding? Yes sir, it was only a matter of time.

Confidential

"Mr. Cruse, I put the files of your new patient on top of your desk. The authorities brought him in late last night. He is booked for two o'clock tomorrow afternoon," my secretary informed me as I walked into my office after having a wonderful lunch with Adelaide.

"Thanks Brianne. What do I need to know about him?" I asked. I didn't really care. I already had the routine memorized. "His mind snapped and he went postal. He killed some people and now needs to be assessed," is what she would say.

"Actually Doctor, all the information is in the envelopes. I have very little information on the guy. All the envelopes, emails, and information you have received are all marked 'Confidential.' However, I have heard he is a very dangerous, mysterious fellow. He has been charged with two accounts of first-degree murder and one account of attempted murder. Earlier this morning, I was talking to Mr. Dillinger and he said he has not had, heard of, or seen an inmate like this in his twenty-year career. He told me to tell you to be very careful. This guy is very convincing and has a way of getting into the mind and twisting thoughts."

Needless to say, her response was a little different than I anticipated.

Mr. Dillinger was the head of the psychiatric ward at Bermingham Penitentiary. He had been there for twenty years now and had seen a fair share of crazy people. For him to think this guy was crazy should have given me a warning, should have caused me to put up my guard, but instead it ignited my curiosity and I anticipated the sessions I was going to have with him. I thanked Brianne, entered my office, and saw the stack of files she had placed on my desk. Sitting down, I took a deep breath, and stared at the mounds of paperwork, all labeled with "Confidential" written in the brightest and thickest of red marker. It was going to be a long night. "Well, this stack isn't going get any smaller just staring at it." I reached for the top envelope, opened it and got my first glance at this mysterious new inmate. "All right my new found crazy person, what do I need to know about you?"

* * * *

"Honey, I'm home!" I yelled as I stumbled into the house exhausted. Nine o'clock was quite later than my usual five-thirty homecoming, but nonetheless I was sure Adelaide would understand why I was home so late.

I then heard her sweet voice carry throughout the halls, "It's about time you got home! What took you so long?" I embraced her with a nice wet kiss on the lips.

"Oh, I just had to stay late and get informed on a new inmate we took in today. Tomorrow I have to assess him and I needed to get to know him through the information I was provided with. It makes discussing things much, much easier."

"What can you tell me about him?" she asked as we went into the kitchen and began boiling a pot of tea. After a day at work, it was our tradition to sit on the sofa, sip tea, eat biscuits, and discuss the ups and downs of our day.

"Well, I have a bunch of information but it is all highly confidential. Besides, I don't want to spend the evening talking about some crazy person that just came to the ward. How was your day?" Adelaide always made the most delicious biscuits. Somehow she just knew the right amount of ingredient. People would ask her what her trick was but all she would say was, "I just followed the recipe." However, I knew her secret. Each biscuit was made with love.

"Oh, it was alright I guess," she replied with a heavy sigh. "Terribly long. There were the finicky customers, the demanding coffee drinkers, and the well-mannered elderly people. You know Brian, as much as I love working with people, the more time I spend with them the more I love them, but at the same time I learn to hate them. It is a really weird feeling."

Unbeknownst to me, I was slowly turning into the exact weird feeling she was describing.

* * * *

After a hot shower, a romantic evening with my wife, and a short fifteen minutes of reading one of my favorite comics, I was still unable to sleep. With his mug shot embedded in my brain, the lazy eyes of Tucker Wilson haunted me. Sure, he was charged for the murder of two people; a grandpa and his granddaughter, but this was not much different than many of the other crazies who came into my office. Actually, it was relatively minor compared to most. Once I had a serial killer in my office who was charged with murder and cannibalism. But, to make matters worse, he had managed to feed the body parts of one victim to the poor at a homeless shelter where he volunteered. Actually, he did more than volunteer there; the homeless shelter was the place where he would target his next victim. However, even this disturbing individual would not keep me awake at night. Through the years, I had managed to sever the tie between my personal life and my job, but with Tucker Wilson I was unable to do so. There was something about the droopy eyes, which were so distant, so lost, so confused, yet so wise, so understanding, and, this may sound bizarre, so welcoming... and familiar.

Sure the reason I did not tell Adelaide about Tucker Wilson was because it was labeled confidential, but that had never stopped me before. It was something deeper than that. The entire situation felt a lot more personal, a lot more intimate than the past assessments I had done. However, I also used the excuse of not telling her because I did not want to disturb her by how frightful and dangerous this man really was. I did not want to stir in her a heart of fear, worry, or anger. I did not want her to have any of the sleepless nights, the paranoia, or the nightmares I was having. Looking back, I wish I had told her what was happening for it may have prevented everything from happening, but for her sake, I could not. I was having a hard enough time convincing myself this guy was real.

According to the report, Tucker Wilson was an eighteen year-old male, who had been unofficially diagnosed as a schizophrenic by a certain doctor and had been given medication to help stop the hallucinations and voices. He had been living with his parents but had run away because he wanted to experience freedom from the voices, the slavery, and from a person named Dorothy, a character who Tucker created to give physical manifestation to the voices inside of his head. Tucker was convinced it was Dorothy who had actually committed the murders, not him. In the report, Tucker claimed to have been whisked away during the middle of the night, and forced to watch the two brutal murders of his friends. As if this was not enough of a stretch already, Tucker claimed to be normal and refused to use mental insanity as an excuse for having done what he was accused of. According to him, he was right and the rest of the world was wrong. The story was ridiculous and I laughed when I first read through the accounts. However, now I do not find it funny, for I know the persona of Tucker Wilson has escaped burning in the lowest, the hottest, and the most frightful place in all of Hell.

Dead.

"Shhhhh," he said as he habitually attempted to hold his pointer finger against his pursed lips, "let me tell you a story." As he said this, he wore a blank expression and sat in the cushioned chair in an upright position with his head straight on his skinny neck. Black rimmed glasses rested on his Roman nose. Curly, unkempt hair danced on the top of his head like seaweed swaying in an undercurrent. Before I could open my mouth, he began to tell his story in a monotone, distant voice. I just sat there, dumbfounded on the descriptive, horrible nature of his experience.

"There in my crib I stood wide-eyed and fearful as I watched the mysterious intruder glide across my bedroom floor. By the shadow produced by the nightlight, I could tell the intruder was a woman. Even in my young age I could tell she was not like my mother, my babysitter, my Sunday school teacher, or any other prominent female figure in my life. With her presence, she brought a sense of horror and disgust, which filled the air and sent all of God's angels fleeing into the clouds of Heaven. My stomach churned inside as she noiselessly glided up and down the floorboards as if she was searching for something. She was whispering to herself but I could not comprehend what she was muttering. It was something about wanting to find a certain object within the perimeter of my bedroom. With a keen sense of curiosity, I stared at the woman wondering what she was looking for. Being a little boy, I had absolutely nothing of monetary value. My shelves were lined with building bricks, action figures, cars, and stuffed animals. An occasional hockey card could be found scattered throughout the floor but even these were of no value. I just sat there on my bed cuddling with my teddy bear, Barns; he and I could survive anything together. However, had I known that this night would be the end of the beginning and the beginning of the end, I would have screamed something, done something, called for someone. But for the time being I could not, I was too captivated in the world of curiosity and imagination."

"My eyes continued to watch her mysterious figure glide silently throughout the room. A light fog had settled over the expanse, not wanting to lift, concealing something somewhere. The fog caused the figure to become even more concealed. By the dim nightlight and the low hue of the figure's lantern, I managed to trace her steps and keep her position. The woman was slowly making her way towards me as she went rummaging through my shelves, toy box, and closet. After several minutes she had finished searching the room but was unable to find what she had come for. The light of the lantern dimly revealed the features of her face but still I was not able to fully gaze upon the face of the intruder. So, I watched. I took slow deep breaths as I stared at the horror before my innocent eyes. My body turned to jelly for her presence was enough for me to know that this was not right. I was hoping she would not notice me and leave without actually having a face-to-face en-counter. However, just as she was about to turn and climb out the window she stopped, lifted the lantern to her face and I saw that her eyes were glued to mine."

"Tucker, that's very interesting but…."

"Wait! Do you see that? The distant features of her horrid face? The frail bones jutting out of her skin? Don't you want to know who this person is? You will never understand me if you don't listen, so just you wait until I am done telling this story." I complied and sat there as he continued. "She stood there in front of the window and stared at me for several minutes. All I could see was her face in the midst of all the fog and darkness. I could not hear any footsteps but the features of her face were becoming clearer and clearer, nearer and nearer. My stomach turned into a knot for I knew she was coming for me. Was it me she was looking for? What had I done? I had never seen this person be-fore; she had the type of face that would leave an impression. Her eyes were twisted in her sockets as they bounced around like a bouncy ball stuck in an oval container. Red streaks of blood shot through the whites of her eyes, giv-ing the effect that there was a great fire underneath, burning behind her eyes. Like a hook on a battle-bruised pirate, her bony nose protruded from her face. Numerous hairs poked out of a nasty wart, which had chosen to plant itself near the tip of her nose. Her defined jaw jutted out from her face and was decorated with random strands of white hair. Each cheek was sucked into her face and green epidermis was slowly beginning to peel off, like bark on a dy-ing tree. Actually, I think I remember seeing her skull. Then she flashed a men-acing smile, revealing all the missing and rotting teeth that had replaced the pearly whites. They were encased in an oval frame of shriveled lips, which were cracked and peeling. Her tongue had changed from a normal pink to a brownish yellow chunk with tiny flakes of flesh dangling by a single cell."

"I didn't do anything. Instead, I just stood there, my whole body shaking like a leaf in the fall wind. My heart pounded in my chest and raced a million miles per second. Slowly, I could feel my heart wiggling its way into my throat. To say I was terrified would be an understatement. I was absolutely terrified! But, there was a certain sense of curiosity around this woman, which was the needle and thread to stitch my mouth closed. Her eyes continued to be glued to mine as she came nearer and nearer. Finally, she was at the side of my bed and she opened her mouth to speak. 'Hello child, it is grand to finally meet you. My name is Dorothy and my master, Fate, sends his warmest greetings,' she whispered in a ghastly long breath. My nose inhaled the rotten stench of death, which floated from her mouth. The knot in my stomach tightened and I felt like throwing up. Her words hung in the thick air, creating a tension, which deepened as she continued to stare. Those frightful red eyes invading my soul and reading it like a barcode. Our eyes were locked; I was the first to break the gaze. In the midst of the tension, I had not realized I had let Barns slip out of my hands, and he was now lying alone on the bed mattress. I bent over to pick him up as Dorothy's eyes continued to pierce through my body. Suddenly, a gasp was heard and her hand flew down like an eagle and snatched Barns just as my shaking fingers were about to wrap around his fuzzy body. A horrible cackle proceeded from her mouth as she held the treasure in her bony, decaying hands. She placed her lantern down on the nightstand and with two hands lifted the teddy bear up to her face. As she stared at Barns she was whispering incoherently, as if doing a chant, calling on someone or something to come to her side."

I tried to keep him calm but Tucker's voice grew to a shout as the climax continued to escalate. "I was horrified as her gross hands tightened around the bear's neck. Barns, my soft cuddly teddy bear, began to fall apart before my eyes. First, it was the limbs. Sure, the sound was simply snapping thread but in my mind I could hear bones breaking. With every limb thrown on the ground, I felt like a part of my heart was tossed out, like a piece of trash. Everything in my room was now in complete disarray. Dorothy moved about the room in fast glides as her rotten hands grabbed all of my toys and began throwing, smashing, and destroying them. Tears began to stream from my horrified eyes as the woman continued to destroy my room. From my mouth came the most desperate, gut-wrenching scream that would alarm anybody but nobody heard. Or perhaps, someone had heard but simply decided not to come. Tears were cold like ice and they froze my feet, causing me to be unable to move. Toy trucks rammed into the wall, and pieces of them flew throughout the room. Her body flailed in rapid motion as she slowly began to destroy the most secure part of my life. Soon my room was a maze of torn creatures, loose wheels, and rolling marbles."

Then, Tucker bent over, and in a cowering whisper said, "Suddenly, she was towering over me, her horrible breath sliding out of her nostrils and invading mine. The tears continued to roll and the cry for help only became more and more desperate. How no one could hear me remains a mystery to this very day. Suddenly her bony hand whipped down and smacked me on the cheek. There was a moment of silence as the slap echoed off the walls. Then, from her mouth came the most terrifying of cackling noises. It sounded like finger-nails being scraped against a chalkboard until there was nothing left except the smooth sound of flesh. In the midst of the cackling, a small incoherent chant was beginning to form. The words were not all clear and the only audible sound was something like a long "e." I watched and listened in complete confusion. Once again she had captivated me, and I could not cry out for help. Actually, I was not sure if I even wanted it anymore."

Then Tucker asked, "Do you like gross stuff Mr. ?"

I laughed, "In this line of work, I have to get used to it."

"So you won't mind if I continue my story?"

I didn't really want him to. I wanted to get on to business, diagnose this fiend, and lock him up for the rest of his life. But I complied and said, "Sure, why not?"

"Ok, good. Anyways, from her sleeve she withdrew a blade and held it in the open palm her hand. It was a rusty old knife with blood-stains on the jagged edge. She simply held it in the palm of her hand and allowed me to examine the meaning the stains. Suddenly, the fog became thicker and thicker and the only way I could see the knife was by the moonlight reflecting off the blade. Everything became shadows for the lantern was dimming and the fog was thickening. In the midst of the darkness, I saw her raise her left arm, as the cackling became louder, the chanting more confusing, and the fog thicker. The jagged blade in her right hand met her left forearm and slowing she began sawing away at the paper-thin green skin. From the cuts came a horrible stench; it smelled like death but there was also a touch of sweetness some-where in the air. Occupied with this stench came the scarlet current. The blood ran down her forearm and began to drip on to the mattress like warm, salty tears. Around my feet I began to feel the warmth of the blood rejuvenat-ing the circulation of life. I was beginning to lose myself. The smell of blood manipulated my mind and began to put me into a mysterious trance. I could not think clearly, all I could do was stand and watch as the woman's blood continued to drip onto my feet. The warmth made me feel so alive."

"My parent's bedroom was right next to mine. Having them so near pro-vided me with the security I needed to have a good night's sleep. Nightmares would flee when they would quickly come to my side when I cried out into the black night. For some reason, tonight was different. They had never heard my cry, or perhaps in my worst nightmare, they had purposefully chosen to ig-nore the piercing noise. Regardless, here I was alone with Dorothy, and there would be no one to save me, no one to even know what had happened that night."

"Then suddenly, the wall across from my bed slowly began to rise, reveal-ing the inside of my parent's bedroom. Dorothy moved from my bed to their bedside, so by the illumination of her lantern, I could see my parents lying there in peaceful surrender to the beauty of sleep. Sure enough, Mom was cuddled up in the blanket and was breathing in a rhythmic pattern, the evi-dence of being in a deep sleep. A light fog was still hovering in the room but from what I could see the space beside her was empty. I wondered where he had gone but immediately I heard the twist of the door handle and the squeak of the door hinges. My father had entered the room. He was a well-built man with handsome features, soft eyes, and a warm smile. His heart was the size of the universe and he lived his life serving those around him. However, tonight he looked like something I had never seen before. His eyes were sucked deep into the dark channels of their sockets as bags of stress hung below. The smile that was so prevalent had been turned upside down and his swollen eyes leaked tears down his cheek. Across his lower lip he bore a cut from his teeth. His neatly trimmed hair spun in wild, greasy circles and his dress clothes were dirty and torn. This was not the man I had known; this was not the man my mom had married."

"In his right hand he carried a hammer which rocked back and forth as he slowly walked closer to the bed, his eyes fixated on the face of his wife of ten years. By his body language, I could tell he was in deep, contemplative thought. As I watched, I maintained an optimistic attitude, but as more tears flowed from his eyes, I knew the decision he was contemplating was now final. He was now at the bedside and was gently rubbing the soft, innocent face of his loved one. His hands caressed her hair and his dirty fingers fondled the lobe of her ear. Slowly, as if knowing this would be their last kiss, he lowered his quivering lips to her peaceful face and gently pecked her on the cheek. A faint smile came across the sleeping woman's face and she whispered a lethargic, 'I love you.' The fog seemed to be getting thicker again and all I could see were the silhouettes of the humans across the room. Somewhere in the midst of the fog, Dorothy continued to stand and watch. I could only tell she was there by the dim light proceeding from her lantern. Squinting through the fog, I saw my father stand up and tap the head of the hammer into the palm of his hand. Obviously he was still contemplating whether or not the decision made was the right one. Thank God for the fog but the sound waves travelled through the air at a lightning fast pace. These sound waves carried the screams of Mom, the sound of a skull being cracked, and the words of my father as he continued to cry, 'I love you,' over and over again. All I could see through the thick fog was the windmill-like motion of my father's arm as he continued to clench the hammer. The fog was beginning to have a red tinge to it and the screaming had finally died off. Now I could hear deep sobs coming from the murderer. In the midst of the gut-wrenching heaves, I heard him whisper, 'I'm sorry, but it had to be done. Sometimes love hurts.' I couldn't tell for sure but it looked like Dad bent down and kissed the now crushed face of his once beautiful wife."

"I heard Dorothy cackle and knew she was smiling with glee. Have you ever heard her cackle before Mr.? Do you like the sound?"

"Actually, no I haven't", I replied, slightly intrigued but mostly impatient.

"Good. It is not a very nice sound. Anyways, the steady beat of footsteps was the next sound to resonate outside of my room and down the hall. No longer could I see into my parent's bedroom, for the wall had blinded me to the sight. I then heard the twist of my door handle and saw the outline of my father against the illuminated hallway. The hammer swung like a metronome as the blood and brains of the woman he had loved for ten years dripped to the floor. He began to move towards me. My stomach turned into a knot as anticipated what might happen next. Frantically, my eyes searched the room for someone to come and save me. My lungs burned with pain as I screamed at the top of my voice. However, the only person who came to my side was

Dorothy. By now my father was leaning over the crib bending over to kiss me on the cheek. I hated the feeling of his dry lips and bearded face. His mouth began to move but there were no words to be heard; they bounced right off the eardrum and fell to the floor like dead weight. Dad patted me on the head and then cocked the hammer. With a glare in his eye, I finally heard my father's voice whispering, 'I love you son, but this has to be done.'"

"Dorothy, as horrible as she looked, now had a certain beauty about her. She was like an angel who had been put through a blender and rejected by God. I knew she was not what I needed, but for the time being, she was all I had. Somehow, even if it was for the worst, I knew she was the only one who could help me. With desperation in my eyes, and a quivering lower lip, I met Dorothy's eyes and she knew exactly what I wanted. From her sleeve, she withdrew her rusty, bloody knife. The room went black as she blew out the lantern and the next sound I heard was the thud of my father falling to the ground. Dead.

"You know what Mr.? After that single moment, I knew my life would no longer be the same. My path was set and henceforth, my life would be defined, if not consumed, by the single thought that love, happiness, Heaven, and Hell are all merely perceptions and vary according to the reality one chooses to create. Eventually, the turmoil of this event would lead me to becoming a Blade addict. And Doctor, I was only six years old."

* * * *

When Tucker Wilson had come into my office, I was surprised at the demeanor of the man. According to the bio of Tucker I had received from the authorities, he was 5 ft. 11 in. and weighed in at about 155 lbs. But, as the officer had led him across the office to the patient's chair, he seemed to be shorter and skinnier. Perhaps it was because he was wearing cheap prison slippers or maybe it was the straightjacket, which was tightly wrapped around his body. It was not too often a prisoner was led into my office by two armed guards, but the straightjacket was nothing unusual. When one, such as me, begins to probe inward thoughts, one never knows how the patient might react. His face was much like the mug shot I had observed. Bony cheeks, Roman nose, droopy eyes, glasses. These features were all the same, but his hair had grown considerably longer and it was evident he had not shaved for several days. The only thing I recognized were the eyes: So distant, so lost, so confused, yet so wise, so understanding, so welcoming… and familiar. Tucker just sat there in the chair with his eyelids half-shut and his mouth hanging open. I knew he was going to be the most interesting patient or the most frustrating patient I had ever had, but I never would have guessed he would be my last one.

I began with the usual way I started the first session with a new inmate, "Hello, Tucker. My name is Brian Cruse. Welcome to the…." Those were the last words I said for the entire session, except for the occasion blurb when he asked me a question. The rest of the time was spent listening to him tell the story I just wrote about. Even though I did not understand the story at all, and doubted that there was any significance (back then I would have never even believed such a story to be true), I decided it would be beneficial for me to jot down random notes about it. I even had the notion to record the conversation. I did this only with the patients that had taken me off guard and there were very few who did. But when they did, I got that gnawing feeling in my stomach, which told me there was more to the person than meets the eye. In this first conversation with Tucker Wilson, I never got a word in edge wise, but there was an instinct inside of myself that told me that the story he shared, as insignificant as it seemed, was actually quite significant. I did not have the time to study the story in the office so I took my recorded version home and decided to study it after Adelaide had gone to bed.

* * * *

"How was your day, Brian?" Adelaide asked as we sat around our small four-person table. She was a beautiful blonde with sparkling blue eyes and the most dazzling smile. Today, for some odd reason, she looked exceptionally beautiful.

"It was good. How was yours?" I answered.

"Oh, fine. Tell me, did you get to meet this new inmate today?" She was always interested in my job. I don't think she was actually interested in my job, but rather she was interested in it because it was a passion of mine.

"Sure did," I replied as I scooped myself some potatoes. I love Southern Fried Chicken and mashed potatoes with gravy. Adelaide makes the best fried chicken in the area.

"How did it go? Was he as bad as the others led him on to be?" she asked as she bit into the chicken.

"I don't know. I never had the opportunity to ask any questions."

She was startled and asked, "What do you mean you never got to ask any question? Isn't that your job?"

"Yeah it is but he decided he was going to guide the conversation. I began the session the way I always do, but then he told me to be quiet and then nar-rated the most bizarre story."

"What was it about?" she asked with genuine interest.

"That is confidential, but it had something to do with his childhood and how a certain event shaped the rest of his life." I was not feeling that hungry, even for fried chicken. There was a nervous ache in my stomach, which made me feel nauseous.

"Sounds interesting!" she exclaimed.

I knew by the tone of her voice and the posture of her body that she wanted to have a small taste of the story. Adelaide was always the type of woman who wanted to be informed on how my day at work was and usually I would share with her about my day. But I was so unsure of what had happened today that I did not want to discuss it. In a way, it felt too personal to discuss with her.

"Never mind it, my dear. I don't want the stresses of my job to stop us from enjoying this lovely meal you have made. You hardly ever make fried chicken and potatoes and I would like to enjoy it in the wonderful company of my beautiful wife, without any thought of the office. So, I think we should plan a camping trip later this summer? After I'm done with Tucker Wilson, I am taking a week off and I think we need to spend some alone time together."

Adelaide squealed with delight. "Yes! Let's go camping up by the Otter River and we can fish, go hiking, have picnics, and sleep under the stars."

"Wonderful!" I replied and we spent the rest of the evening planning our camping expedition to the Otter River. In all honesty, I hated camping. It was a highly uncomfortable pastime, but I decided I could sacrifice my own desires for her sake. After a couple hours of planning, Adelaide retired to our room but I stayed up and continued to dwell on the new inmate Tucker Wilson. Finding my briefcase, I took out the recorded version of our conversation, grabbed my notepad and began to take notes as I listened. I listened to the story a couple times, and jotted down different things that might be deemed important to the symbolism behind the story. For the life of me, I could not figure out what he meant through the story. There was a great mystery wrapped in it, and I was going to crack the code and discover the meaning. I could not come to grasp any understanding of what Tucker was talking about but I was completely baffled and mystified when he said, "…that love, happiness, Heaven, and Hell are all merely perceptions and vary according to the reality one chooses to create." Deep inside, I had the feeling that this single sentence was the key to Tucker Wilson's mind… and mine.

Self-perception: Skewed. Miserable Bliss.

Most inmates took multiple sessions before I could actually diagnose them accurately, and in my mind Tucker would be no exception. I intended to show him who was running the show and get down to the nitty gritty details. But I knew that if other sessions went like the first, it would be a very long time before I would actually know what was going on in his mind. He had already been diagnosed with schizophrenia and I had no doubt in my mind that he suffered greatly from it but there seemed to be more. There was something deeper, something no one else could understand but something I wanted to understand terribly bad.

I could feel the effects of staying up too late last night. My head pounded, my body ached, and I had a terribly hard time keeping my eyes open. Previously, I was able to make little headway into the mind of Tucker Wilson but I was excited to have him for another hour in my office, but being overtired was not going to work in my favor. I had a plan and by it I hoped I would begin to make headway in this case. In the files I had read on Tucker, he was given medication for his mental illness and had been taking it since he had been arrested, which was at the time, only a couple weeks ago. I hoped he would be somewhat normal today so I would be able to gain an understanding into his background with questions, which would circulate around his family, his enjoyments, and his religion, if he had one. I simply figured his previous story was a result of the schizophrenia.

Right on the strike of two o'clock, my office door swung open and one of the prison guards led Tucker Wilson to the chair. He was still trapped inside the straightjacket but his eyes were not so confused, not so lost, not so distant... but still familiar. They were a sparkling blue and seemed so curious and lively. There was energy and life running through his face and the pale complexion of last week had been replaced with an array of healthy colors. Tucker scanned the welcoming walls of my office and stopped as he quickly scanned my bookshelf. I was not much for decorating, but I did have a picture of the Great Sphinx on my wall. Egypt was a place I had always wanted to visit. To me there was nothing more intriguing than the ancient pyramids, the gods, and the temples. Going to such a place as Egypt was on my bucket list, but now I know I'll never get there. Despite having very little decorations, I had to have books, lots and lots of books. There was something about having books that made me feel like there was more to life than the simple mundane structure, which so many people lived by. There was an entirely different world out there waiting to be created and explored. Most of the books I had never read and never would, but I still kept them because a person just never knows. Besides, it made me look smarter than I actually was.

"Hi Tucker. How are you today?" I asked.

"I am quite fine, thank you. How are you?" his voice was warm and friendly.

"Oh, a little tired from a late night last night, but other that I am having a great day. However, I am a bit confused on our session the other day. Can you explain yourself?"

"Doctor, I actually want to apologize for my rude behavior last session. I don't actually know what came over me. Stuff like that happens quite often, and sometimes it is quite scary. I hope I didn't hurt anybody or cause any damage."

"No, you were in a straightjacket, so you couldn't go anywhere or do anything. However, you told a weird story about someone visiting you late at night when you were six years old. Do you recall telling that story?"

Tucker gasped and a look of horror came over his face. "You told me you wanted to hear it didn't you?"

"No. As soon as you entered the office, you hushed me and began to tell that story," I replied defensively.

"What! I swear you asked me! Someone asked me and told me if I didn't tell that story they were going to come and get me." Tucker was quite worked up and there was a deep look of fear in his eyes.

"Get you?" This guy really was crazy.

"Yeah, that's what the voices told me! I needed to tell that story in order to feel free!"

"Tucker, just calm down. No one is going to hurt you. Now tell me, what voices?"

For the rest of the session, Tucker told me about when the voices had captivated his mind and made him their slave.

* * * *

"I was a young boy when that story happened. After that, her gliding shadow haunted me day and night; Dorothy's seductive presence never left my room, always by my bedside waiting for me to call upon her. Even though the psychological terror of this event consumed me day and night, I never told anyone. It was a deep, dark secret buried beneath the floor-boards of my soul. To find it, someone would have to destroy the soul then maybe, just maybe, they would discover the nightmares I kept locked away." He laughed. "However, if anyone ever discovered any of my secrets I don't think they would have been able to handle the horror. At least Mari and Mr. Johansson weren't able to. You wouldn't believe how scared I was, Doctor. That night would be the ground by which the rest of my life was rooted in and the tree from which my apples would blossom. On the outside they were a healthy, appetizing green but the truth was they infected with worms and rotten at the core. One thing that really scares me is that I don't know whether what happened is real or not."

"Tucker, I know you are scared, but we have to talk about this. Let me ask you, are you ready and willing to tell me about these voices so I can help you?" I asked.

Tucker sighed and continued. "I would be but the voices told me not to talk about them because it would scare people. I've lost a lot of friends, you know, and I don't want to lose anymore. Besides it could be dangerous. Look what happened to me!" Then he laughed as he looked around the room, at the straightjacket, then at me and replied, "But it seems as though I don't have much of a choice, hey?"

"We always have a choice, Tucker."

"No Doctor, we don't. At least not when the voices tell you what to do. There is absolutely no choice."

"What voices? Tell me about them so I know what you are talking about," I suggested very confused, getting frustrated, and slightly concerned. I was beginning to think Tucker was a little more disturbed than what had been assumed.

"I can't tell you right now, but maybe I can one day," he said as his eyes shifted back and forth is his skull.

"Then what can you tell me, Tucker? I am trying to help, but you need to talk if you want this time to be beneficial. Do you want to change?"

"Oh, there is no changing me. The only one who will change at the end of this is you. I am only here because I am forced to be. My lawyer insists I file for mental insanity but I really don't want to. There is nothing wrong with me, this is just who I am. However, I will admit this to you: I have many problems. But, you see, Doctor, my main problem is that I always get my dreams confused with reality. And I remember it all started with the perception of myself."

"Explain."

"It's a very long story."

"Oh, don't worry about how long it will take. I have you for as long as I want."

He sighed. "Ok. Well, on the outside I was calm, cool, and collected. Several times my friends would remind me how funny, smart, and witty I was. Above the rest of the group, I stood on a pedestal, which I did not deserve. I remember one day a good friend of mine said I could get any girl I wanted. All I would have to do is smile, swing my magic wand, and she would faint because of my charm. This always made me laugh. Girls were not something I wanted to spend my time chasing or getting to know. They were too intimate, too personal, and too perceptive. They might ask questions, which would slowly loosen the floorboards. Besides, the girls might have thought I was charming, funny, and handsome, but as soon as they began to know the real me they fled to the comfort of what they know. Doctor, girls are like cats. One minute they are purring as they beg to be loved and then the next minute they turn their tail and walk away. I could never tolerate such attitude and I could never ever risk feeling such rejection. My thought was, 'Why enter a fire when you knew you were going to get burned? Avoiding the flames is so much easier.'"

"Because my friends saw me as a man full of wisdom and advice, they would come to me with their problems; they would seek my advice, for they knew I would listen. They knew I would help them because I would never let a friend stand alone in the midst of the storms of life. I lived with the philosophy of keeping the needs of my friends above my own and because of this, I could never be honest with the hell burning in my own mind. If I did, the clouds would only thicken and we would become lost at sea together. This also translated into how I conducted myself within my family. Being the oldest in my family, I was always told to be mature and act in a way, which would set a positive example for my brothers. My desire was to be a brother who would be worthy of respect, a brother who would be a positive role model, a brother who was fun and was considered to be a good friend. So, leveled with fear of failure, I masqueraded and pretended I did not have a care in the world. I walked through life with my head held high, confidently acting out perfection. It was my only choice; I had to keep myself together in order to help my brothers and friends maintain a solid foundation for their lives. What if they followed in my footsteps? I would be to blame. What if I failed them? I would lose respect. I could not, for any reason, allow weakness or struggle to be revealed. After all, the young always follow in the footsteps of the old. There was no way, in God's holy name, was I, by the lifestyle I chose live, going to be a bad example to my brothers and friends by leading them down the path I wanted so badly to go down, but could not because I loved my brothers too much."

"I knew my parents loved me. Every night before I went to bed they would tell me so. I believed them for I knew that a parent would always love a child no matter what he or she ever did. However, I was not naive and I knew that there was a huge difference between liking someone and loving someone. Recognizing this difference, I desired so strongly for my parents to not only love me but also like me and take pleasure in who I was and what I enjoyed to do. Again, this translated into masquerading. I would behave in such a way, which warranted expressions of pleasure rather than expressions of disappointment. I would not do certain things just to make my parent's happy and I would do things just so they would like me more. It was all a lie; a simple act to ensure I was not rejected by the very ones who had given birth to me. The darkness slithered inside my skin but I could not and would not allow it to be revealed. I lived in constant fear of being discovered, of being rejected, of being hurt."

* * * *

Journal Entry #1

Everywhere else will just lead to emptiness and more confusion. That is a good word that describes me: confused. My mind feels all twisted and trapped. It needs to be set free. I need to be set free from the pain of my past. But, again the question remains, what pain is found in my past? I need to uproot it and deal with it. How? I don't know. I could talk to my parents, but I am, for some odd reason, uncomfortable with that. Why? To be honest, I feel that when I have aches and pains in my life that they cast a judgmental eye on me. Why do I feel this way? Because I feel that they expect perfection. I know they don't but that is how I feel. I feel that the pain in my life is not acceptable and is not allowed in this household. I'm sure that is not true but that is how I feel. I bring up my pain in subtle ways to them and they don't catch on so in that way I get the sense that they don't care.

* * * *

"To the world, I appeared to be the ideal teenager. I received praise from numerous people about how good of kid I was. Once I remember getting a card from a family that said how much their boys looked up to me. I smiled and laughed, for I knew they were simply respecting someone for something he was not. That was a blunder by the parents. The only person who truly knew me was my worst nightmare: Dorothy. She knew who I was and was okay with my anger, hatred, selfishness, and darkness. Such things were acceptable and I knew she would never reject me. Dorothy seemed to understand my hatred for everything and everybody. I loved my family but at the same time I hated them. I loved my friends but hated them at the same time. I knew who God was, but hated Him because I could. I did not have a reason to love a God who could not love me because of who I was. He was a selfish slave driver, sitting in the sky waiting to smash every dream and aspiration of mine to tiny little shards of sharp glass. In essence, I felt as though God had rejected me, the very person He claimed to have created in His image. I felt like my life was a mirror and at any moment it would be smashed by a single word, a single glance, or a single assumed thought. He who smashed the mirror would not be cursed with seven years of bad luck, but rather I would be the lucky recipient of that curse. This curse would not only last seven years, but it would last for the duration of my life unless I was able to make sense of the hell, which was invading my body and was slowly becoming evident in the way I lived out my life. From the heart comes the actions of a man. My heart was a black cloud of heavy smoke and the smoke was slowly beginning to leak out of my veins. In my subconscious, Dorothy was creeping around and beginning to look more and more pleasurable."

* * * *

Journal Entry #2

I am bound by chains. Chains of guilt. These chains are keeping from being who I truly am. I need to be freed. Freed from the chains that hold me. The chains of lies are also wrapped around my neck and they are the ones doing the most amount of damage. The Devil is hand feeding me lies about myself that I am devouring. These lies are poison to me. They are ruining my life, ruining what I had planned for myself. I have come to believe that who I am is nothing special. My words, my actions, my smiles, all seem to be fake. They feel like plastic. It feels like someone has taken a shiny little blade and carved a smile on my face. My words seem to have no emotion but are monotone and meaningless. I feel like I keep my emotions bottled up inside so no one can see what I am feeling. Why do I do this? Why does everything seem so fake? So cheap? So plastic? I feel emotionally detached. My mind always feels as though 50% of it is shut off. That 50% contains the areas I do not wish to explore. Areas of emotion, events, regrets, guilt, and scary thoughts that I don't want to begin to explore because of what emotions they bring. The emotions that they bring feel wrong.

* * * *

"It was becoming harder and harder for me to live at home. All I wanted to do was curse God and die. (Dying was not physical but instead it was surrendering to the sound of Dorothy's enticing voice). The fear of failure and the fear of rejection was enough of a vehicle to transform myself into an object in my room. I would hide out there for hours living in my own imaginative world where everything made a little bit of sense. On several occasions my mom would come to my room and tell me I needed to do something else, to come out of the furthest corner of the basement and get some sun. I would adhere to her wishes simply to make her happy, so she did not begin to loosen the creaky floorboards on which I stood. As much as I wanted to give up on life and abandon God, I could not for I knew that there would still be some sense of purpose to my being. My mind was not easily convinced that there was a God who actually loved me but my mind was also not easily convinced that there was a God who did not love me. I figured, due to the season of my life, He was simply disappointed in who I was and hated the part of me that clung to Dorothy. I never wanted her to leave my side. Doctor, I hated her too. Because of all the hate, I became a restless wreck of anxiety and nervousness. Like the invasion at Normandy, depression swept through my mind, putting to death all the joyful thoughts and liberating the thoughts I had once taken captive. It was easier that way; the darkness made a whole lot more sense than the joy I was seeing around me. I may have had a smile and twinkle in my eye but deep down in the crevices of my mind, I was swimming in a sea of despair, loneliness, hopelessness, and rejection. I could not reveal the darkness to anyone for I was afraid of what they would think of the person I was. In short, I assumed rejection from all."

* * * *

Journal Entry #3

What am I so mad about!?! I just don't understand! I hate it! I'm too sensitive and take things way too personally and it sucks. I just feel like withdrawing myself from all humanity. I feel as though every person, whether they know me or not, is keeping a watchful eye on me just waiting to pounce on a stupid, pointless, innocent mistake. I feel as though it's me against the whole world. I feel like all humanity is against me and working to bring me to destruction. I know that isn't true but oh how true it feels. I was out of my darkness for a day and a half, but now I'm being covered again. How hopeless! I'm alone in this world: Me and my thoughts, me and my demons, me and my god. I feel as though I'm stuck in a coffin and one by one the nails are being hammered down. Most of the time I care but I don't do anything about it. Then there is the odd time where I'll kick with all my might and some of the nails will pop off and a ray of light shines in. But then right away I'm drowning in black. I continue to hear the nails being driven into the wood. Obviously, I need some outside help but by whom? Who will come and save me?

Why do I feel this way? I want to be free. I want joy.

There is no joy, no joy, no joy, no joy down in my heart, down in my heart, down in my heart. There is no joy, no joy, no joy, no joy down in my heart, down in my heart today.

I wish there was. I feel lost.

* * * *

"Then, one beautiful spring night, I decided I must take action towards these feelings. The daily battle was becoming too much and I was having a hard time containing Dorothy within the confines of my skin. My attitude was progressively becoming worse and the growing hatred in my heart made me lash out in vulgar, unnecessary fits of rage. I was becoming scared of the monster rising inside and I needed to unshackle my mind and begin to walk in the path of freedom. So, I realized I had two options. First, I could confess and seek the help I so desperately needed, or second, I could run as far away as I could and hope for the best in regards to myself, my friends, and my family. As far as God was concerned, He would still be there with His hammer. The decision was easy to make. For several weeks, I would lie awake late at night contemplating what the best course of action would be. The realization that I needed to continue being an example to those around me, forced me to decide to run; it was the only solution to the problems I had. It was the only way to escape the failure, the assumed rejection, and it was the only way I could experience freedom. Running away would be easier and a whole lot less painful, at least for my friends and family but that was a sacrifice I was willing to make. By running away, I could ignore my past and simply live for the future and be free from expectations, disappointments, and failures. I would live a life of rejection but I was okay with that for I knew that the darkness is so much more real and so much more genuine than the light. Frankly, the darkness is what I deserved. I had done nothing to deserve the light of joy or the gentle, warm blanket of peace. Because of this, I knew that the darkness was for me and the light was for those who were more fortunate than I, a damned soul. I was one of the many God had chosen to reject. Oh well, my life would be one of rejection and there would be a smile on my face and joy in my heart. After all, it was what I deserved for failing everyone around me. It was what I deserved for not having the courage to bring my struggles into the light. I was to be exiled like a political dissident who had betrayed his country. Like the dissident, I would tread with my head held high and a smirk on my face."

"And the voices told you all this?" I asked.

"Yes, but not all at once. One whisper a day was enough to keep the truth away because I listened to what they had to say. You're a smart man and one who makes his decision based on logic because that is the only way things makes sense. If there is not logical answer then you, like me, become anxious because you don't understand your world. Am I right?"

"Yep." Now I was uncomfortable. I was supposed to be the one getting into his mind, not him getting into my mind.

"The voices were logical. They made sense. And because of this I listened to them even though I felt the way I did. Looking back, I see how I would have rather believed a lie and have the perception of understanding rather than believe the truth of who I was and live in the realm of faith."

How things have changed.

"Were there any other reasons you would have wanted to leave home?" I asked.

"Well, ultimately I wanted to be free from Dorothy and I thought that if I left, she would not follow me. You see Doctor, that horrible wench haunted me every day and night. She would never let me sleep, and she only riddled my life with more fear than I already had. Every night she would come out of her closet and beckon me to enter into her world. I never could though. The path she proclaimed would only lead to temporary freedom and temporary relief. It sounded enticing but I wanted to be completely free and I knew the more I sold my soul to her the tighter her chains would become. Eventually, if I gave in even once, I knew she would be the wind in my sail, the gas in my tank, the breath in my lungs, and the reason my heart beat. That was not freedom! That was merely a mirage in the desert of life that I would continually leave me high and dry: a shriveled raisin on a paved road. Dorothy and the rest of the voices would have to die before I had any chance to experience freedom. I did not want to kill her, so I thought I could just run away and she would never be able to find me. Or, perhaps if I was lucky, she would move down the street and haunt some other damned soul, but I highly doubted that."

"Already my future was not very bright. I knew I would enjoy the freedom of running until I became so infected with the cancer that I would simply commit suicide and then I would, hopefully, know absolute freedom. It seemed to be the logical conclusion to my decision. When one does not seek help for depressed behavior, the conclusion is pretty obvious. The chains never get looser; they only become tighter and tighter, resulting in the disgustingness of realizing that there is nothing to live for. Everything a person does simply tightens the chains, which hold you captive to yourself. Also, the voices only get louder and more persuasive. I could see a fire on the horizon and I was not going to endure it. However, I would attempt to escape the flames while I still had a fighting chance. Not only would I be saved from the flames, but my family and friends would not have to endure the pain of knowing who I actually was and what the reality of who I was looked like. It is better to sacrifice one for the restoration and betterment of others. I took that philosophy from the Bible. Yep, I knew God loved me.

"With these thoughts racing through my mind, I decided the decision was obvious: I would run. Like the wind, I would be an invisible force, which travelled the world unappreciated and rejected. Wherever I went I always brought storm clouds, but as long as I was moving they would always be with me. That night I began to plan my runaway. My parents would not find out I was gone until the morning. Actually, it probably wouldn't be until early afternoon when they finally decided it was time for me to get up. Then, much to their joy, they would find my bed empty, a note, and an open window. Usually they went to bed around 10 p.m. so I had no fear of them intruding on my escape. They would remain oblivious until I was no longer to behold. Then they would panic, realize how much I meant to them, and wish they had treated me differently. I do not know how they would have treated me differently. If anything, the relationship I had with them was the result of my own decision to neglect them and not be willing to build into their lives. So, I grabbed my notepad, and quickly jotted down a note for my parents."

* * * *

"When that night came, my greatest fear was Dorothy. I had not felt her presence for a couple of months now and I hoped that she had gone to haunt the little girl down the road. Imagine a little girl curled up in the corner screaming her lungs out as Dorothy slowly and noiselessly advanced. The blade. The blood. The horror. Result: Slavery. I laughed, for I actually enjoyed the thought of someone else going through the same torture I was going through. Such a thought brought a strange peace to my mind and calmness to my soul. I was not the only one among the unfortunate. I just hoped the night of my escape was not the night when Dorothy decided to reappear and remind me of what had happened in the past, which was the very thing I needed to escape from. Inside my heart, I could still feel her wondering around and keeping my self-perception at an all-time low. It was a nagging feeling like something was not right, something was on the horizon; a storm was brewing. Like an old person

with arthritis who can tell what the weather was going to do, I could tell
when Dorothy was coming closer or when she was being lost in the distance.
Sometimes she felt lost in the distance, but I always felt there was a storm on
the horizon. But this is my reality and maybe I am wrong. After all, everything
is just in the head, right Doctor? We all create our own realities and my reality
could never exist if Dorothy was not, in some minute way, involved. I would
have prayed to God, if He had been listening. I thought, 'God, You better be
listening but then what have I done for you to lend Your holy ear to such un-
holy, worthless, lying lips.' So, I withheld my prayer. After folding up the note
and placing it on my bed, I moved towards the window. The night was mine;
the whole world was mine and I would discover, no matter what the cost,
what I earnestly longed for: the truth of who I was."

* * * *

"Doctor, the voices told me I had to leave. They said that the situation I found
myself in was hopeless and that there was no way of fixing it. Fate had simply
dealt me a bad hand and now I had to choose what I was going to do with it. I
decided to take life into my own hands in hopes to find the freedom I so desperately longed for."

I Am I Am

Many evenings, when I would come home, my body aching, and my head pounding from exhaustion and stress, I would see nothing but a single light illuminating one window in our two-story house. I would enter the room and see Adelaide curled up in the covers, reading a good book, or perhaps, and more probable, journaling about something in her day, a dream, or some new creative idea she had. There was one evening where I got home and I asked her what she was journaling about. She replied in a dreamy voice, "Oh, I am just journaling about the names we are going to give our kids and what fun we will have with them. How do you like the name 'Jordan' for a boy or 'Anna' for a girl?"

What kids? All her dreams would have come true if we ever had kids, but we never had any. And I was the problem. Perhaps she eventually did have kids and I am just not the father. I don't really know because I haven't talked to her in a while. You see, in the three years we had been married, Adelaide and I were unable to have kids. Oh, we tried and tried but there were never any results. Thinking she was the problem, she had herself tested only to discover that all her parts were functioning on a normal level. That left me. Hesitatingly, I went to the doctor, he ran his tests, and informed me, due to complications, I was the problem. Even though I did not want to tell her I had to, her dreams were only becoming bigger with each passing day.

"Adelaide..." She was cuddling in the blankets as pen scrawled thoughts onto paper. The light from the lamp added serenity as she looked up at me with such peaceful eyes. "I have something to tell you." Immediately, by the seriousness of my voice she knew something was not right. I had told her I was going to see the doctor sometime but I never told her when. That day I had gone without telling her because I did not want her to be too anxious about the whole situation.

"What happened? Is it Tucker Wilson?" Her voice was full of worry and fear. She was never the most emotionally stable woman and had the tendency to become worked up before hearing the entirety of a situation. Oh, she was a handful, but at the time, I would have never traded her for the world.

"No, it has nothing to do with Wilson. Babe, I went to the doctor today," there was quiver in my voice and I could not look into her eyes. I could feel tears welling up and soon they began to drip down my face.

"And?" There was a sense of excitement in her voice as she straightened up in her bed. At that time, I never would have imagined that her lips would be kissed by someone so unclean, her body fondled by dirty, perverted hands, and her hair stroked by him. I would have never imagined an innocent girl like her could do something so wretched. Her life goes to show that no one is innocent and that such decisions have their consequences, especially when I am god. Now, thinking of the whole situation makes me sick to my stomach.

"I...," I didn't know why I was telling her this. I could have just led her on to believing that for some reason, though both of us were without complications, we were unable to have kids. I could just play the God card but I did not want to be dishonest so I finished my sentence, "...am the problem." There, I said it, and I knew by her facial expression she had heard me loud and clear. She tried to mask the disappointment but it was too deep and she began to cry. I too cried, and she wept in my arms as my tears soaked her blonde hair and my shirt began to get wet from her tears. It was a tough night but things only began to get worse. She never made love to me again.

* * * *

"So the voices told you to leave home, hey?" My skepticism towards this man was beginning to grow and I was beginning to think there was nothing to what this guy was saying but rather he was simply leading me on a wild goose chase. Through the entire time I had Tucker Wilson, I hoped the goose would lay a golden egg and she eventually did. But I had to put the pieces of the puzzle together before I truly understood what he was talking about, which, because of my narrow perspective, was extremely difficult.

"Yes sir," replied Tucker. "I did not know where they wanted me to go, but I had to step out in faith and trust the voices. You know Doctor, faith is not an emotion but rather a decision and I decided I had to do what they told me even though it was not pleasant."

"Tucker, can you tell me about the night you left? Do you remember it at all?" I was shooting in the dark but I was hoping I would be able to get a glimpse into what these voices were.

"Oh yes! I remember it as though it was last night. It was very late, probably two in the morning, and I quietly crawled out of bed and looked out the window up into the night sky. Clouds were beginning to cover the glowing moon but the layer was just thin enough to produce a soft silhouette of the celestial being. Occasionally, the sound of an owl hooting and hidden crickets croaking travelled through the air and floated through the open window. I gently, carefully, cautiously, slid out of my bedroom window and onto the shingles of the roof. The moment I stepped out of the window onto the shingles of the roof, I could feel the storm moving in. The winds of my soul were picking up and I could feel the darkness of Dorothy closing in on my bedroom. I thought I heard the door squeak open and then being shut gently. My head would not turn to look who it was. If it were my parents then they would yell at me as I disappeared into the darkness. But if, by some unfortunate turn of events, it was Dorothy I knew I was already as good as dead. She never liked it when I did not tell her where I was going; she always wanted to come. My heart rate accelerated as I continued to scramble out the window. My backpack got stuck on the ledge and I just about fell off the roof as I struggled to tear it free. As I stood near the eaves trough, I finally had the courage to look behind me, expecting to see someone sticking their head out the window or perhaps climbing out to come and capture me. Thankfully it was just a hole of blackness from which I had come. The banister pole became my ladder as I shimmed down, balanced on the deck rail and then finally jumped to the cold earth. Freedom. With the intention of conserving energy, I decided I would walk for the first couple of miles and then when daybreak came, I would begin to jog. Like I said, Mom and Dad would not notice my absence until early afternoon. But then my ear picked up the breaking of a twig from the nearby bushes. My mind panicked and I bolted off into the unknown of the darkness."

"I knew someone or something was chasing me. It was as though I could feel its very breath slipping down my back and raising the hairs on my neck. The breath was warm and came in a steady rhythm of 1-2-3-4. Its eyes must have been piercing through the back of my skull for I felt as though every thought was being scanned like a barcode, which relayed the message of panic to the alert desk of my mind. The pursuer must have known of my plans so no matter where I went he could always find me; there was no hiding. My mind was now like Pearl Harbor after the Japanese had attacked. Both of us thought we were safe with nothing to fear but then tragedy struck and it was hard to regain composure, never mind claim victory. Behind me I could hear the rustling of grass and the quiet pattering of feet. Was it my imagination? Was someone actually chasing me? I didn't know. I was nearing a clump of bushes and impulsively decided to hide there with the hopes of the pursuer running by. Climbing into the brambles I waited… and waited… and waited. The only sound I could now hear was the pounding of my own heart against my chest. I waited for another ten minutes and still no one passed by my hiding place. Something still did not feel right. It still felt as though someone was watching my every move and just waiting for the opportune time to take full advantage of me. Remember Doctor, I am a young person with arthritis."

* * * *

"So, Doctor, what do you think comes after we die?" Tucker asked me with great concern on his face and in his voice. There was a look of confidence as he asked this question as if he already knew the answer. I didn't know the answer but I thought I would make up something. I was an educated man, but spirituality was never something that really interested me.

"Well, I really don't know. Quite frankly, I personally have come to the conclusion that I really don't care. But some believe they will go to Heaven while others will go to Hell. Then there are also those who believe in reincarnation but I think majority believe there is nothing after death. Why do you ask?" Pretty good answer for off the top of my head, I thought.

"Cause, I'll tell you what happens when we die: nothing. A person takes one final gasp of this world's air and then is no more. He simply does not exist anymore just like before they were born. I know this because this is what god told me."

"This is what God told you?" I asked in great curiosity. "Why do you say that?"

"Well, during the summer when I was 14 years old, Grandpa Lucas would invite me and Dylan, one of my best friends, to spend the day fishing with him on the Colin River. Armed with fishing poles, wearing straw hats, and lathered in sunscreen, the three of us climbed into the fiberglass canoe, and began paddling down the Colin. What beautiful days those were. The sun was hot and not a blemish could be seen against the bright blue sky. The gentle breeze, just strong enough to keep the bugs away, was like a fan, cooling us off as salty sweat began to drip from our brows. When we found Grandpa Lucas' favorite secret fishing hole, we tossed in our hooks and chewed seeds waiting with breathless anticipation for a nibble. With his long handlebar mustache blowing in the wind, he would tell us story after story and answer our many questions. I'll never forget him sitting there with a pipe in his mouth and a fishing pole in his hand. That was Heaven. Grandpa Lucas was a man who had a huge heart for people, especially young people like us. He showed genuine interest in both of us and asked us what our dreams and aspirations were. We talked about girls and he gave us relational advice, which was backed with 50 years of experience. I even told him about the girl I liked. Never will I forget the twinkle in his eye when I revealed that secret. Dylan told Grandpa Lucas, who he liked too. I did not even know who Dylan liked! Actually, Dylan and I had never been the best of friends. We hung out occasionally but always in a group and never intentionally. However, after that day and thanks to Grandpa Lucas, we became the very best of friends.

"There were many memorable moments throughout the entire summer. Once during the course of a trip, Grandpa Lucas lost his balance as he was trying to reel in a giant fish and ended up falling into the cold river water. At first Dylan and I looked at each other with concern as his body disappeared into the blue water. A couple minutes passed and he was still not surfacing. Just as we were about to dive in, we felt the canoe rock and before we knew it, we too were falling into the river. When we surfaced, we first saw the tipped canoe floating upside down and we could hear laughter. Behind us, waiting in the water was Grandpa Lucas laughing so hard he was beginning to cry. "Got you guys good!" he proclaimed. Dylan and I looked at each other in confusion, shrugged our shoulders, and began to laugh at and along with Grandpa Lucas. Instead of fishing, we spent the afternoon swimming in the cold water of the Colin River."

"Sounds like he was a very lovable man," I said.

"He was. The most caring, loving man I had ever known. But then one night my family and I received a phone call from Dylan's mom who informed us of Grandpa Lucas' death. According to her, Grandpa Lucas was out fishing, had a heart attack, and fell into the Colin River. His dead body had floated up on shore and was found by a couple of hikers. The news hit me like a brick. That night the voices were worse than ever."

With pen ready for action, I asked, "Do you remember what they said?"

"'If there is a God why is there so much pain? If God really cared about you, and more specifically, Dylan, then why would He let such a tragedy strike? You know why, Tucker? God hates you. He hates you, Dylan, Grandpa Lucas, and every idiotic soul on the planet. He's out to get you.' I never wanted to believe the voices but as the next couple of days unraveled, they were confirmed."

"Ok. Go on." I was trying to take notes but I did not know what to take notes on. There was too much to communicate on paper. My brain had to sift through the wads of information and pull out what was important and what was useless. At that time, I felt something inside of me, which I had not felt for years. It was a small yearning, a small yearning for something greater, for something more significant, for something of meaning, but something I did not understand.

Tucker continued. "Three days after Grandpa Lucas' death, Dylan and I found ourselves as pallbearers at his funeral. It was a beautiful funeral with several pictures of him hanging out with his family and fishing. There was even one of Dylan and me with him when we had gotten back from canoe tipping. The preacher, a bald, skinny, pale fellow with telescope glasses, stood behind the pulpit and spoke on the topic of death. On the pulpit laid a big Bible from which he spewed out verses about the afterlife. It seemed as though he believed there was a Heaven and Hell and depending on what a person did with Jesus would determine where he would find himself after death had struck its final blow. It made sense, kind of. The preacher even had the audacity to proclaim, from the pulpit, that Grandpa Lucas was, at that very moment, burning in Hell and being tortured by the Devil himself. 'This is the will of God,' the man said, 'for he who refuses the free gift of salvation will be eternally condemned to the flames of Hell.' But Grandpa Lucas was a good man who put the needs of others above his own. He was always willing to help, listen, or offer some solid, moral advice. 'Being good isn't good enough,' was the truth according to the preacher.

"I turned my head to see how Dylan was responding to what the preacher was saying. His eyes were sunk into the back of his head and he stared straight ahead with a blank expression. There was a fire in his dark blue eyes and I could tell his mind was racing with questions, anger, and utter confusion. The words of the preacher were not healing the wounds of death but instead they were causing a brutal infection. After the funeral, I never had the opportunity to speak to Dylan. He sat with his immediate family, a stone in the midst of a waterfall of tears. Much to my sadness and dismay, Dylan and I never spoke to each other again. His mind was in complete disarray as he continued on the downward slope of depression. He would sit alone for days in the darkness of his room, refusing to eat and scrawling word messages onto the walls with his fingernails. To this day, absolutely no one knows what they mean or their cause, except for me. Dorothy had found him and he had given into the voices. The wench had come into his life and began slowly tearing down the world Dylan once knew. The reminder of his father was too much for Dylan to bear, yet that was the very pill Dorothy was shoving down his throat. You see, Grandpa Lucas had been a father figure to a fatherless boy. The truth was that Dylan was not actually his grandson, nor was I. 'Grandpa' was a term of endearment given to a man who was worthy of all the respect and honor he could receive. Now Dylan was truly fatherless.

"You know how the brain works Doctor, and you would understand why our young minds could not tolerate the death of such a beloved, respected man. Things would never be the same after his funeral. Dylan committed suicide a week later. He never left a note explaining his reasoning, nor saying good-bye to those he loved. Those he loved were already gone and the only one who should care did not care at all. I never went to the funeral. Of course, I loved my friend but he was now gone and ceased to exist. I knew it was going to be the same old ugly preacher and his same old hopeless message about Heaven and Hell. The thought made me sick. I was not going to buy the program the preacher was selling. What he spoke of was his reality and I wanted nothing to do with it. Who is he to say that my two best friends were now burning in Hell? Who is he to tell the world of what actually will happen when we die? Is not the afterlife left up to the imagination and belief of the one whose life Death steals from him? I am not going to believe in somebody's personal reality! This was several years ago and on the day of Dylan's death I made another absolute in my reality: Heaven and Hell are lies. When I am god everyone dies."

* * * *

Journal Entry #4

And now, here I am, 18 years old, and running away from myself in order to escape the darkness and find freedom. I was breaking free of the prison that had long been established by the pain of the environment I found myself in. Not only were the expectations too much for me, but the memories were something I needed to be liberated from. Success was already being granted to me, for I was out of the cell, and now all I had to do was reach the fence without being spotted by my parents or Dorothy. A canvas of darkness was the only thing I would run into which, ironically enough, was the very thing I was running from. I would run. I would run long and hard until I became lost and forgot about the world behind me. The reality I had formed in my mind was something I no longer wanted to experience and I was going to transform it. After all, reality can be changed as long as one thinks long and hard about it. The reality, or what I created as reality, so often would change into the center of my mind as a dream. I could then excuse myself from the consequences and responsibility of that reality because of the simple fact I had changed reality. I can change reality and I will change reality.

* * * *

"Still nothing had passed my hiding place so I decided it was time to continue. By the light of the moon, I could see the silhouette of the highway. Knowing where this highway led, I followed it at a distance and by the protection of the forest on the side of the road. My mind began to wander down memory lane as I continued to walk, tripping over sticks and being slapped in the face by branches. I had believed in God and Jesus as a very young boy. The significance and meaning of my decision was something I was not aware of. My parent's said I would burn in Hell and I did not want to be there forever. I smirked. Again, this was just what my parent's believed and I did not want to surrender to the reality of my parents. I was out to create my own world, be my own god, and ultimately decide what would happen within my reality. The god my parent's served, who supposedly was the God of the Bible, was a mere pup-peteer in the sky, playing with the lives of those He had created for the purpose of seeing His will be carried out. I do not make it a habit of buying junk and I certainly was not going to buy into a God who would not love me for who I was and delight in the very person He, Himself, had created. Screw Him! I could feel the passion brewing inside of my chest cavity. A defiant, rebellious emotion of not caring, giving up to ignorance, and proclaiming myself as god. After all, everything I had believed, ever since I was a little boy, was no longer real, it didn't exist; it was just a dream. I had been sucked into someone else's reality because of my ignorance and innocence. I swore at the next branch that slapped in the face and tore it from its life-giving source. The pain in my heart was becoming too much. It was like a hand squeezing, clenching, squishing the life right out of me. Not only was it an emotional sensation, but it was also physical. I literally felt like my heart was snapping in half. This brought on a fury of explicit words pouring out of my mouth like a faucet opened completely. I cursed my Dad, I cursed my Mom, I cursed my brothers, my friends, and all those I knew. Tears started to well up in his eyes and soon they began to drip down my cheek. I bit the bottom of my lip, trying to hold back the tears. I cursed again but this time it was directed towards God Himself. 'You know what God! I don't need You!' I screamed into the silence of the night. 'Who put You in charge? Who gave You the right to make all the decisions? You're just a dream. You are nothing but a slave driver hidden beneath the banner of religion, which is slavery! I am not going to be a slave to a God that does exist! You don't exist! NOT ANYMORE!'

"You see Doctor, I wanted freedom. I wanted freedom from everything and everyone. Looking over the wreckage of my family, my friends, and society, I had a sinking feeling that He who claimed to be the very source of freedom was actually lying. Cynicism quickly invaded my mind and it brought me to a place where I could find a reason to hate everybody and everything. 'God, I hate You! Little slave driver in the sky! Screw You! All I need is me, myself, and I. I can do this on my own by creating my own version of freedom. Nothing matters anymore. I can do this on my own. I will not lose my life but instead I will rebuild what You have destroyed!' I kicked at the ground and stubbed my big toe on a rock. This incident just fanned the fire of anger inside of my heart. I grabbed the rock and tried to pick it up but it was too heavy so instead I spit on it then continued on my way. My eyes burned from the salt of my tears and my face ached from the tension of my facial muscles. In fact, my entire body ached from being caught in the tension of fear, despair, anxiety, anger, and cynicism. I tried to convince myself that all that had happened in the past was nothing more than dreams and the further I ran away the more likely they would be just as I imagined. As I continued to walk through the godforsaken forest, I pondered what life actually was. I realized that life, in and of itself, was a dream inside a dream. There was no bigger picture, there is no God, and Heaven and Hell are lies.

"I was just walking. Where I was going still remained a mystery to me. The small town of York was only a couple of miles from my parent's acreage but that was too close to home for me to stop running. How was I going to lie? Being the popular kid I was, someone in town was bound to notice me and begin to ask questions. For now, all I knew was that I was leaving my home, my family, and disappearing from the world I knew and hated. I would be free from the captivity, the pain, and most importantly, Dorothy.

"Oh, and Doctor, have I introduced myself? Of course, I haven't. How silly of me! Well, now that I know who I am, allow me to do so. My name is Tucker Wilson and I am god."

Warning: Danger Ahead

"Brian, how are things going with Wilson?" It was Mr. Dillinger. His broad frame and tall stature cast a shadow into my office as he stood in the doorway.

"Well, I have only had two sessions with him and it has been interesting, very interesting. He thinks he is god and that he has the power to change reality according to how he wants to perceive it. Also, he told the most bizarre stories, which seem to convey some kind of meaning to him but I cannot make sense of what he is talking about. They seem so fictional yet he is convinced he has actually experienced each event. And he is always talking about this woman named Dorothy who haunts him. It is so bizarre. Tucker is a really, really strange character."

"Certainly sounds like you have your hands full. Brian, are you still all right taking this guy on? I don't want you to become attached to this man on a psychological and emotional level. You have a scary obsession in such bizarre men and I do not want it to consume you to the point of you becoming like them, especially one like Tucker Wilson." There was a sense of genuine concern in his voice and at the time I was too arrogant to heed his subtle warning.

Looking back, I now see that his warning was too late. Even if it had been earlier it would not have changed the outcome.

I replied, "Thanks for your concern, Mr. Dillinger, but I want to stay on this case. We've only had two sessions and the complexity of his mind is shattering my world. Besides, I think he is warming up to me. The last session went really well and I feel as though we made some headway. Don't worry about me, I'll be fine."

"Ok. I guess you know best. But if you notice things changing let me know and we'll put someone else on the case."

"Thanks boss, but that won't be necessary." Mr. Dillinger left the room and I continued to pour over my paper work. One of the downsides of being a clinical psychologist was the enormous responsibility of signing papers, which would play a major role in the outcome of the sentence a criminal received. If deemed mentally unstable, the criminal would receive a lesser punishment but if deemed mentally stable, and therefore fully responsible, one could be locked up for years, if not life. This was my least favorite part of the entire job. Diagnosing was very enjoyable but the responsibility of labeling a disorder greatly disturbed me. Especially sense I believe each of us is sick in the mind.

I truly appreciated Mr. Dillinger's concern for my mental health but it really was unnecessary. While it was true I was completely enthralled by the person of Tucker Wilson, there was absolutely no need for one to be concerned that I might become like him. I was a psychologist and because of this I thought I was capable of protecting my own mind against the power of his. But, like I said, each of us has a mental disorder and it is just waiting for the perfect breeding grounds. Or, perhaps we are not even aware that even during the times we are normal, we are actually the very victims of the cruelest and most shocking forms of mental disorders. Normality is insanity.

* * * *

Adelaide was already in bed when I got home from the office. I did not think it was as late as it was but when I saw the illuminated numbers on the alarm clock I was amazed to see it read 1:30 a.m. I had intended to only spend a couple hours after work reviewing my notes from that afternoon's session, but obviously a couple hours had turned into several. I just desperately needed the mystery of Tucker Wilson's mind to unravel. Had I known the consequences of my labor, I would have not have worked on the case with such diligence. Or, better yet, I would have handed the case over so someone else but I cannot change that now.

* * * *

"Morning," my wife said, sleepily as she rolled over into her side.

"Morning," I replied as I rubbed the sleep out of my eyes. I yawned. My body told me I had spent another night barely sleeping. What it told me was true. I had gotten home at 1:30 a.m. but laid in bed as my mind spun webs through the information I had on Tucker Wilson. Indeed, it was going to be a long day.

"Late night again?" her voice was distant and unengaged.

"Yeah. I intended to be home earlier, but I got studying my notes and became so involved in my review that I lost track of time." She was sitting up and her hair stood in a mess, a wild, beautiful mess.

"I know you are mystified by this guy but you could have at least called. I stayed up quite late, worrying about you." I hated when she used her mother voice on me. It drove me crazy.

"I'm sorry. I won't let it happen again." Little did I know that this was the beginning of the downfall of our relationship. I should have seen it coming, I should have stopped, I should have done something, but I was too wrapped up in Tucker Wilson to take note of the changes that were happening in my personal life. Much to my regret, my relationship with my wife became lower and lower on my list of priorities. Had I known the outcome, I would have changed my ways but hindsight is always 20/20.

After showering, dressing, and eating breakfast, I went back to the office for another day. Today I would have several inmates in my office but none of them seemed to matter to me right now. I would go through the general procedure, label their disorder, and sign the papers. Then, after a week of monotony, Tucker Wilson would be sitting in my office, dressed in a straightjacket, and hopefully with the same set of vibrant eyes he had the other day.

* * * *

The paranoia, the nightmares, the haunting shadows - my mind is the imagination station.

The Trash of God

Journal Entry #5

I am God's trash. A miserable piece of art, which will one day be burned by the angels as they do their victory dance. Who will be my company? I am not sure if I will have any. Most of the people I see look like God's little treasures, which He has poured out His blessings on. To me they are a bunch of smiling little creeps who don't understand what it actually means to live. Living means to struggle, to wrestle, to feel the pain of seeing the world for what it actually is. I laugh, swear, and cry when I see the majority of people thinking they are living life to the fullest. Life is not happiness. Life is pain. The daily gut-wrenching feeling of worthlessness, anger, hatred, and bitterness. I do smile but they are as fake as the idea that life is happiness. Happiness is just a figment of the imagination; the reality of life is pain.

* * * *

"I will always remember that night just like it happened yesterday. The memory is etched in my mind like the hieroglyphics on the walls of the Egyptian pyramids. I walked for hours upon hours. Leg muscles screamed out in pain as I plodded along through the forest tripping over sticks, trees, and tall tangled, twisted, mangled, green grass. Occasionally, I would stop and sit amongst a thick layer of underbrush; such a stop was just long enough for me to catch my breath, but just short enough so I would not become too comfortable. My watch told me I had left four hours ago and I was beginning to see the lights of York illuminating the endless black horizon. Within the next hour I would be walking through its streets. I was not going to stop. 'York 1 KM' read the sign as I grew nearer and nearer but further and further away. During the rest of the way to York, I never once heard the haunting footsteps behind me. I guess I must have lost my pursuer in the darkness of the night. Or maybe, just maybe, it was not a physical being chasing me at all. Perhaps it was something in the spiritual realm. An angel? I laughed. If anything was going to be following me it was going to be the demons of my past. To think I had an angel! Ridiculous!

Regardless of what it was, I continued on my trek through the woods. It was encouraging to see that I was actually succeeding in my runaway. York was approximately 30 KM from my parents' acreage. My mind told me this was not a comfortable distance and I knew full well it was not but as I entered the town fatigue engulfed my body.

"Suddenly, I could feel every muscle in my body. My arms, my legs, my lungs, my head pounded with exhaustion but the control panel in my brain would not let me stop. 'Run' was flashing across the screen in big, bright red letters. I could hear sirens and someone yelling, 'Emergency! Emergency! Save yourself!' But, as I slowly made my way through the trashy backstreets, the garbage dumpsters and park benches were beginning to look like queen-sized beds with plush feather pillows and a soft, heavy blanket. My body was beginning to win and my mind soon became weak. The bright letters were becoming dim and the yelling was reduced to a mere whisper. Because of the increasing fatigue both on my mind and body, my walls of stubbornness, ignorance, and defiance began to crumble and soon the consequences of my decision was beginning to be brought into the light. I asked myself, 'What are you doing, stupid? What are you trying to prove? That you don't care about anything? That you can do your own thing? That you're all grown up? You're an idiot!' The logical self was rising from the dead. I had killed him a couple years ago but had kept his face in my back pocket so I could wear it as a mask whenever the need arose. I reached into my back pocket and pulled him out. Into the eyeless sockets I stared, wondering, contemplating, and questioning the reasoning behind my present action. Was it wise? Maybe confronting the pain would be easier. Maybe, by the grace and mercy of a hateful God, my life would become the very thing I wanted it to be. Maybe, just maybe, I would feel good about myself. Or, maybe and most likely, I never would. Running was so much easier. However, easier is not always better but at least it does not hurt. At least not at the moment. 'Yep,' I said to the face in a defeated, tired, exhausted tone, 'I am a stupid idiot but I am okay with that.' With that, I threw the mask onto the street and was crushed by an oncoming car. 'Good. Now he is gone forever,' I said, rubbing my hands together with satisfaction as I rebuilt the walls of stubbornness, ignorance, and defiance. The bricks were light and the work was much too easy.

"Unbeknownst to me, thick, dark clouds had gobbled up the starry sky and the wind was beginning to whistle through the lighted streets. It was a cold, icy wind whose fingers slithered up my spring jacket and massaged my vulnerable skin. Within minutes, I began to feel cold drops of rain on the top of my head and the tip of my nose. 'To be expected!' I said to myself in bitter cynicism. 'Now God is spitting at me.' I continued to prod along through the streets, not relenting on the decision I had already made. God would have to send a lot more than rain to stop me from running. Thunder then began to crack over my head and lighting brightened the sky. Great! Now God was relaxing with His angels around an exciting game of bowling. When I was a young boy, Grandpa Lucas told me that the sound of thunder was the crashing of the bowling pins. In this moment, the thunder sounded a lot like collapsing of ten pins. Strike! I wonder if God used human pins. Perhaps that is why my life always gets smashed to pieces; I am always the head pin standing boldly, proudly, and with great fear in my heart anticipating the next blow. It was not long after these couple cracks of thunder that the rain began to fall in torrents; it was like a sheet placed before my tired eyes. I knew that within minutes I would be a soaked rag so I scanned the area for shelter. Park bench? Nope. That was giving a cold the perfect opportunity to kidnap my health. I had once seen on a movie where there were homeless people curled up in the shelter of the entrance to a shop. Looking around, I saw many shops but none with the type of entrance that suited my needs. My cramped legs continued to push on in the midst of the downpour. Then I noticed, down a gently lit back alley, that there was a garbage dumpster. My heart raced and I ran towards the dumpster. Two plastic lids covered the trash and I lifted one of them up to climb inside. 'Thank God!' I exclaimed as I opened the lid. Placed inside the dumpster were folded up boxes and other pieces of cardboard. The mysterious aroma of cardboard filled my nostrils and I eagerly climbed into my semi-dry bed. Drops of rain bounced off the plastic lids and caused quite the racket but I was so tired I did not mind. I grabbed a piece of cardboard and pulled it over my body like a blanket. The feeling and warmth of cardboard was nowhere equivalent to a wool blanket but it did prove to be the protection I needed to feel secure. I looked at my watch and it was 6:00 a.m. and the next thing I knew, I had fallen asleep.

"I was fast asleep and having a wonderful dream, which was suddenly shattered like a mirror by the sudden squeal of the dumpster lid and a startled gasp of an intruder. My heart pounded as my eyes flew open to see who had discovered my secret hiding place. The blinding sunlight inhibited me from seeing who it was. Around the silhouette of his head, the sun gave the appearance of a halo above the person. Maybe it was an angel who had come to rescue me. I rubbed my eyes as they slowly adjusted to the bright sunlight and pinched myself to be sure it was not just part of the dream.

"'Hello there,' came a raspy, worn voice. 'What are you doing in this dumpster?' Nope, just by the sound of his voice I knew he was no angel.

"'Oh, I just needed a place to stay for the night,' I said, hoping that would be enough of an explanation. It would probably just raise more questions.

"'Here, let me help you out,' he said as he extended a withered hand down into the dumpster. Grabbing his hand, I soon found myself out of the dumpster and onto the cracked pavement of the back alley. I teetered back and forth as my cramped legs slowly began to loosen. Dumpsters were not a very comfortable hotel room. I looked at the man who had intruded on my sleep. He was a thin, gaunt man with long, thick, greasy strands of grey hair, which ran past his shoulders, settling in the mid-section of his humped back. His hair was matted down by a worn black toque. A salt and pepper beard hung to his chest and blew in the warm summer breeze. I could not even see his mouth. When he spoke all I could see were some subtle movements of hair and then a gaping black hole. His shirt was worn down to its final threads and it seemed as though the snip of a single strand of string would make the whole shirt fall to the ground like a snake shedding its skin. It was caked in dirt and had several holes in it. His red, knobby knees stuck out of his jeans like Pinocchio's nose. Old worn out sneakers barely covered his feet. They looked like someone had walked a thousand miles in them. Holes in the toes, no laces, and worn out soles, peeling back like black banana peel, gave me this impression. He was no angel but rather a bum. A homeless person. Probably a person running, kind of like me.

"'What's a young kid like you doing in a place like that?' he asked as he pointed at the dumpster with his lips.

"'Like I said, it started raining and I needed shelter and this was the only place I could find,' I replied as I straightened out my wrinkled t-shirt.

"'Don't you have a home, boy?' his voice was not demanding or even threatening but it had a ting of genuine concern mixed with curiosity.

"Dang! Tricky question. I did not even know the answer to that. Home is where the heart is and my heart was in my chest, therefore I was home. So, with this as my logic, I hesitantly replied, 'Yeah I do.'

"He looked at me with an air of disbelief and said, 'Oh. So instead of going home to a warm bed you decided to lodge in a dumpster where you had to use a folded cardboard box as a blanket?' I knew he was onto my game. The tone of his voice told me he knew I was up to some sort of mischief.

"'Yep,' I replied as I nodded my head and swung my backpack onto my shoulders. This was done to indicate that I wanted to end the conversation immediately.

"'Might I say my boy that you are a weird one. I would much rather have a warm bed, soft blanket, and a family than the freedom of sleeping wherever I wanted to. But hey,' he shrugged his shoulders, 'that is just my personal preference. You would obviously prefer to be cold and lonely, curled up in this here dumpster than be warm and loved.'

"'What do you know?' I scowled, underneath my breath but the old man had better ears than I expected and he asked, 'What do I know? Son, I do not know what you are up to and neither is it my business. How you construct your reality is up to you. However, I do know this: Running only makes things worse. Believe me, I know.'

"'How would you know?' I asked with clenched teeth.

"Compassion filled his voice as he replied, 'How would I know? I know because I was once just like you.'

"'You ran away too?' Dang! I let my secret out. Now he would probably phone the police who would then come and take me to their station where my parents would be waiting all teary eyed and disappointed in me. They would take me home and demand to know what I was thinking. Then they would probably put me into counseling in order to fix all my problems but I would simply use that as a Band-Aid to mask the wounds. Once they thought I was under control again, I would run away again and this time I would never stop. At least not until I was sure I could never be discovered. Or maybe, and more probable, I would just kill myself.

"'Yep. Except when I ran away I was twenty-eight. Do you have time to go to the park and listen to an old man tell his story? That is unless you have any appointments you need to be at today,' he said in a sarcastic voice.

"I laughed. 'I had a haircut appointment today but I think I can miss it,' I replied with the same amount of sarcasm but slightly hoping he would believe me. Laughing, the old man replied, 'Perhaps after my story we can both get our hair cut together.'

* * * *

"The clouds had been erased and now there was only a beautiful clean slate of crystal clear blue sky and the rays of the bright yellow sun. Cheerful robins were jumping on the ground pulling up earthworms and singing the most beautiful of tunes. The grass seemed greener as a result of the fresh rain and the smell of wet earth penetrated my nose and stimulated my brain. What a beautiful day! Mind you, every muscle in my body ached and my stomach was growling, but it would be an ideal day for traveling. The old man and I found a park bench and sat upon it. There he began his story.

"'Well, let me start by introducing myself. My name is Jeremiah. I am fifty-eight years old and have lived on the streets since the age of twenty-eight. I have not always been a vagabond but this came as the consequence of several bad decisions I made as a young man. The worst decision was to run. Run from my problems, run from my fears, and run from the pain. Actually, it all circulated around one specific individual who I was in love with. Her name was Katie Fraser. However,' Jeremiah said in a very matter-in-fact manner. 'Before I begin I must use the washroom. Excuse me.'

"'Her name was Katie Fraser.' His words echoed through my mind. I have always had a wild imagination and started to wonder who this certain girl was. A long lost lover? A sister? His wife? A prostitute? Or perhaps she was nothing more than a girl in the centerfold of a porn magazine. Regardless, I was itching to hear the story. Finally, after what seemed like an eternity, he was back.

"'Alright. Where was I? Oh yes! Her name was Katie, Katie Emaline Fraser....'

* * * *

"'At the age of eighteen, I fell in love with a beautiful girl by the name of Mary Anne Joseph. Oh, she was the cutest creature I had ever laid eyes on. Her hair flowed down her shoulders, yellow, like ripe fields of grain. Blue, diamond eyes sparkled in her perfectly oval eyes. Like a picture frame, her strawberry lips lined the picture of white sheep grazing on a hill. She hardly ever frowned. Her giant smile would cause wrinkles to appear at the corner of her eyes and produce little, cute dimples, which sat on both cheeks. I will never forget her laugh. It was like the sound of a babbling brook on a hike during a quiet summer day. It was smooth, pleasant, and relaxing. At first we just hung out casually but soon I was finding myself spending more and more time talking to her. We would go to the local restaurant and spend hours talking and laughing over burgers and milkshakes. What I appreciated the most about her was how I could simply be myself around her and she accepted me for who I was. Tucker, there is nothing worse than having a girl who wants you to change for her. This shows she does not actually like the person you are but rather is attracted to the wrapping paper. Anyways, we would talk about anything and everything. She would laugh at my stupid jokes and smile when I stuttered over my words or accidentally choked on my hamburger. Mary Anne delighted in who I was and I delighted in who she was and because of this we became the best of friends. Two years later, I asked Mary Ann if she would marry me. I will never forget how I did it. You see, I enjoy playing the guitar even though I am not very good at it. But I wrote a song for her and sang it to her when we went on a picnic in the woods. As I let the last chord of the song ring, I reached into my pocket and pulled out the ring. She screamed with delight and shouted an emphatic, 'Yes!' Six months passed and on the thirteenth of March we said our vows and joined lives to become one flesh.'

"'Our married life was absolutely wonderful! After our honeymoon, I started my own mechanics business and Mary Anne started working as a cook until she became pregnant with our first child. I'll never forget when she told the wonderful news. One day, I was changing the oil in a vehicle, when I heard the sound of my wife's voice. 'Jeremiah,' she called, 'I have something I need to tell you.' My natural inclination was to assume the worst so I replied with a concerned, 'What is it?'

"'You are going to be a father. I'm pregnant,' she announced. There I was stuck underneath a rusty vehicle covered in oil and my wife, standing so beautiful against the greasy, messy background, just told me that we were going to have a child. That I was a father! I climbed out of the bottom of the vehicle and found Mary Anne standing there with a giant smile on her face and tears running down her eyes. I stood up and was greeted by my beautiful wife who gave me a giant hug and a prolonged, sloppy kiss. There she stood in her red and white polka-dotted dress now covered in grease from my coveralls. We held hands and stared into each other's eyes and we talked about our excitement and our fears. To be a father was something that both excited and scared me. I was excited and thrilled at the thought of having my own flesh and blood that I could raise with good morals and a heart for doing good. However, I was scared that in some way I would harm the poor child and as a result he or she would forsake the family and run. Throughout the nine months of pregnancy, Mary Anne and I spent hours planning for the child. I actually built a cradle for our child. It took me many hours of concentrated work but I enjoyed it for I could meditate on the fact that I was going to be a father. Both of us had many names for the child but there were two which stuck. If it was a boy we would name him "Derek," and if it was a girl we would name her "Katie." A year and a half later our child was born and we named her Katie; Katie Ema-line Fraser.'

"'Katie was the cutest baby I had ever seen. As I held her in the hospital for the first time, I had never experienced so much joy, pride, and happiness at the same time. It felt as though I could crush her tiny body in the palm of my hand. I held her close to my heart and kissed her naked forehead. As I held her, I whispered to her how I would protect her at all cost, provide for her needs, and be the Daddy she needed regardless of what would happen to my personal pride. Mary Anne lay in the bed exhausted from childbirth but nevertheless refreshed and reenergized by the beauty of her new baby girl. There were no complications in Katie's birth. Katie was perfectly healthy and would grow up to be a healthy woman. Likewise, Mary Anne recovered quickly without any complications and within a couple days I was driving my family home. My family! My pride and joy, flesh and blood. Tears of joy rolled down my eyes as I continued to drive the car down the highway. I felt Mary Anne's warm hand slip into mine and we never said another word for the rest of the trip. There was none to be said. We reached the house and carefully, Mary Anne laid Katie down in the crib I had made for her. She was wrapped in swaddling clothes and laid there, an innocent bundle of pure beauty.'

"'Mary Anne and I never saw it coming. We were both above the world, proud parents of the cutest baby girl on earth. One month after Katie's birth, our lives were turned upside down and shaken like dice in a cup. It had been an extremely peaceful Sunday night and both of us were able to receive seven hours of solid sleep. This was irregular for us; we averaged about five as we took turns caring for a crying, upset baby. That night we thought maybe she had finally broke her bad sleeping pattern. Monday morning came and I got ready for work in my usual way. Breakfast, a hot shower, packing a lunch, a quick kiss and an 'I love you,' before I was off to the shop for another day of twisting wrenches.

However, this Monday morning as I was brushing my teeth, I heard a horrifying scream from the bedroom. My heart stopped and I dropped my toothbrush, racing in desperation to the bedroom. There Mary Anne lay, col-lapsed on the floor beside Katie's crib. In the fetal position, she rocked herself back and forth as tears and snot ran down her face. She was having a hard time breathing as she lay there gasping for breath in the midst of deep anguish. I as-sumed the worst and my pessimism immediately took over my mind and I raced to the side of the crib. There lay Katie peacefully wrapped in her blanket, just the way we had left her last night when I kissed her on the forehead and pinched her rosy cheeks. However, she looked too peaceful... much too peaceful. Quickly, I bent my head down and placed my cheek just above her mouth to feel her breath. Mary Anne was muttering something in the midst of gulping for air and deep sorrowful cries. She was pulling at her hair as she rocked back and forth. I could feel no air against my freshly shaved face. I did not want to admit the worst so I gently pressed two fingers against her chest, desperately hoping it would feel the rhythmic motion of her lungs filling and then collapsing.'

"'Her lungs had collapsed, Tucker.' I squirmed awkwardly in my seat as he stared off into the distance reflecting on the horrible incident. Tears were welling up in his eyes.

"'She's dead! Jeremiah, she's dead!" she screamed as her eyes bulged from her head and the veins on her neck swelled. "And it's entirely my fault." She fell again into a crying fit and gasping for breath. Her hands began tearing out chunks of her beautiful blonde hair. I grabbed her by the head, stared into her swollen eyes, and in a cold tone said, 'I know' and shoved her to the ground where she rolled around in anguish.

"'How desperately I wish I could tell you I continued to be a loving husband. That the death of our daughter drew us closer together, rather than further apart. I wish I could tell you we had four other daughters who I was able to protect, love, and cherish. I wish I could stand before you and say that I fulfilled my vows to Mary Anne and that today we are happily living together in a tightly glued relationship. Tucker, this was not the reality I chose. I chose a different reality. A reality that looked freeing but only brought me to where I am today. We never understood the cause of Katie's death. The doctor's told us her heart had failed but neither of us believed them. Mary Anne blamed herself for the death of Katie and so did I. After Katie's death, Mary Anne fell into a deep depression and was put on anti-depressants and sent to see a professional counselor. Within the next couple months she was on her way to recovery and she began to function as a normal human being again. I was happy for her but my heart was shattered and beyond repair. To see her so happy made me more angry so one night I never came home from work.'

"'It was a selfish decision of mine but it was the only one that made sense at the time. Going home, seeing the empty cradle, and sleeping through the quiet night was too much for me; I could not handle a house empty of the precious bundle of joy. And now here I am. A bum who has lived the last thirty years of his life on the streets because he was scared to be a man and tough out the pain.'

"I looked into his brown eyes and could see the depth of regret so deeply etched on his heart. 'Why don't you go find Mary Anne?' I asked.

"'Are you kidding? There is no way she would ever love me again. I've screwed up way too much. She deserves something much better than me. No,' Jeremiah replied as he scanned the streets, 'this is where I belong. A piece of trash that because of Fate, has been destined to be blown about the streets along with the rest of the invisible. You will soon realize, kid, that no one likes a man who deals with pain. He is too much to handle. He's like a never-ending thorn in their side. They would rather he run away and pretend everything was all right and be blown around like trash. Then they would not feel guilty about not doing anything. No Tucker, I am, actually we all are, the trash of God.'

"'But...' I started before he cut me off.

"'No 'buts' Tucker. This is my reality. This is the truth of who I am. I deserve what I have been given because this is all I am worth. Remember, Tucker, pick your reality very carefully. You will live in it as long as you breathe. You should carry on though. I wouldn't want you to be late for that hair appointment. You desperately need one.'

"Looking at my watch, I realized it was noon. I shook hands with my new friend and watched him hobble off down a back alley. He may suffer because of his choice but my path was to freedom and I knew it with all my heart. Jeremiah never understood; no one ever would. I had over welcomed my stay in York and it was time for me to continue on my journey. And Doctor that was when I heard the voices again. They were so convincing, so seductive, yet so horrifying and attractive."

"Do you remember what the voices told you?" I asked Tucker.

"Oh I could never forget. It was actually the words of Jeremiah, which triggered their response. 'You piece of trash,' they said. It was in a loud, scolding voice and it sent shivers down my spine. 'What are you? A wanderer being blown throughout the woods like a neglected piece of newspaper that gets tossed aside and trampled on. No one ever picks up a piece of trash unless it is annoying them. Trash is an eyesore and that is exactly what you are. Oh, and Tucker, don't forget that trash always gets burned.' Then they told me to hang myself in God's dump. What the voices said were true, there was nothing to me.

"So, that day I walked for hours upon hours not stopping for anything. I marched on and on staying hidden in the trees as I continued on my way to some godforsaken place where nobody knew me, and where nobody could find me. The only reason I would stop was to go to the washroom. My mind had become a narrow tunnel with only one thing in mind and that one thing was to press on until it was no longer possible. Unlike the previous day, the sun was now scorching hot and seared my skin, which caused beads of sweat to pour from my brow. My brisk walk turned to a normal walking pace, which then shifted to trudging along which then resulted in me dragging my feet along a new trail.

With shoulders slouched and head down, I forced myself to go on. My tongue felt like sand paper and a glaring headache came as a result of dehydration. I had packed a few snacks but had eaten them with Jeremiah as we sat on the park bench. Stopping for a moment, I took off my backpack and checked to see if I had brought my hat. Nope. There was not anything except a couple extra pairs of clothes, personal hygiene, and my journal. I sighed and forced myself to push through the beating sun. Not only was the sun scorching hot but the bugs had come out in droves. The little buggers swarmed around my head and sang their annoying song as they tried to land on any exposed limb. My arms flailed back and forth as I attempted to keep them off my face and arms. It was no use. There were way too many of horrid little creature. Most of them were mosquitoes but in the mix were big black flies and little sand-flies. The sun, the bugs, the dehydration, the cramps - All these nature demons were making the trek a whole lot more difficult than I expected. But I was like a donkey and would not stop when I had my mind set on something, especially something as valuable to me as freedom. Putting my head down, I forced my feet in front of each other as they screamed for mercy.

"I saw that everything was not good and evening and morning were the first day."

Mother Nature, Cigarettes, and Caterpillars

"Oh, Doctor, did I ever tell you about the caterpillar named Roger?" His eyes had that lost look again and he just stared straight ahead as if he was staring at nothing. Rather, he was staring right into my eyes and it was beginning to make me feel very uncomfortable.

"Um, no you didn't," I stammered. I did not really know what to think of this guy anymore. He was truly beginning to scare me. There was something about him, something so dark, so mysterious, and so disturbing that I wanted him to leave and never enter my office again. However, as much as I wanted him to leave, there was something about him, which made me want him to come back again and again. Maybe it was his honesty? Or perhaps the sheer curiosity of what was happening in his twisted mind.

"Roger wasn't actually his name. I don't know what his name was but that is what I decided to name him. He looked like a Roger to me. Do you like that name, Doctor?"

"Yes. It is a very nice name, Tucker." These were the days where he got that so confused, so lost, so distant look in his eyes and he would tell the most bizarre stories, which were laced with unique characters and seemingly unreal and fictional situations. Each time Tucker told such a story he insisted everything actually happened. Sometimes it seemed familiar.

"You see, one day I was soaring high in the sky above this miserable world with the white puffs of fluffy clouds. Below me spun the world and on it the people were like ants that were searching, probing, and praying for a successful day on the crumby dirt of the earth. I laughed. They looked so desperate, so eager to make sense of what they were doing. This must have been how God felt as He stared down upon mankind, just laughing at the realities we are creating. I would laugh. I am laughing. From where I floated I could see what was lying in their path. I could not change the circumstances but I could watch with a cruel sense of pleasure at what was out of my hands. After all, was not the world simply a ship set sail and taken in whatever direction the wind of choice blew? I watched one woman, a real fat woman, who must have just started chemo because she was half-bald and the rest of her hair hung in thin strands, was rounding the corner of the grocery store, pushing a cart when she was suddenly smacked by an oncoming vehicle. The groceries flew in every direction and she popped twenty feet into the air and smacked the ground with a very audible crushing of the bones. Had I been there I would have been upset and probably would have vomited but, because I was god, I liked to see other people writhe in anguish. It felt good. Real good. Too good. Up in the sky, I felt no desperation, no panic, no worry, no nothing. Just pure joy. I smiled as I took giant gulps of the cool fresh air. I sometimes wonder if this is what God is like. Probably was. Do we create our own realities or is it already known? I don't know. Does He have the ability and power to prevent specific situations from happening? Yep.

Suddenly, the smell of cigarette smoke climbed my nostril hairs and I coughed. "Here," a raspy, desperate, panicked voice, which continued, "Take these. Hurry!"

I looked and beside me there was a horrid skinny caterpillar huffing and puffing from the exercise he had just received. My eye curiously scanned the breaker of my blissful world. He was green in color with twelve different segments, which started small, swelled in the middle, and then narrowed at the end. On his head sat two beady red eyeballs, which bounced around and spun in circles. In the middle was a little black dot that looked like a bull's-eye. Two brilliant red ears jutted out from his head and acted like horns. I could not actually tell whether they were horns or ears. Tucked behind his ears (or horns) was the rim of a black bowler's hat, which had a wilted red rose stuck in the band. Several of the dried petals had fallen and landed on the brim of the hat. From his mouth hung a half-smoked cigarette, which had an orange illumination on the tip. He was sucking on a cigarette, which was disappearing fast as he breathed in through the mouth and blew the smoke through his nostril like a dragon ready to fight an oncoming knight. He stood on his hind feet and had six tiny forearms outstretched towards me. There was nothing in his hands except a wooden handle. I stared at the creature curiously.

"Here! Quick! I stole this from God. Take them and run before He finds out they are gone," the caterpillar said in a panicked whisper.

"You stole these from God!" I exclaimed in horror.

"Hush, Tucker! You must speak quietly. God and His angels were bowling the other day so I had the perfect opportunity to sneak into His office and steal these from His stage. I thought I would help by giving you the opportunity to take control of your life instead of leaving the handle in God's hand. You deserve better than what you are receiving Tucker. Why leave your life in the hands of a God who is only shattering your reality?"

"What exactly is this?" I asked in a skeptical voice as I examined the handle.

"They are marionette strings. Before you were simply an actor on God's stage, every move was scripted; every word was memorized. Quite frankly Tucker, you were a slave, even though you thought yourself to be God. However, now you possess the power to take absolute, complete control of your life."

"Ok," I replied, still skeptical of both the character and situation. "And you want to give them to me?"

"Yes! Now hurry so we can get out of here. God is going to notice they are gone at any moment now!"

Before taking them I looked around to be sure nobody was watching. "Thank you!" I exclaimed in a low whisper. "Maybe one day I will be able to repay you."

"Oh, I am sure there will come a day," the caterpillar whispered. "Until then, good luck." Roger took another deep inhale of the cigarette and blew out a huge cloud of grey smoke. With that, he began to ascend into the cloud of smoke. In the smoke he was carried up until he completely disappeared. I watched with wonder as Roger disappeared into the blue canvas, trying to grasp something about what he was, where he had come from, or where he was going. Finally I decided it was not worth my time so I stared at the controls in my shaking hand.

"I was like Adam in the Garden of Eden when Eve had given him the sparkling red apple. Like Adam, I contemplated what I should do with the strings the caterpillar had given me. Should I indulge or should I refrain? Either action would have its ensuing consequences but which consequence did I want? Did I want to put the controls into the hands of a God who would prevent me from enjoying life because of the limited freedom He gave me? Did I want to lose control of my life only to discover it in the hands of Someone I could not trust? Mind you, the human mind is weak and understanding is limited but with control comes understanding or at least a perceived sense of understanding. Whether or not this understanding was real or not did not matter at all. In my reality, it was not a perceived sense of understanding; control equals understanding. I now possessed the key to the tree of life I wanted. The fruit I would bear would be the tastiest, the most attractive, and, most of all, the freest. Sure, I was already god but now this would put me in total control and give me complete understanding of who I was. After all, then I could control and limit the amount of control and understanding I wanted in my reality, and therefore I could always perceive my life as something that was bound to nothing. When I am god, I understand my reality in its entirety because I am its creator. So, I folded the handle up and shoved it into my back pocket."

"And god saw everything that he had made, and behold, it was very good. On the seventh day he rested."

Then.I.Found.My.Cottage.

Over and over again I worked overtime and Adelaide became more and more frustrated with my bad prioritizing. This, mounted with the stress and disappointment of not being able to have kids, was becoming a wedge between our relationship and things were beginning to change very quickly.

One afternoon, I was sitting in my office and my co-worker Carson came in with a look of concern on his face. He started the conversation by asking a question. "Brian, how is Adelaide doing?"

I was extremely focused on my work and didn't even look up at him as I replied, "Fine. Why do you ask?"

"Well," his voice had a nervous quiver in it, which made me stop my work and pay attention to him. His head hung low as he continued, "I went to pick up a coffee at Jimmy's and I saw Adelaide having coffee with some guy."

My heart stopped. "Do you know who he was?" I looked up from my paper work as my stomach began turning, my mind racing in a thousand directions.

"No. I have never seen him before."

I took a deep breath and ran my hands though my hair. "Okay. Thanks Carson."

"You gonna be alright Brian?" his voice portrayed genuine concern.

"Yeah. I'm sure it is just a misunderstanding or lack of communication on her part. Don't worry about it. Thanks for the heads up though. I appreciate it."

When Carson left my office I dropped my pen and paced the room. Adelaide had not told me she was going out for coffee with anybody. When she or I had to do something like that, it was strictly for work related reasons and we were very open about the conversation, where we were going, with whom, and what we were going to do or did. This was out of character for Adelaide. At the time I was confused on why my wife would go for coffee with a strange individual, at least strange to my world. But when I found out who he actually was I should not have been so surprised. I should have seen it coming. After all, he did say, "I'm sure there will come a day." I thought about calling her but then realized I did not have time for the clock read 1:50 p.m. In another ten minutes Tucker Wilson would be in my office. I bottled up my confusion and pretended to work but my mind was lost in space thinking of all the possible scenarios while trying not to imagine the worst.

* * * *

"I slowly began to realize that walking was not the most productive means of transportation, so I decided to hitchhike. There I would stand on the side of the road, looking like a complete idiot, with the thumb sticking up in the air. Some vehicles stopped but majority would just zip right by and continue on to their destination. I could not blame them. Who would want to pick up a complete stranger on the side of the road? You would have to be a bigger idiot than the hitchhiker himself. Majority of those who stopped were truck drivers who were probably looking for a drug dealer, a pimp, a whore, or even a homosexual. But I, being none of those four, would climb into the cab, buckle up, and be riddled with a barrage of questions which, when reading between the lines, all pointed towards illicit activity. So I sat, squirmed, or slouched in a smelly truck cab with some greasy truck driver listening to '80s hair metal, choking on cigarette smoke, and extremely uncomfortable with the bunk bed and the magazines lying on the floor. Out of the two of us, I was definitely the bigger idiot."

"The worst driver of them all was a man by the name of Morgan Jones. To this day, I am baffled that I survived a seven-hour ride with him. It was dusk and the sun was just beginning to set on the horizon when a semi-truck whipped by me but then pulled on to the shoulder of the road a little ways up the road. I was extremely tired from another long day of walking but I still had enough energy to run to the truck and see if I could hitch a ride. Climbing up the steps, I tapped on the window and he rolled it down."

"'Can I get a ride?' I asked. I wanted to get right to the point. Small talk with random strangers, especially greasy truck drivers, has never been a talent of mine.

"'Yeah,' replied a monotone voice. Because of the darkness, I had yet to see his face. But, as soon as the interior light flickered on when I opened the door, I wanted to trip down the steps and run for the woods. There was something different about him. Something that I was attracted to but at the same time there was something I was horribly disturbed by. This man looked like the typical trucker. He wore a trucker's hat, which encased a brown mullet and probably covered up a developing bald spot. Bushy eyebrows grew wildly above his almond eyes and were connected at the middle. A long handlebar mustache covered his upper lip and brown stubble had begun to grow on the rest of his face. For a shirt, he wore a plaid button up, which had its sleeves rolled up to the elbows revealing tattooed arms as a couple undone buttons exposed long stringy chest hair. He probably weighed 250 lbs. with his round beer belly and thick fatty arms. In his mouth hung a lit cigarette, which produced a steady stream of smoke. With the amount of smoke I breathed in on that trip, I would not be surprised if I was a victim of secondhand smoking. My stomach was like dough being kneaded; my nerves were acting up again. Should I go or should I stay? I could hear the cushioned seats beckoning me to enjoy their comfort and my exhausted body pushed me forward. So, I climbed in, fastened my seatbelt, and began the ride of my life."

* * * *

"An awkward silence hung in the air. Someone once told me that you know who your best friends are by how long you can maintain silence before feeling too uncomfortable. For obvious reasons, this man and I were not the best of friends so there was a heavy awkwardness in the cab of the truck. I decided to start a conversation.

"Not really knowing what I was going to say, I attempted to start a conversation, 'So... um... how's it going?'

"'Cut the crap kid!' came a harsh reply. Dang it! Wrong way to start a conversation. 'Do you want the truth?' he asked in a bitter tone, which dripped with anger. 'Most people don't care about the truth. They are just trying to be polite.'

"'Um...' I did not know how to respond, so I said, 'sure.'

"'Pretty dang crappy!' his tone was biting and angry.

"'Oh', was all I could say. And then there was silence. More silence. Greater silence. Heavier silence. Thankfully the radio was on and there was the noise of '80s metal pervading the air. But still, the silence between us was more obvious and was beginning to make me feel terribly uncomfortable. So, I used another method to create a conversation. 'My name is Tucker Wilson. What is yours?' Oh, that sounded weak, pathetic, and very childish. I may as well tell this stranger what my favorite color is, whether or not I eat my veggies, or what age I was finally potty trained at.

"'Morgan Jones.'

"'Um...' my brain searched for a follow-up question, 'how long have you been driving truck for?'

"'Twenty years. Where do you want to be dropped off?' Man, this guy was not interested in conversation, but simply wanted to get to the point and get rid of me, a failed vehicle for his addictions.

"'Um... I don't know. I guess at your next stop.'

"'Where ya headed?'

"'I do not know. Until I feel like stopping.'

"'Ya runnin'?'

"'Dang!' I replied. 'Yep. How did you know?'

"'I ain't stupid kid. When a person hitch-hikes it shows there is a problem in his life. Hitchhikin' is a desperate attempt to get away. You in trouble? Runnin' from the law?'

"'No. Just running from home.'

"'Why ya doin' that kid?'

"I proceeded to tell him the reasons for why I was running. Knowing I had to make my story sound really good in order for him to feel sorry for me, I exaggerated on some details and made my life sound a lot worse than it really was. Personally, I thought I had done a good job of making my life sound as terrible as it could sound without actually making up non-existing conflicts. Waiting for a sympathetic response, I saw a little smirk come to his face and he replied, 'Your life ain't that bad punk! I'd say life has been good to you. By running from home, you're leaving a pretty good life behind.'

"Now I was getting upset. How dare he say I was running from something good! How dare he say I had no problems! 'How would you know?' Now my tone was biting and angry.

"'How would I know?' Morgan sounded offended. 'What kind of dumb question is that? Tucker, let me tell you how I know. Tell me, do you got an abusive father, you got an alcoholic mother, you got a dead brother and another one who hates your guts? You ain't got that man! Does your dad beat your mom? No! Your mom and dad are still together. My father would beat me every day in a drunken stupor. Do your friends stab you in the back? No! Your friends respected you! You live like a king. You're fine kid! Why the heck ya runnin' from all that? You're an idiot! If I had all that there would be no way I would ever leave it. I'd stay man. I'd love to hear my mom say, 'I love you,' or my dad say, 'Son, I am proud of you.' Instead, I told I was worthless, a mistake, a burden, a stupid son of a bastard. Kid, you're runnin' from everything I ever dreamed of; you're runnin' from every kid's dream. Right now, my biggest dream is to feel loved. It will never happen though.'

"'Why not?'

"'Because! It's gone man! It's gone! My mom is dead, my dad is in prison for murdering my mom, my brother hates me and I hate him and the other one has been dead for the past five years. You think I can just go to my dad and he will all of a sudden love me. Your world is small Tucker. You live in this little box you call your world and you think it has mistreated you. Man! Fate has blessed you but you're runnin' from what many people only dream they could have. You won't realize what you had until they are dead and gone. Then comes the regret and it will eat you alive. Quite frankly Tucker, you are an idiot who should be ashamed of himself. Ya ain't got problems, kid! Open our eyes, take the lens off yourself, and then you will notice that the biggest problem is yourself. Don't give me that crap about how sucky your life is! You don't know nothin'!'

"Nothing like having a strip ripped off my back and then poison put on the wound. But it did not matter because my mind was set and there was absolutely nothing that was going to stop me.

"This conversation happened within the first hour of a seven hour drive. Needless to say, the rest of the trip was driven to the sound of '80s hair metal bands. And silence. Morgan was not much of a conversationalist and I did not want to initiate any more conversation. I was angry at Morgan for how blunt he had been to me. No one had the right to say such harsh things to me! Especially a stranger! Smoke seeped from my ears like the end of Morgan's cigarette and my mind spun webs of anger and put up walls to protect myself. I had excuses. And I used every one of them to combat the words of Morgan. The truth in my reality was that my life did suck. It sucked rocks. However, in Morgan's reality, it did not seem as bad because his experience and perception of life had formed his own reality by which he interprets the rest of world. I would stick to the truth I knew and that was this: My life sucked and was worth running from in order to find freedom. No one understood! But, then again, neither did I.

"We drove through the night and at 2 a.m. Morgan decided to pull into a secluded truck stop along the highway. It was a sketchy place with street lights gently illuminating the dark parking lot. The lights of the diner were dimly lit and a red open sign hung dangling in the window with its colors running red. Considering how late it was into the night, I was surprised to see another truck pull in shortly after us. The parking lot looked like a carton of eggs. Each truck was nestled into its own little parking lot as it quietly sat there. Its driver curled up in the bunk beds sleeping a long day of driving off. As soon as Morgan killed the engine and I heard the click of the door locks, I opened the door and climbed down the steps. I never even looked at Morgan because I was still frustrated and angry with him. In the distance, I could see the lights of a town. I had no clue where I was but I was beginning to feel like I was far enough away from everything I knew. I climbed out of the truck to reclaim the darkness, but in it I heard a monotone voice fly through the air. It was still harsh but there was a level of sadness to it, which I had not heard before. It said, 'See ya kid.'

"I did not reply.

* * * *

"I walked for another hour but soon exhaustion overcame my body and I curled up in the tall grass for the night. All of me wished I could say I had had a restful night and a peaceful sleep, but it took me a long time to fall asleep. Morgan's words kept playing over and over like an annoying song stuck on repeat, 'You ain't got it that bad kid! The biggest problem is you.' Oh, how I hated that man! Eventually I dozed off and found myself in a half-sleep/half-awake trance, which made me even more frustrated and angry. Minutes dripped by like cold molasses; every minute felt like an eternity. I kept looking at my watch, but the short hand never seemed to move. Only the incessant ticking of the second hand moved in a repetitious circle. I just wanted the night to end so I could continue trekking through the woods in an attempt to find somewhere to settle down. Forcing the words of Morgan out of my mind, I filled my empty thoughts with rancid rants about how much I hated life, hated myself, and hated the rest of the world. Such peaceful familiarity lulled me to sleep and I dreamed about taking a gun to Morgan's head and pulling the trigger. At the time it was quite satisfying.

"The morning sun soon came, and I was greeted by the chirping of birds, and the waving of the tall grass. My head pounded and my whole body was sore from sleeping on the godforsaken earth. The stupid birds were making my headache worse and I cursed the robin sitting in her nest protecting her young ones. I rubbed the webs out of my eyes and squinted as the sun slipped through the cracks of my eyelids. Again, I had absolutely no clue where in the world I was but I thought I would continue walking seeing how I had nothing else better to do with my time. I remembered seeing the lights of a town on the horizon as Morgan and I pulled into the truck stop so I decided I would follow the road heading in that direction. I walked and walked until I noticed a little green shack nestled in the tall grass, weeds, and overgrown trees. I stared at the little house for a couple of minutes and then decided to check it out. "Perhaps," I wondered out loud, "I could stay here for awhile." This is when life became a living Hell.

Can-cer

"As I walked forward, I did not see the fallen barbed wire fence, which had one time protected the home and I tripped over it. I cursed and scraped myself off the ground and continued on my way. "I guess I'd better be more careful. Who knows what kind of traps are around this place," I said in a bitter tone. In its prime, the house would have been a cozy little place, which would have been the home of a small family. I could just imagine the smashed, jagged windows once cheerfully allowing the sun to warm the home. The door, which now creaked as it swung in the gentle breeze, would have had a warm "Welcome" sign on the front. The scraggly trees, which grew along the side of the house, would have been nothing but innocent saplings anticipating the day the kids would be able to climb on them. Fresh shingles would have guarded the roof instead of peeling pieces of rotten wood and the hole would have been fixed by the caring hands of a loving father. But now, the beautiful home had been reduced to a mere run-down, dirty, old shack forgotten in the deep, dark woods. Behind the house I could see a couple of other buildings, which looked like tool sheds and an outhouse. I continued on my way but this time a little more cautious of what may be hiding in my path. Soon I reached the entrance and stepped into the little house. The floor creaked and I heard the pattering of a mouse against the wooden floor-boards. I was in what I assumed was the porch. It was a dark room that had no windows and gave little way for movement. I noticed that there were a pair of shabby shoes, a couple needles, and a hospital bracelet sitting jumbled in the corner. 'Just a little creepy,' I thought to myself.

"Just in case there was someone living there, I knocked on the wooden door, which stared menacingly at me. I rapped my knuckles against it but no one answered. I knocked again and still no one answered. Twisting the doorknob, I decided I would enter the house regardless of whether or not somebody lived in it. The whole house was like one giant room. Nothing divided the kitchen and living room but they were naturally fused together. In the living room sat an old rocker, which was tangled in a mess of spider webs and painted by dust. To the right of the rocking was stacked a few pieces of old firewood that would have been used in the old rusty cook stove. On the stove sat a cast iron frying pan, containing burnt food particles. Empty soup cans were strewn around the kitchen and other random pieces of garbage lay about the room. The room looked like a city, which a bomb had been dropped on. There was only one tiny bedroom in the whole house, which contained a small metal spring bed frame with a worn out, pee stained, moldy mattress. The entire floor was covered with the wood shaving, which had once been the insulation for the home. One of the walls had partially rotted away and the shavings had fallen on the floor making a nice, cozy home for the mice.

"I continued to explore the house and decided to go upstairs and see what I could find. A set of creaky, cracked, crumbling stairs was all there was so I carefully began to make my ascension. Stop! I thought I heard the sound of a muffled cough coming from the attic. I slowed my pace, slouched, and crept up the remaining stairs as quietly as I could. However, the stairs were like a never-ending tattletale and with each gentle step came a horrifying scratching of the nails and creak of the board. Reaching the top of the stair-case, I peeked my head above the edge and peered over the room. A mess of old mattresses, an old fan, vacuum, among other wood particles and miscella-neous garbage, were strewn all over the floor. And the smell! So musty and thick that I could feel the dust particles latch onto the sweat of my skin. I would not have been surprised if I found a rotting body someone had buried underneath all the trash. As I started to walk down the stairs, I again heard the sound of a muffled cough. However, this time it was a bit louder and I could tell I was closer to where it was being produced. But, it still sounded as though it was coming from upstairs. I climbed the few stairs I had gone down and peered over the edge again. My heart stopped. My breathing quickened and I could feel my stomach turn to a lump of lead.

"The light from the hole in the roof was like a spotlight that focused on a rusty hospital wheelchair, which was the home of an emaciated body. All I could see was the pointy shoulders underneath the hospital gown and gangly, naked ankles, which protruded from the bottom of the gown. A bald head hung in shame and I could see every vertebra in the neck. There must have just been a thin layer of epidermis. I could not tell whether the person was breath-ing or not until I heard an exhausted whisper quiver and travel to my ears, 'My name is Edward. Edward Robert Pursee. What is your name young chap?'

Silence.

"'Do you not know your manners? It is rude for you not to introduce yourself.' Pursee spoke in a tired, exhausted, worn out, scolding voice.

"'Oh... um... my... my name is... Tucker... uh... Tucker Wilson,' tripped my tightly tangled tongue.

"'What are you doing here Tucker Wilson?' he asked with great curiosity.

"'I just saw the house and thought it would be a good place for me to find some shelter. I'm sorry for trespassing on your property. I knocked several times but no one answered, so I just let myself in.' Somehow I hoped Edward would find it an innocent reason to pardon my trespass.

"'Oh,' Edward whispered as he drew out the word in a curios drawl. He continued, 'Do you know where you are Tucker Wilson?'

"'No.'

"'Do you know who you are Tucker Wilson?'

"A pause.

"'I am...' I started but was abruptly interrupted.

"'Wait! No! Don't leave!' Edward reached out a scrawny arm and tried to stretch out his bony fingers as if reaching for something in the sky. He continued, 'Kiss it all better! I'm not ready to go! It's not your fault, love. You didn't know! Don't leave! It's not your fault I am sick! Darling, no! This is unnecessary!'

"He suddenly calmed down and I replied, 'I am god,' in a cold-hearted, defiant tone.

"'My! Aren't you an arrogant fellow. Listen, young man, call my lover. Tell her not to worry about me. Tell her to bury me in all my favorite colors for it won't be long.' He lifted his head to the sky and I caught a glimpse of his hideous face as the sun shone through the cracks of the roof. 'Hello, Deborah? It's me, Edward, Edward Robert Pursee. Do you remember me?' A pause. 'Yes, yes. The walk, the picnic, the song. I am he, the one you once called, "Sweetheart".' Another pause. 'I know I left, but it was not your fault. It has been so very long and I miss your diamond eyes and sparkling smile.' Yet another pause. 'No, Deborah! You cannot see me!' Still another pause. 'Why not, you ask. Let me tell you, my love. I'm awful just to see. My hair has abandoned me and my body is a stack of bones wrapped in paper. My lips are chapped and faded: a thin line of chalk on a pale, lifeless skull. Rawboned, hollow cheeks jut out from my face and my eyes have lost their color. Baby, I'm so soggy from the chemo.'

"I interrupted the conversation. 'Where am I?'

"'I'll tell you where you are young man. You are inside of yourself; this house is your soul and I am a reflection of the life you are leading.'

"'You're crazy! What happened to you?'

"'I came here when I was young and remained here until now. I will never be able to escape now. The cancer brought me here and I will not be free until it lets me go. But that will never happen.' He looked up again and started yelling, 'Love, will you not be true? Don't leave me! It's just a sickness! Will it not pass?' Silence. He must have been listening to her reply. 'Yes I know but the hardest part of this whole thing is leaving you.' Listening. 'Of course you are dear to me but you cannot come. You cannot see me this way! I am ashamed of the sickness, Deborah. It will scare you! You will turn and run but the images will haunt you day and night for the rest of your life. Baby, it is not easy saying this but until I am better you cannot come see me.' Again, Edward had his head tilted towards the sky as he listened intently. 'I know we are in love but I cannot let you see my sickness. It is too much! I am a shame.' Pulling the IV out of his arm, Pursee tried with trembling strength to stand but collapsed back into the wheelchair.

"I stared in solemn silence. A sick side of me rejoiced in seeing the man in such despair.

"'Deborah! You are coming! It is not my fault! You do not understand! I have to stay in this sickness for this is who I am. I am a cancer patient. You will never fix me.' Listening. 'Call the doctors? Never! I have been to so many and all they do is pump me full of chemo and give me drugs. They do not help just like everything else. I am lost, babe. Even if you could find me you would not know who I was. I am not myself; I do not even know who I am anymore. The sickness has stolen my identity and replaced it with the cancer. You can see the evidence on my hospital identification bracelet.' Holding up his shaking wrist, he screamed, 'See!'

"'You were in love?' He turned his head from the hole in the roof and looked at me.

"'Yes my boy. But I lost her when I chose to live with the cancer. It replaced her. Actually, it replaced all the relationships in my life. My father and my mother would be ashamed to see me now even though I receive letters from them on a daily basis saying how desperately they want my company. See, I have all their letters hidden in the left breast pocket. I have read them to the point of them falling apart. I have every word memorized and I treasure each stroke of the pen but that is all. I've lost them Tucker Wilson.'

"'No you haven't. You, yourself have said they want to see you.'

"'I know but I am too ashamed.' A breathe of silence and then, 'Oh good God! It's come! I see the light at the end of the tunnel. The cancer, flying with the wings of an angel, coming, coming to take me home with her. Oh beautiful, seductive lover, how I have longed to see you! Finally, my life is complete! Here, come closer and wrap your arms around me. There, there now let us not get too excited. We are in the presence of a guest. But please, dearest cancer, take me with you. Take me to your bed where you and I will become one just like it has been destined to be. No! You cannot take him with us.' Edward's bony finger pointed at me. 'He is still young, innocent, and naive. He is lost but I am sure he will find his way. But lover let us fly for the day is long and the night is short. And I do not want this night to end.' A pause and he began to cry. Then, bowing his head he began gasping for breath. 'Love has finally killed me Tucker. If you ever see Deborah tell her the hardest part of this is leaving her. Promise me!' I'll never forget the pale face, tired eyes, and gaunt features.

"'Um, ok, I promise.' I once heard that the best promises are always the one you never intend to keep. This was such.

"In his last breath he whispered, 'Thank you, Tucker. Now, goodbye. Perhaps I will see you on the other side.'

"During this whole exchange, I remained on the steps with only my head peering over the edge. I waited several minutes and then decided to advance towards Edward as he sat slouched and lifeless in the wheelchair. His body was filled with pale white scars and runny red lines. Maggots were festering in his wounds and worms were beginning to surface on his skin. They were thick nasty critters with six legs and teeth like a bat. Finding a shovel, I went behind the house and dug a six foot hole right beneath the attic window. I then went back to the attic, pushed Edward over to the open window and dumped him into the hole. He hit the ground and his weak skin could not withstand the impact. Bones pierced through his body and he laid there, a pathetic pile of bones and flesh. It did not take me very long to refill the hole. I never put a marker on his grave for he will never be remembered. His legacy would never live on in the mind of anybody because he chose to be a poor, pathetic man. He chose to be invisible and would therefore never be remembered. After I buried Edward Robert Pursee, I decided the shack would be a fine place where I could find the freedom I so strongly craved. Then, I took my journal, and began getting high off the smell of pen and paper while I wrote about Robert Pursee "

* * * *

Cancer. It is a disease, which invades the body and completely transforms the life of its helpless victim. I met with a cancer patient today. His name is Tucker Wilson. It was the strangest and most curious experience. I wonder if I will ever get cancer. If I do, the greater question is, "Will I die from it?" But then I shook my head and reminded myself, "I am a psychologist. Nothing can harm me."

F. Air

Adelaide never told me about the coffee date she had with him. That night when I got home she was already in bed and all the lights were out. When I got to the bedroom and asked her how her day was she gave me a short response and then silence fell on the room again. The entire time she had the covers pulled over her thin body and had her back turned to me. She didn't even raise her head to give me a good night kiss. I then asked her what she did after work and she said she did some grocery shopping and then came home and cleaned the house. This part to her story was true for the fridge was full of fresh food and the house was clean. Actually, it seemed pretty much spotless. I decided not to press the matter and trusted in the integrity of my wife. Needless to say, my mind was still disturbed by her having coffee with this random guy. Until now, I never knew why she would not tell me what was bothering her. If only she had told me what she was struggling with. I now realize she was trying to the whole time but I never lent a listening ear.

Actually, the day I decided to come home early from work was one of the biggest mistakes of my life. The events of that day make my stomach turn and cause great anger and bitterness to rise to the surface, even though I pretended it was all a dream. It was still early enough in the evening that the sun continued to shine and illuminate the world. I pulled into the driveway and was quite excited to be able to have the evening off to spend some time with my wife. Candles. Romance. The soft feeling of her lips. I imagined us reconnecting and talking late into the night about our wildest dreams, about how much we loved each other, and the week we would be able to spend together. I even stopped at the local flower shop to pick up a dozen red roses. Roses were her favorite flower and I could just imagine the squeal of delight, the giant smile, and the smothering of kisses I would receive. I thought everything would be better as I walked to the front door and rang the doorbell. Knowing the door was not locked made ringing the doorbell look foolish, but I wanted to surprise Adelaide.

DING DONG.

30 seconds passed.

DING DONG.

Maybe she wasn't home.

To my surprise, I heard the click of the lock and the door swung open. Adelaide, there she stood, looking exhausted yet full of life and energy. There was a red tinge to her cheeks and her hair was laid straight down and looked a tad messy. She was dressed in a bathrobe and walked around in her bare feet.

"My! You're home early!" she exclaimed. Looking back, I remember the tinge of nervousness in her voice, but at the time I did not take note of it. The narrow-mindedness of my excitement was like a blind over a window.

"Well, I thought I would surprise you and come home early for a change. Here, I brought you these." I pulled the flowers out from behind my back.

"Wow! My! This certainly is a surprise!" she exclaimed as she awkwardly put her nose in the flowers to inhale the aroma.

"Why are you dressed in a bathrobe?" It seemed highly unusual for 5:30 in the evening.

"Oh." Again I remember her looking a bit nervous. She couldn't make eye contact with me. "I just had a bath. That is why it took me so long to answer the door. I couldn't come down naked you know."

"Well you could have waited for me," I said in a seductive tone and gave her a sloppy kiss on the lips.

"Okay there, Brian. Come inside and I'll find something for us to eat."

So, I went upstairs to the bedroom in order to change. A gentle summer breeze floated through the open window. What a beautiful summer day it was! I breathed the air in deeply as I scurried around the room looking for my sweats. That is when I noticed the sock. A sock is to be expected to be on the floor of a bedroom but this was no ordinary sock. I liked wool socks, even in the summer, and this was an ankle sock. I hated ankle socks! I never thought much of it as I went to the bedroom bathroom to wash up. That was when I noticed no wet towel, no wet floor mat, and no wonderful aroma of flowery shampoo. A piece of garbage lay on the floor and as I stooped to pick it up I realize it is a condom package. "I went to pick up a coffee at Jimmy's and I saw Adelaide having coffee with some guy." Carson's voice rang through my head. I mentally combed through the evidence and realized what had happened was what I most dreaded. I ran to the window to see if the pervert was still in sight. Nothing.

My mind was spinning in circles but came to a sudden halt when Adelaide's deceptive voice floated up the stairs, "Are you coming Brian?"

"Yep," I yelled back as I folded up the piece of garbage and tucked it away in an envelope, which was then placed in my dresser drawer.

This was the second time I felt rejected by a woman. The first time was because she was scared of who I was and what I struggled with and the second time was due to an affair. I remember the first time I was rejected, which actually, upon reflection, was not that bad. I was depressed for a few days but quickly got over it. However, I never really knew how much she had actually hurt me until all the stored anger overflowed into a very tragic event. I never meant to do what I did to her and her grandpa but it seemed like the logical conclusion. There was so much pain there, so much anger, so much bitterness, and so much confusion that I did not have a choice. When it happened I never even believed I did it. I am now convinced I made the decision on my own free will. God would never allow me to do that... or would He? I thought I had properly dealt with the array of emotions but I never have. Why am I only now starting to realize this? Until now. Also, Adelaide never told me about her affair with him until we were on our camping trip. When we were alone, I pressed the matter and she broke. Man did she ever break. I never heard a woman scream, cry, or groan as much as she did. Not even my first girlfriend.

* * * *

Roses are red,
Bruises are blue,
Soon you'll be dead,
I'll kill you.

The Mystery of the Outhouse

"Tucker, with all the voices inside of your head, did any of them ever tell you to commit suicide?" I asked.

"Hush Doctor. That is a bad, bad word. The voices don't like it when I talk about that. Heck! No one likes to talk about suicide. Such a topic is too real. Everyone, in some minor way, wishes they could meet death and have her bring them to their eternal home. I am convinced it is the fear of the unknown, which keeps people alive. When people have nothing to live for but themselves they are missing out on so much of life. How empty! How meaningless! How purposeless! I too have been swimming in the seas of meaninglessness, death only a call away. To answer your question, I would like to tell you a poem. Do you have the time?"

"Tucker, I do not want to listen to any more of your ridiculous poems or nonsensical stories! Just answer the question!" I was getting angry. I was sick and tired of always hearing about how the voices told him not to talk about something or told him to do something. Tucker was screwed up, and though I had enough evidence to give him a ticket for mental insanity and a couple years in the crazy house, there was something I still needed to discover. I hate admitting this, but my job in diagnosing him had now turned into a personal journey and it was I who needed to know what was wrong with him... Or what was wrong with me. If I could not figure him out, I knew I would not sleep another night. Thoughts of him already haunted me every day and night.

His mouth closed and he just glared at me. I apologized. "I'm sorry Tucker. I should not have gotten mad at you. You are just obeying the voices. Please, tell me this poem."

He looked at me hesitantly but then proceeded. "It is not a very pleasant poem but this is the only way the voices will let me tell you. But, before I begin, let me tell you something Doctor. As you listen to this poem, and even with the rest of the stuff I tell you, there are two levels to what I am talking about. There is the level that the average person sees, which is basically what the eye perceives and what the ear hears. However, there are also people like myself, who see past the initial perception, the stereotype and dig deeper, looking for what it really means. Everything has meaning, even though everything is meaningless. To understand what I am talking about, Doctor, you need to stop thinking and start believing that not everything is as it seems. Do understand what I am saying?"

I laughed inside my head. I had no idea what he was talking about but I could not tell him so. "Ok. Tell me your poem." Tucker's eyes began to look so lost, so confused, and distant as he began to tell me the following poem:

Two boys, each thirteen,
One persuaded a girl to come,
And one waited to accomplish their task,
Met at a secluded spot now known as The Horn.

A white-washed outhouse, the scene of the crime,
Stood in a patch of fresh, green trees.
The grass was green, the air fresh; it was summer time.
Days were bright and made life pleased
With every little breath.

Each entered the depilated outhouse
Standing on dead grass amongst a patch of dying trees.
After they had shut the creaky door one bolted it.
Then, with evil in their eyes, they glared upon the victim
Who trembled like a leaf in a breeze.
From his eyes, one withdrew a dagger.

Outside the sun shone warmly.
Chickadees sang their song,
A mother deer bathed her fawn.
It was perfect, nothing was wrong.
Innocent thoughts drowned the reality of evil.

Like cats they pounced on the prey,
Piercing her in the heart.
The girl tumbled to the floor, screaming unintelligible words,
Trying to withdraw the dagger.
After pulling the knife out, she threw it aside

And began to frantically clog the wound with the rotten wood,
which had separated from the floor.

Beside, in a tree, a sparrow slept
Without disturbance for in its mind
Peace, harmony, love was being kept.
Hate is sometimes covered but to find,
Undo that sweet, hypocritical dream.

Exhausted, she then lay down in a puddle of her own blood.
Not satisfied with the results,
The boys retrieved their daggers and went for another round.
One arm, the other arm,
One leg, then the other leg,
All slowly and painfully sawed off.
Blood-curdling screams filled the summer day,
But there were no knight to come and rescue the princess.

A breeze whispered throughout the forest,
"Peace, harmony, joy. Peace, harmony, joy.
In this we shall forever rest."
A lie, like a cheap plastic toy,
Was all it was and will ever be.

The gore only made the boys want more
So they began to chop the now deceased girl into tiny fragments.
Every slice was made with the utmost care,
Every piece was made the exact same size.
Finally, after accomplishing this pleasant task,
The boys scooped the pieces into their shirts,
Went to the hole and threw them down to rot with human feces.
Knowing that their deed was done,
They unlocked the door and ventured off to find their next innocent victim.

* * * *

He smiled and asked me, "You don't understand it do you?"

I shook my head, "No."

"Didn't think so. Nobody ever does. Anyways, after that I felt like a hero but that evening when I got home from Bruce's house a different feeling came to me. The high of the pictures had worn off and I was now brought back to reality, my own reality that is. My heart felt defiled and dirty. I felt as though I had violated my mother, my female friends, and myself. Most of all, I knew I had disobeyed my parents. If they ever found out about what I had done I would be in deep trouble. I could not imagine disappointing my parents. I wanted them to like who I was. I knew God was disappointed in me (but I didn't really care), I knew my parents would be disappointed in me (this really bothered me), and I was disappointed in myself (which made me hate myself with a deep, dark passion). That night I went to bed as usual but as I made my way downstairs I could feel the darkness closing in. Heavyhearted, I climbed into bed and waited for Mom to come and say goodnight."

"How was your time at Bruce's today?" asked Mom as she tucked me in.

"Good," I replied.

"Did you stay out of trouble?" she asked as she lifted an eyebrow and turned her friendly tone into a very serious one.

"Yep. We just hung out and worked on the fort." Liar, liar pants on fire.

"Good. Let's pray. Dear God, I thank you for Tucker. Thank you for blessing him with a good day with Bruce. Please give him a good night's sleep so he can be rested up tomorrow. And please give him good dreams. Amen. Goodnight, love you. See you in the morning." She kissed me on top of the cheek and then quietly left the room. As soon as I heard the click of the door, I went to the closet, shut the door, and curled up in the darkness with all my demons. With my head in my hands, I let the tears fall out of my eyes, soak my hands, and then drip between the cracks in my hands. Nothing felt the same anymore. I felt as though there was nothing left, no one cared, and that God was glaring at me in disappointment and judgment. I had chosen to look at these pictures and indulge in my senses. I could have prevented the situation but I chose not to for this was the reality I wanted to create. It was to intriguing, to exciting, to stimulating. 'God cannot forgive you for what you have done. He is very, very disappointed in you, Tucker. Actually, He hates your guts,' whispered the demons in my head. 'And just wait until your parents find out. Oh boy then comes out the stick. But that is not the worst of it. They will be terribly disappointed in you. They might not like you anymore.'

"To this day I tell myself this never happened, that it was simply a dream and was like chalk which could be erased. But this was the reality I only wished to believe. Perhaps the reality is that I wanted it; I cannot remember for it feels as though it was all a dream. Actually, the situation felt more like a nightmare. Regardless, I thought that maybe the guilt was just a figment of my imagination. Perhaps all of this was just in my head. But how can that be when the outhouse stands in the same place today as a symbol of someone's reality. Not mine though. In my reality, the whole situation never happened; a nightmare was all it was and all it will ever be. But if this was all just a nightmare then why do I still feel so guilty? Maybe I am feeling guilty for something I am not even responsible for. Did this actually happen? Did I actually steal that magazine and see a naked woman? I do not know. I do not remember. I always get confused between dreams and reality. From this situation I began to construct my own reality."

"You began to create your own reality? What do you mean by that?" I asked in utter confusion.

"Remember Doctor, I am god. Because I am the god of my reality, I can choose to create it as I wish. We all create our reality based on the god we serve. If I idolized academics then I would create my reality around an academic world where my world would be based on the ideas presented in scientific and mathematical works. Take yourself as an example Doctor. You are a psychologist and therefore you create your reality based on the god you serve which would be psychology. I am god, therefore I serve myself and construct my reality based on what I think and how I feel about myself. Do you understand?"

I was greatly confused, lost, and frustrated, so I brought the conversation back to its origin, for I could not see how this poem answered my original question, and asked him, "So what happened when the voices told you all these things?"

"Well, several months passed and I could not confess to anyone what had happened in the outhouse. I continued to go to the outhouse but my family and I moved away a couple months later. Now it was such a horrible memory that I wished it had been nothing but a dream. I forced myself to admit that it was just a horrible dream, which I was not responsible for and would never have to bear the consequences of. Soon, my reality changed and I began to view that event as nothing but a dream. 'It wasn't reality,' I told myself. Reality is something each one perceives from his own eyes. I forced myself to erase the reality and live in a dream. A dream that told me everything was okay, a dream that told me I could believe what I wanted, which would therefore be my own reality.

"I was thirteen years old when Dorothy came and visited me once again. Actually, she was not there physically, but rather she had invaded my mind and was whispering lies, which I chewed, swallowed, regurgitated, and then chewed some more, then swallowed again, like a cow chewing the cud. It was just before supper as I shook with nervousness, sitting on my bed as I continued to scrawl what would be my final piece of communication with the physical world. There was not a single sound except for the scratching of the pen and the rhythmic and predicable patterns of my parents on the upstairs floor. By the sounds of their feet, I knew exactly where they were in the house. Therefore, I could time everything according to plan and I would be dead, long before there was time to stop the bleeding or call an ambulance. Beside me lay the jackknife I had received for my eleventh birthday. It was sharp and was ready to fulfill its destiny. But the letter. I had made up in my mind that there was no way I could simply cut off life without leaving a valid reason. So I wrote...

Dear Mom and Dad,

Several months ago I committed, what I thought, was the most grievous and wretched of sins. Dragging myself through every day, I have been living in constant fear of you finding out the truth about me. Anxiety, fear, worry, and depression - These horrors plague my mind and steal every ounce of what I consider to be valuable in life. I was waiting with frightful anticipation for God to open your eyes and reveal my wretchedness to you. He has yet to do so; I have decided to take initiative for I can no longer live with this burden on my heart.

I know you two love me. You tell me this every night before I go to bed, every time I leave the house, and at random intervals throughout the day. Your love for me is doubtless and unquestionable. However, there is an enormous difference between loving and liking someone. Of course you are going to love me; I am your child, your very flesh and blood. To not love me would be in some bizarre way not loving yourselves. I know with full confidence your love knows no bounds towards me. But the contrast between loving and liking is so crucial it has brought me to where I am today. I question whether or not you actually like me. To like someone is to take delight in and enjoy their company. To like someone is to show genuine interest in whom they are as a person. Through my disobedience, I feel as though you will no longer find delight in the person I am. I have failed, I have let you down, and I now suffer the consequences of my decision.

Because I have disappointed you, I now feel like a failure. I cannot live with this feeling anymore. I have been fighting it for months already and it is getting nowhere. Mom, you always told me things were in my head and that is so true. My head is a place where I am not even comfortable exploring. Everything happens in the head for in our heads we form our realities. My reality is one of failure, disappointment, and fear. This reality is not something I want to live in forever; I want to be free.

I love you both of you very much. My appreciation for you is boundless and I wish I could list the qualities I see in each of you. However, there are too many to count. My love has driven me to where I am at right now. Don't cry for me, I am not worth wasting your tears.

With much regret,

Tucker Jeremiah Wilson

"The guilt had eaten me up and I was not prepared to deal with it in any way. So I decided I would no longer be a physical being but instead I would be a soul, burning in the flames of Hell. This was the reality I wanted. I wanted to wake up from this miserable dream and lose myself in whatever was on the other side of death. My fingernails were bleeding from chewing them much too short due to the tremendous amount of anxiety I was experiencing. I did not feel as though my life was meaningless; actually, the exact opposite was true. The future was a tremendous mystery of blackness, which slowly unveiled as each second ticked by; kind of like the mystery of the outhouse but this mystery was never going to be revealed. The note was done; the time had come. Slowly, I reached for my jack knife, trying to enjoy the pleasure of waking up from this dream. The handle was made of cheap plastic but it felt warm against my quivering fingers. So much control was found in the handle of a knife and I would play God and ultimately control the duration of my life. The sharp edge was now against my wrist and I was about to slit my veins but then there was a knock on my bedroom door. Quickly, I hid the knife under my blanket and grabbed a book and pretended to read. 'Come in,' I said. I tried my best to disguise the nervousness in my voice. It was Dad. 'Suppertime,' he said. I followed him up the stairs and left the note and knife under my covers. Later that evening I decided it was not time to pop the dream for there was too much to look forward to. I shredded the note and put the knife back in my dresser drawer. 'Maybe another time,' I said as I laid it to rest. Little did I know that the seed was now planted and would be nourished as is sat buried in the back of my brain. Unbeknownst to me, its fruit would bear itself in another way, at another time. The world is full of possibilities."

The End of Part One

Land Mines

"I don't know who I am anymore..."

these
landmines
i plant
always
EXPLODE!
in my face.

"And I deserve to harvest the very seeds I have sown."

My name is Tucker Wilson and I am a very confused man. I have been charged with two accounts of first-degree murder and one degree of attempted. Presently, I am being held in the psychiatric ward at the Bermingham Penitentiary. For the last couple weeks, I have been assessed by a psychologist by the name of Brian Cruse. He is a nice man who listens to me talk on and on about what goes on in my head. Even though he acts so nice, I am sure he has some dirty secrets of his own. Often he will sit in his chair and fidget as I tell my story. The voices tell me there is something terribly wrong with him. Almost like he is living a lie he is refusing to admit and uncover. I like him though, I think he and I have more in common than he knows.

I was back in his office wrapped in the sweaty straightjacket and being escorted by an armed guard. There he sat in his leather office chair as he looked up as I entered into the office. There were bags of stress under his eyes and he looked like he had not had a goodnight's sleep for multiple nights. I saw him once a week and I would be extremely surprised if he had slept a wink since last I saw him.

I sat down and asked him, "Something wrong, Doctor?" I meant my question in complete concern for his well-being, but he seemed to take offense to it.

"Tucker Wilson," he started in a stern, loud voice. "I am the one running this show, not you. Therefore, I will ask the questions and you will simply answer them according to what you know. Is that clear?"

"Yes Doctor.",I hung my head in shame.

"Now Tucker," he started as he scanned his notes to see where he had left off, "tell me more about this house you found in the woods. Can you describe it? Was there anything specific you remember about it?"

"Oh Doctor, let me tell you about the place. My heart pounded with excitement at the thought of having my own, secret place where I could just be by myself and escape all that I knew. I felt as though I, Tucker Wilson, was free. Absolutely and completely free from everything. For the time being, I had my own shack where I would spend the summer and hopefully by winter I would have a warmer place to stay. If not, I would survive. I would survive because I was god and I could tell myself whether I was cold or warm, hungry or full, tired or energized. Fear would not prevail for I would conquer her and slit her throat with defiance as my knife and ignorance as my cup, which I would use to catch the draining blood. And I would make that blood the symbol of all I once knew; all would be dead to me.

"The place was extremely messy, so I spent a large amount of time trying to make the place somewhat livable. I brushed as much sawdust as I could out the door and onto the lawn. Readjusting the tipped over table and chairs, dusting off some spider webs, and clearing all the trash made the place look a little more livable. They say all demons live in Hell and the shack was a constant reminder of the demon inside of me. Besides, in this hell I had created I was free. Free from God (I had replaced Him), free from authority (I was my own), free from who I used to be (I created a new man), and free from the past (I had erased it). I decided Hell was a rather inappropriate name for something I had worked so hard for, so I decided to call the shack 'Salome.' A place where there is no suffering, no rejection, and where one is released from what he once knew. Here I would recreate the reality I had destroyed and resurrect a new man. It would be a grand and glorious adventure, which would leave me deeply satisfied and free. I was home.

"One evening I decided to go and investigate the sheds behind the shack. I still had to be terribly careful of any fallen fences, covered wells, or random boards, which stood threatening me with their rusty nails. The first building was an outhouse, which was leaning to the left like the Leaning Tower of Pisa. I reached for the handle and pulled the door open, but the door snapped off its hinges and was left hanging in my arms. Leaning the door against the building, I looked inside and decided it would be good enough for me to use. It definitely was not ideal but beggars cannot be choosers. The next building, an old tool shed, was decorated with rust nails, screws, and other carpentry related items. It was good to know they were there for they might come in handy one day. I closed the wooden door, latched it shut, and began wandering around the rest of the overgrown yard. Surrounding the buildings and buried in the tall grass was a bunch of rusty machinery, which included a banged up lawn mower, a couple of old tires with rusty wheel rims, and a shopping cart. How the shopping cart found itself in the middle of the woods remains a mystery to me. Maybe Edward used it to haul his personal items to the shack.

"I remember the sky burning red and yellow as the sun barely peaked through the branches of the trees, when all of a sudden I heard a noise. To my right I heard the rustling of grass and I thought I had seen something slip behind one of the tall oak trees. Stopping in my tracks, I waited patiently to see if what I heard was simply the wind and what I had seen was a figment of an overtired imagination. I waited and waited but I neither heard nothing nor saw anything. Convinced I was still alone, I continued on my way back to the shack. I was tired and deserved a good night's rest. I spent many nights on the hard ground.

"Then, with ears like a radio antenna, I began to pick up a sound wave that came in a gentle whisper: The rustling of grass, the crack of a stick. Immediately I looked behind me to where I had heard the sound come from earlier, but there was not a physical manifestation of the producer of the sound. All I could see was the red and yellow sky hiding behind the arms of the trees. The forest looked like a large gaping mouth and seemed to be advancing, coming to swallow me whole so they could stick their roots in my veins and suck out all my blood. 'Get with it Tucker! Man, you really need to go to bed!' I said to myself. I shook my head trying to clear it as I convinced myself that there was nothing whispering incoherent words other than my exhausted mind. I continued walking towards the shack but then it felt like there were two eyes observing every step I made. The feeling reminded me of the night I had run away from home. My heart rate increased, my breathing quickened, and all my senses were on high alert. Another sound came from behind."

* * * *

Journal Entry #6

Don't the days when you feel like you are worthless suck? When everything you do seems useless, pointless, and stupid? I hate that! I feel that way much too often. I don't know what it is but it just sucks. I try hard at everything I do but I feel like I fall short every time. I know I don't

fall short of my parents expectations but I think I fall short of my own. Because I am internally motivated this kills my motivation. When I feel I have fallen short or the things I do are worthless, I feel like giving up on everything and not doing anything with my life. But there are those days, every now and

then, when I feel like I could conquer the whole world. Why I fluctuate be-
tween these feelings I don't know, but I wish I could just stay on that emotion-
al high forever.

The ground I now stand on is so shaky. Any minute it feels as though it
will split and I will go plummeting in to the depths of despair. And I will
dwell there, in the deep caverns of depression, for several months. I'm like a
dying leaf hanging on to the branch of the tree. The wind comes and blows
but still the leaf clings to its home. How long can it last? Not very long. How
long can I last? Not very long. At any time that leaf will blow away and sail to
its new home. Anytime I will blow away and sail to the caves where the voices
live. I'm walking on a tightrope. Too much weight either way and I'll go crash-
ing down. It sucks. Why is this happening? Where are these feelings coming
from? I hate who I am. It's reality; it sucks. I know there are good things about
me but I am afraid to admit them for fear of them disappearing and leaving
me with nothing. I tend to focus on all the stuff I hate and dislike about my-
self.

* * * *

"Was someone following you? Had you seen anybody that day or found any
trace of human activity?" Mr. Cruse asked with a great amount of interest.

"Don't interrupt me, Doctor. Let me tell you the story according to my
reality. You just sit there and listen." This seemed to put Doctor Cruse in his
place and he did not look very impressed with me running the show but I
didn't care. He would just have to listen. "Anyways, I whipped my head
around to see who, if anybody, was watching me. Again, nothing. 'This is
stupid! I am just tricking myself.' I told myself this but the increasing heart
rate, shortness of breath, and the feeling of two eyes piercing through the back
of my head convinced my mind otherwise. 'But there is no visible person following me!' Then, out from behind a tree, stepped a figure. Because of the
burning skyline, shadows, and invading darkness I could not see exactly who
or what it was. 'Remember me?' whispered the creature. 'My name is
Dorothy.' I screamed and swore as she continued to move closer. The voice
was all too familiar, full of seduction and enticement. Slowly Dorothy made
short, deliberate steps towards me. They were confident steps and she seemed
to be savoring each one of them like it was a delicious dinner. I could still only
see the silhouette but I could see hips swinging in a very confident, defiant,

convincing manner. I ran. My feet pounded against the dirt earth as I headed for the shack. Occasionally I would stumble over a tangle of long grass, a piece of wood, or a rusty piece of metal but I kept going. I did not know how much the shack would actually protect me. Most of the windows were broken and the door could easily be smashed in but I figured I had a better chance hiding in there than getting lost in the woods. But then warm, soft hands wrapped around my neck and my breath was cut off by the solid grip of a mysterious hand. I cursed and wondered how Dorothy had managed to catch up to me so quickly. Then again, it was Dorothy and nothing seemed to be impossible for her. After all, she had found me several hundred miles from home and not once did she show her face. Not once did she even leave me a hint that she was following me. My legs spun like tires stuck in mud but I tried to keep going but then collapsed to my knees and gulped in buckets of air as Dorothy began to circle me. I could not look up but I could see the legs going round and round in a mocking dance. And the sky opened up and God said, 'Tucker Wilson, I hate you.' Looking up into the fading light, my eyes met a horrifying surprise.

"The last time we had met she was a horrid witch destroying my bedroom and taking everything I loved away from me. But this time she looked different. First, I met her bright red eyes flickering beneath eyelids painted a light green. Her lips were like strawberries and her face was like a dolls. It was unblemished and caked in makeup. Her rosy cheeks were dimpled as she smiled at the sight of me gasping for breath on the cold earth. Dorothy had the torso and limbs of a human being but from her back protruded butterfly wings, which were colored a silvery blue. They were outlined with a trim of white and had small dots which reminded me of eyes. Like a cat's ears when he is irritated, the wings folded behind her. She was dressed in a tight black skirt and fishnet stockings pulled over her skinny legs. Two antennas were extended upwards from the top of her raven black hair. Staring into her eyes, I let out a faint smile but she ignored it completely and continued to circle. This time her silvery blue wings beat back and forth like a metronome keeping count for a pianist. The house was only meters away and there I could hide somewhere. I watched her with my head down observing her red high heels in order to understand where her location was. Once I knew the path to the shack was clear, I bolted forward and ran with all my strength. I reached the door and tried my best to block the entrance. After pushing the table against the door, and stacking some chairs on top of it, I frantically searched the house for the darkest corner. It was still light enough that not many of the corners were covered in complete darkness but I found one which would somewhat hide me from those piercing red eyes. Next, I heard the sound of the knob turning. Quiet. Footsteps. The shattering of glass. Dorothy was coming! In the darkness of my corner, I shivered with fear as I huddled there curled up in a ball of anxiety.

"She began to speak, saying, 'You want freedom, Tucker Wilson. I have come to give you the freedom you so strongly desire,' she whispered in a seductive, low tone. 'Stop running, child, for I have with me the key to everlasting freedom, something very few people find because they are bound to different forms of slavery. Your greatest form of slavery is yourself. If you can lose yourself, you will be free.'

"I saw her standing in the doorframe of the shack and I held my breath in hopes she would not be able to discover me. It was now dark enough that she would not be able to see me so the only thing that would give me away would be my own sounds. Needless to say, I did not move a muscle.

"She continued in a seductive whisper, 'Crawl out of the corner Tucker and stretch out your hand and let me give you the key. You know you want it. You yourself said this shack is your freedom but you're missing the key. Here. Take it. Let this give you the freedom you deserve. Severe the rope which ties you to yourself and become lost.'

"In her elegant hands was a piece of glass from the shattered window. She stretched her arms out towards me and motioned me to take the sharp glass into my hands. Thoughtfully, I grabbed the piece of glass, examined it, and then threw it against the wall were it smashed to small particles. I jumped out and screamed at Dorothy, 'No! None of this is truth! It can't be!'

"'What is truth?' Dorothy asked in a low voice as she raised her right eyebrow.

"'I don't know! Quite frankly, I do not care because I am god!' I was still screaming at the top of my lungs.

"'You're God? Tucker, don't be so ridiculous. How can a person like you be God? There is nothing to you; you have absolutely nothing. All you did have is now hundreds of miles away and your family, your friends, those who you thought cared for you have probably all forgotten about your existence. Remember, you are living a lie and God does not lie. You are not God, Tucker.

No. God is invisible. He refuses to show His true face because He is too holy for scum like you and me. He wants you to believe your worth something, He wants you to believe you are valuable but in the end all He wants is you to use you to further His kingdom. He wants to set you free so you can only become a slave to Him. Then, God will grab His whip and beat the crap out of you when you disobey. He will look at you with disgust and disappointment, tears running from His angry eyes. Do you want to risk being rejected by God?'"

"'You believe in God?,'" I asked, stunned by what she had just said.

"'Don't be ridiculous! Of course I do. But just because I believe in him, does not mean I need to surrender to becoming His slave. I can still believe in God and be god. But in the end believing will not set you free.'"

'I believe in God but I am god too,' I meditated on the thought.

"'Tucker, do not surrender. Instead, let me give you the key to freedom. If God hates you, then you will not find freedom in Him. Here...'" Dorothy had picked up another piece of glass held it in front of my face with an open palm. It was the size of a can of tuna and had sharp, jagged edges, which threatened like the teeth of a hungry lioness. It definitely would be sharp enough to cut away the binding ropes. With quivering fingers, I reached for the piece of shard glass and let my fingers gently envelope the sides. For several seconds I stared at the key in my hand and during this time Dorothy somehow slipped out of the shack without me noticing. However, there was the constant hum of something. It was like a song being stuck on repeat or an annoying little brother constantly asking what you were doing. I tried to make out the words but they were too distant, too quiet to understand clearly. The moon had now come out and now peaked through a shattered window and its rays gave the glass a glistening edge. 'Freedom, freedom, freedom,' the whisper was becoming more distinguishable. Unzipping my pants, I pulled them down just far enough to bare the upper part of my left thigh. Like a knife cutting through soft butter, the glass pierced my epidermis and ran a couple inches across my leg. I did not know what I was feeling. Actually, I was not feeling anything; a sudden serenity covered my world like a mother gently pulling a blanket over her sleeping child. My mind was put into a trance as the words hypnotized me. They pounded through my head like a hammer pounding in a nail, 'Freedom, freedom, freedom.' A monotonous record being played."

--Cut--

My world was fine...

--Cut--

Everything was all right...

--Cut--

I was god...

--Cut--

Freedom....

"I was left floating through the air with only the cute fluffy clouds. But then to my left and right, in front of and behind me there started to float a variety of sharp objects. Kitchen knives, scissors, razor blades, and metal scrapers all danced before my eyes. Something inside of me wanted to marry each one of these lovely shiny silver blades. To march down the aisle with a blade holding my wrist seemed like such a delight and pleasure. Perhaps once we were wed she would fix all my problems. She would definitely be able to free many of the different nooses I caught myself in. I soon came down and the world became black and all I could hear and feel was the pounding of my head."

"I have to get out of here!"
"This is not right!"

I ran out the shack.

"Dang barb wire!"
Blackness.

* * * *

"It was quite the experience, Doctor."

"I imagine it was. I have never experienced self-harm but I have done a lot of research on the issue. The statistics for those struggling with self-harm - whether it be cutting, anorexia, bulimia, burning, or any other form - are startling. However, you are the first client who has actually admitted to have harmed himself. Most of the time I have to sift through wads of information to finally discover issues with self-harm. Why are you so open with it?"

"It is not easy to talk about, Doctor. I'm always afraid of what people will think of me when they hear what I struggle with; you never know how someone is going to respond. Believe me, I have experienced it." My struggle with self-harm was nothing I was proud of. I had scars on my legs and on my forearms from to many nights of listening to the voices and obeying them. Even though the cutting has stopped, I still have the evident scars, which cause people to ask many difficult questions. And harming still is an option.

"You experienced it? What do you mean?" the Doctor asked. Now Doctor Cruse was starting to control the conversation again and I needed to retake the wheel. I had him hooked on the story and now all I had to do was hook him long enough.

"I'm not ready to talk about that experience. It hurts a lot and I need to fill you in on more details before it actually makes sense."

"Okay then, continue with what you were saying." His pen and paper were ready to go.

"It was not until the morning when I finally regained consciousness. The events of the night before were lost and I could not remember what had happened. Then I saw the barbed wire slouching in the wind and remembered tripping over it as I was running. I sat myself up and looked back at the shack. The other day it had seemed so beautiful and exciting but now my stomach turned at the sight of it. Broken windows glared at me as the door hung open like a gaping mouth. Then I notice a large, deep red spot had stained the upper part of my jeans. I did not know what it was. Licking my finger, I tried rubbing it off but then I realized the spot had glued my pants to my leg. And pain ran to my brain when I rubbed. I unzipped my pants and pulled them down until I could feel the tension between my skin and the fabric of the jeans. 'What the heck!!' I exclaimed. With one quick tug, I ripped the jean from my skin. 'Ouch! Man that hurts!' Blood has started to flow so I quickly found some leaves and pressed them against the reopened wounds. After the blood had quit running, I spit on my hand and tried to clear away the dried blood. Then it all came back -The broken glass, Dorothy, the high. I stared in disgust at the mess I had made: | | | | | | |

"My mind raced like a machine and the motor began to sputter, I could not believe what I had willing chosen to do to myself or, even greater still, how this whole mess was created. Had I created this? Was this the end result of creating my own reality? A terrifying fear moved into my heart and my stomach turned to knots. I had not eaten for a day so when I threw up a couple chunks of granola bar along with stringy, yellow bile rained down. Then I reminded myself: This was all a dream. Like religion, like God, like forgiveness - it was all just a figment of my imagination, something I can choose to erase and ignore. What had just happened never really happened but it was simply a very graphic and rather disturbing dream. Nothing more. But then I felt where I had cut myself and the pain was too real. If this truly was all a dream then why in the world was I experiencing pain? Why in the world was I sick to my stomach? Then I saw the stain of blood against my blue jeans. If this were all a dream there would be no blood, there would not be any pain and, most of all, I would not have this empty, sick, dark feeling stirring inside my soul. Something was not right, something was dreadfully wrong; something was out to harm me. I shrugged my shoulders and told myself, 'This is just a one-time deal. This will never happen again so just get over it. I had a weak moment like we all do. What happened actually does not exist because it is all made up in my mind. Just get over it, Tucker, and do not let it happen again.' This was the message my thoughts were sending to my brain but my heart was telling a different story. As it beat inside my chest it said, 'No. This is merely the beginning.' I swore."

"The whole situation was a flash, a simple scene in the great scheme of life. The voices said, 'It's all right. This is a good thing to do. It's healthy.' I looked down at my leg and saw the red lines running parallel. It was a horrible mess. How can this be right? I looked up to see who was speaking to me. The person had disappeared. Maybe it was my mind. Maybe it was truth. Maybe it is alright that I cut myself - it could be the right thing to do."

Not-In-Special

"Doctor, don't you hate the feeling when your mind caves in and you no longer know what you are thinking? It is like being controlled by a robot. Honestly, those were the times when I hated everything. My mind spun in circles and I could not control where my thoughts were going or their destination. You know how the anger just grabs the wheel and takes its occupant on a wild ride, which only ends when the mind calms down. I did not know how to calm it down and neither did I want to. Do you know what I mean Doctor?"

"No, I've never experienced such confusion." He answered the question with confidence, but there was a strange look in his eyes like he was trying to cover something. I know I should trust Mr. Cruse but there was something about him that made me very nervous. At the time I did not know what it was but he seemed to be too perfect.

"Really? You are a very lucky man. It is a terribly crappy experience if I do say so myself. But such an experience has its benefits. Have you ever been depressed, Doctor? Have you ever done something like I have and regretted it?"

I could tell Mr. Cruse was getting irritated and he replied in a seething, stern voice, "My life is of no concern to you. I am the one who should be asking the questions, not a criminal like you. Besides, what do you know? You're a schizophrenic who is going to be a jailbird the rest of his life."

"I don't know much, Doctor, but I do know this: Not everything is as it seems. I have built my reality on that single idea."

"Is that so? Well, quite frankly I don't care what you build your life on! Now continue your story or we'll call it quits and have you locked up for life." I had never seen the Doctor so mad.

* * * *

Mirror:
Reflect
the
Defect
of
the
Subject
and
make
him
Perfect;
a well made china doll.

* * * *

I continued to tell the Doctor my story as he sat there listening, not taking any more notes and it seemed as though he did not care anymore. He already knew I was crazy, but there was something about what I was saying which glued him to my words.

"So, out of utter confusion and complete anger, I grabbed the frying pan off of the stove and smashed every remaining piece of undisturbed glass. The sound of the shattering, the falling, and the clanging brought joy to my heart and I continued on my quest for destruction. I went up to the attic and found Edward's wheelchair and rammed it against the wall. Across the room I threw it as I swore and cursed God. At that moment I could find a reason to hate anything, anybody, and everything. They may not be legitimate reasons but what my mind told me was enough because that was the truth about my reality. The truth was, I hated everything, including myself. I sat on the attic stairs, locked my jaw together, ground my teeth together, and dressed my face in an angry scowl. I had lived in the shack for several weeks already, but my life was not getting any better. Here I thought I had found freedom but actually maintaining it was becoming harder and harder to do. Much of the place I had managed to renovate. The shattered windows were replaced with pieces of plywood, which I had found in the attic. Now I would have more windows to repair, less light, and more shattered glass staring up at me with the gnashing of teeth. 'If this is freedom,' I said through clenched teeth, 'then why do I feel this way?' I punched the wall. I had no obligations, no one to come home to, no pressure, nothing except the thoughts of my mind, which were the one thing I wanted to indulge in. But now I was realizing that the thing I hated the most was my own mind. How ironic is that? I needed to get out that godforsaken hellhole so I decided I would go to town and hopefully lose all the adrenaline that was pumping through my veins. 'I hate this place!' I said as I began to follow the path to town. 'It is such a crap nest.'"

"Actually, the town of DeMonte was only a couple of miles away but it usually took an hour and a half when walking. It was not a grand town by any means but was simply the typical small town with a crappy little grocery store whose groceries were way overpriced, a stuffy post office, which had miserable, slow service, a rundown bar that had been closed for the past year, a coffee shop where the demon Gossip lived, and a small country church, which was full of a bunch of little angels (I mean that in a biting, sarcastic way). I had only been to town once prior to this outing but had mainly stayed hidden in the shadows. The first time was for the purpose of adventure, and to buy some much needed groceries. My whole world was new and exciting and I wanted to enjoy the freedom I had. At that time the town had looked beautiful, a cute little town nestled in the midst of healthy green trees. However, with the change of perception, I already imagined it to be nothing but a miserable place full of miserable people who simply cared about nothing but their own beautiful selves. Oh well. I needed groceries again so I did not have much of a choice but to put up with the people and risk the possibility of being discovered for who I truly was. I had absolutely no desire to talk to anyone. I wanted to be miserable inside my own head and stay there while the rest of the world spun on in their realities.

"Money was scarce so I would have to survive on another two weeks of outdated white bread, brown bananas, sour milk and anything else that was either discounted, outdated, or on sale. Not exactly the fresh home cooking of my mother but it was enough to keep the hunger cramps at bay. As I walked to town, my mind rewound and reminded me over and over again why I hated everything. Life was a crap factory and the sooner it was over the better but, as much as I hated my life, I could not commit suicide for I felt as though there must be beauty somewhere in life, even in the midst of all the crap."

* * * *

"Doctor, did I ever tell you about the first time I met Mari?" I asked. I think I had mentioned her in passing but I had never elaborated on the person she was.

"No, I don't think you have. Tell me about her."

"Mari was one of the first girls I actually felt I could love. This has not happened to me very often even though all my friends think I am a big hotshot chick magnet. Most of the time I am floating above the clouds and unaware of the girls who are attempting to flirt with me. Quite frankly, Doctor, I don't care. Never have cared about the giggly ones who wish to attract attention to themselves. I like a girl who is genuine. Anyways, I first saw her at the De-Monte General Store that day when I stormed off and went shopping for groceries."

* * * *

"Have a great day!" a pretty brunette girl exclaimed as her latest customer turned to leave the store. Being polite, I held the door open for a complete stranger and awkwardly stood there as the customer said some final words to the clerk. 'Hi,' she said to me with a cheerful smile, 'how are you today?'

"'Good,' I said as I gave her a quick smile, which suddenly vanished. Like I had decided, I was not going to be friendly to anybody, which included cute girls. All she was looking for was a fling. Besides, if I was friendly she would simply ask more questions, which would then make me look suspicious. She seemed like the type of girl who liked to talk and those were the kind I always avoided. Girls like her had a way of squirming their way into a man's heart to discover his secrets. My secret was the shack and I was not going to let her in on it. I would rather put a gun in my mouth and pull the trigger.

I went through the aisles looking for anything that was on sale that I might enjoy, even a little. Like I said earlier about the grocery store, everything was overpriced. So, I went to the cooler and grabbed the sour milk, went to the bread shelf and grabbed the moldy bread, sifted through the discount bin and found some ancient cookies and a couple cans of tuna. 'Well,' I said to myself, 'beggars can't be choosers.' I went to the counter with my groceries and was greeted with the much too enthusiastic voice of the very pretty girl. 'Rough night?' she asked in a sympathetic tone as she started ringing my groceries through the till. 'Dang!' I screamed inside my head. Doctor, I was so embarrassed! I was such a mess!" The Doctor looked at me funny as I laughed at myself. "Oh, Doc, my white V-neck was stained with dirt and grass, my pants were torn at the knees and there still was that dark stain of blood. Can you imagine the big, black bags hanging eyes, which clearly showed I had not slept well for the last couple days, if not weeks? My hair was really greasy and standing in every direction and the stubble on my face looked totally nasty. I had also lost a lot weight so my cheeks looked like I had a vacuum shoved down my throat and it was sucking my cheeks back. Oh, it was a sight to behold."

The Doctor was looking at me with questioning eyes.

"Yep," I replied as unenthusiastically as I could. I did not see any point on putting on a fake smile. If anything, this girl was probably just faking her way through life and was attempting to get another guy, this time me, to fall for her stupid little games. I would give her absolutely nothing to feed off of. However, there was something different about her. Sure, she smiled like everybody else did, but there was something different about hers. Her smile seemed to come from the depths of her heart and was actually a genuine result of being happy with where she was in life. 'You smile all you want, dear. Just wait until He finds you and He'll smash your world to little shreds of glass. You will be left on your knees in the puddles of your tears. There will be no smile then, there will be no enthusiasm; all that will be left is a hatred for everything and everybody.' Well, I hoped she would stay high on whatever drug she was on but when she came down I hope it hurt, I hope it hurt really, really, really bad. 'A little taste of reality princess!' I laughed. But that was reality in which I created and lived, it was the one I had invented. Maybe hers was different. Maybe she had created one with the perception of everything was innocent; everything was as it seems, and everyone was okay. Puke in a bucket is all that is. But who was I to say her reality was wrong and mine was right? Perhaps every reality is okay and it is what we do with the reality that matters. My train of thought was suddenly broken with, 'Is that everything for you?' Those words simply brought me back from outer space and I asked her to repeat what she had said, 'Pardon?'

"'Will that be everything for you?'

"'Oh, yep.'

"'Your total is $22.76.' Like I had said, small town groceries stores are overpriced but I did not have much of a choice, so I pulled out my wallet and paid the clerk. The door had those annoying bells above it, and it rang its miserable tune when I left the store. Like the usual typical small town, there were a couple wooden benches in front of the store. But then I noticed a coffee shop across from the store and I decided I would go and loiter there for a while. I laughed. I did not have much to get to the shack so I decided to loiter in the coffee shop would not be such a bad idea. At least I would not be alone and stuck in the crevices of my own mind. I crossed the street and found an empty table."

"So, what ever happened to Mari? Did you guys get married?" Just by my story, I could control the Doctor. Interesting....

"Just you wait, Doctor. That part is coming. Something else happened on this trip, which is worth noting." I'm sure the Doctor would not care about the following event but it spoke buckets of truth to me. You see, I have always been skeptical about relationships. In the past, I have been burned by too many people who have caused a lot of mistrust and lack of intimacy.

I was sitting at a table when a big burly woman who had a little apron wrapped around her wide waist came and asked, 'Want a menu kid?'

"'Um... no... just coffee please.'

"I watched the woman waddle across the floor and disappear behind the doors. Within seconds the door swung open and she was back out carrying a cup of coffee in her chubby hands. She placed the cup before me and a little drop of coffee popped out, ran down the side, and landed on the plastic table-cloth. I hate coffee stains on the table. "Thanks," I said as the waitress clumsily wandered to the next table and asked how the meal was. I let my body slouch into a relaxed position and watched some people come in and out of the restaurant while others sat around tables conversing with each other.

"There was something about the human animal, which I found both intriguing and disturbing. I always wondered why people did what they did. What made that woman drink her coffee so carefully? What is she thinking about as she sits there with her chin rested on her wrinkled hand? Was she thinking about the past? A heavy burden, which has never left her? Or maybe she was planning a big surprise for a member of her family. What made the little boys stop and look at me so quizzically? There was something deep about the human being, so deep that it was not something any philosopher could ever understand. Oh they definitely tried. They tried with all their might to explain the meaning of life, to explain the 'whys?' to make sense of the senseless but most of their words were just senseless jargon, which many people bought. Stupid, naive people! Sooner or later they would understand that the human is merely an animal with the unique ability to form relationships,

106

which usually were senseless and pointless. Actually, I would go as far as to say the most dangerous part of being a human animal is the ability to form relationships. Life and death hinged on whether or not people were accepted by their peer group, a significant other, or a family member. Through relationships, individuals were made vulnerable and many would seek to blackmail each other with the secrets of oneself. The sooner a person realized that relationships were like a gun to the head, the sooner people would be able to find freedom. The risk of a relationship was one of those things, which enslaved. It was one of those things God used to make people drawn to Himself. Relationship is God's design to enforce slavery and I would never buy such an obvious scheme. I laughed when I saw the complete despair of a billion different realities trying to fuse together to make one substance, which they like to refer to as "life." Life is a crap shoot at a circus."

"'…and did you see the shirt she was wearing? I was like 'Oh my gosh, are you for real? Girl, that does not make you look any thinner.' It made her look fatter than usual.' A couple glitzy drama queens were sitting behind me drinking soda and deeply involved in an important conversation. At least that was how it seemed."

"'I know, right? At least if she wore a looser shirt then we would not have to see the jelly bounce when she laughs.' Her large hooped earrings bounce off her shoulder as she laughed and nodded her head in agreement. I decided to call her "Loopy." It seemed to be an appropriate name and would reflect both her earrings and her mental health.

"They laughed.

"'The other day,' started the other girl, flipping her hair back in a proud, confident manor. Her name, I also decided, would be, "Flippy," because of the annoying flip of the hair. I always hated when girls did that. It made no sense to me. All they were trying to do was attract attention to themselves by pretending they were hotter than they really were. 'I saw her laughing while she was talking to Heather in the mall and I could not believe how much her boobs and fat jiggled. It was so funny! I thought it would all pop out and fall on the floor!"

"'If you ask me, what she really needs to do is go on a diet,'" said Loopy.

"Flippy replied, 'I agree but do you really think that would help? After all, imagine all the extra skin that would sulk around in loose clumps. She would be like one of those dogs with the extremely wrinkly faces!'"

"Laughter.

"'She's the biggest slut I know,' announced Flippy.

"Loopy gasped and asked, 'How can you even talk about her like that? I thought you guys were friends?'

"'Oh, we are, but it is only because we grew up together. I have moved on but if I left her she would probably have a hissy fit. Besides, she is a friend with benefits. She makes me feel good about myself. Every time I see her I feel like a queen and she the beggar. She makes me feel smart, beautiful, sexy, and worth something.' Flippy ran her fingers through her blonde hair and ended with an exaggerated flip of the back of the hair and continued. 'When I see her I say to myself, "Girl, you truly are beautiful."'

"'And to think she likes Bernard! Girl, like, she is not worthy of even thinking about him. He is a pure god!' Loopy said in a dreamy tone. I could just imagine her eyes looking up towards the heaven as she dreamed of this god ascending from the sky.

"'Uh! I know. So gross! Imagine, a flabby girl walking with the hottest guy in the whole school! That would be the greatest sin of all!'

"Excited, Loopy slapped both hand onto the table and exclaimed, 'Oh! Guess what? He was checking you out the other day!'

"'What? You're kidding! Bernard?" she yelled, looked around, then she lowered her voice. 'You're kidding right?'

"'Nope!'

"'No! Explain!' Flippy said as her voice continued to build with excitement like a bomb waiting to explode.

"'Remember the other day at school when we were in the lunch line?'

"'Yeah!'

"'I was already sitting down, waiting for you to join me. Bernard was a couple people behind you and I was watching him very closely to see where his eyes would go. Girl, as you were walking away his eyes went to your butt and he watched you all the way!' squealed Loopy.

"'Oh dear! I hope it looked small and tight!' her voice was both worried and anxious.

"'Don't worry about it. I'm sure he liked it," she replied, and I could just imagine the wink that went along with it.

"'Do you think I have a chance?'

"'Well, you have a better chance than that slut.'

"They laughed again. Suddenly one of their cellphones rang and the girl with the big earrings answered it with a chirp, 'Hello?'

"There was silence. A long silence, and then a gasp from her. 'Oh my gosh! You're kidding right?' More silence. 'Thanks for calling. See you in a bit.' She hung up her phone and then said solemnly to her friend, 'Heather just committed suicide.'

"That day Doctor, I left town with two certain, concrete thought and that was this: Small town grocery stores are overpriced and the staff is much too friendly. Also, our realities interact, creating others and relationships are a bullet to the back of the head."

The World Is a Sugar Bowl

Journal Entry #7

I used to be such a burning example, I used to be something people would look up to and respect. I was like a burning flame, which though disguised, led people to pursue something worthwhile. There was something about who I was that greatly attracted people and they were drawn to me. Complete strangers knew who I was simply by the name. I was a spreading flame; a flame which all could see and some would follow it like the Israelites in the desert. I was their excuse, I was their reason, I was the weight behind their argument. However, the flame was becoming extinguished by the tears of God as He watched me live out my daily life. My life was full of contradictions of thought, philosophy, and belief. No one could see the hypocrisy except God. For the longest time I was not aware of the product I had created with my own mind. At one point, I thought Dorothy was just something in the back of my mind, but now I knew otherwise. She was like a cancer that spread and now she was such a part of me that she consumed me every step of the way. I could hear her cackling in the back of my mind, teasing me and manipulating me to let the darkness out through my veins. "Only that once," I would tell her, "and never again." I do not think she believed me for the horrid, gross laughter was something I could not help but be captivated by. I was no longer a burning flame but rather smoking ashes which were becoming cool very quickly. Soon the wind would blow and I would disappear without a trace and no one would remember me. No one would remember the hypocritical life of Tucker Wilson. I would merely be a bad nightmare, a figment of the imagination.

* * * *

"The depression was becoming much, much worse. My world was a sugar bowl spinning on a straw from which I would take spoonfuls of sugar. However, the sugar I tasted was not something delightful but it was something bitter and gross. It made me want to throw up. It made me want to rip open my stomach and expel all the sickness, all the disease, all the sugar from my inward being. The straw on which the bowl spun was becoming feeble and worn. I could feel the weakening of the plastic, the slight collapse of one side, and the earthquake, which ensued. At any time that straw was simply going to snap and down would tumble the sugar, my life, the purpose of existence. I needed something to fortify the straw and make the sugar taste a little sweeter. Even if I could just get the straw to stabilize I would be full of joy. Life does not have to be sweet but the bitterness is much easier to cope with when the rest of the world is spinning on in confidence. I no longer knew what to do with myself. The pages of my journal began to fill with random, meaningless poems, bizarre, pointless artwork, and the occasional paragraph of happiness, which was spattered sporadically throughout the pages. My days consisted of me lying around doing nothing but wasting space and oxygen. It was a good thing I was out in the woods all alone, because no one knew that my useless life was simply being wasted. If they did, they would probably euthanize me for the betterment of my family, my friends, and ultimately society.

"Quite frequently my mind would wonder how my family was doing. Did they miss me? Had they even attempted to find me? Maybe they had forgotten about me? Or, did they just hope for the best knowing I was a man of independence and strong will? I wondered if they experienced any regret. Maybe now they would have a greater appreciation of who I was and what I did. I could always go home. I laughed at the thought. In the Bible there was the story of the prodigal son who, after pursuing a life of worldly pleasure, was welcomed back into his home with open arms. His father even had the fattened calf killed in order for his family and neighbors to have a giant welcoming party. There would be no welcoming party for me when I got back home. Instead, there would be a barrage of questions like, 'Where were you? What were you doing? Don't you know we love you? How could you do this to us? Are you okay? Maybe pray a little more and all these thoughts and feelings will go away. It is all in your head so don't dwell on it and it will go away.' This would only be the start of the interrogation. Then there would be crying, anger, disappointment, and, quite possibly, rejection. Rejection was the bullet I feared the most. I could handle the rest but as soon as I was rejected then life as I knew it was over. It was such a painful experience and I did not know how to handle it appropriately.

"And my friends. I did not exist to them anymore. To them I was now just a long lost memory, a simple shadow in the distant past. I still remembered them but it was with painful memories. We had several good times but they are all erased by the regret of me not being what they needed me to be during the hard times of their lives. I failed them on many levels and for that reason I hoped they would forget about me. But it is always easier to remember the disappointment as opposed to the good times. So, for that reason, I had no doubt they would ever forget me.

"All these thoughts were not helping my state of mind. If anything they just confused me more and sent me on a spree of cynical thoughts, which caused me to hate everything even more. I hated EVERYTHING!!!!!! I wanted to burn, destroy, kill, and absolutely obliterate anything and everything I saw, everything I did, everything I said, every single fruitless thought. Looking through my journal I scoffed at the pathetic excuse for poems I had written. They were the crappiest pieces of literature ever written and, even though they revealed my heart and helped me process different emotions, I hated the themes, I hated the rhymes, and I hated the imagery. "What do you think you are doing?' I screamed as I hurled my journal against the wall. 'This is meaningless! This may be what you think, this may be what you feel, this may be how you perceive the world, but it is time to get real! No one cares! Not a single soul! So just stop!' I ran to my journal, picked it up again and threw it against the wall a second time. Nothing made sense! I wanted something but I did not know what! I needed something but I didn't know exactly what it was I was craving. A million thoughts swept through my mind and I could not focus on a single one. They were like a stupid frog a little girl was trying to catch but it always eluded the welcoming hands. I wanted to welcome the thoughts but I wanted to embrace the ones, which would build me up and not tear me down but those were the slipperiest ones. Continually I was being battered down by the thoughts that I did not want, the thoughts I tried to refuse but in the end they were the only ones I had left. So I grabbed them and hung on to them like life itself. These thoughts were my life. Everything else made no sense! Everything else was a confusing map of incoherent thoughts and words that all slurred together to make one giant word soup.

"I stood pounding the wooden wall in frustration. Breathing came in heavy gasps as my chest began to tighten. I have never had good nerves but I could feel them giving way as I continued to stand there. My hands began to shake and my knees began to feel weak. Then came a whisper, 'Death.' The horrid ugly creature who had claimed so many of those I loved. It was the in-evitable ending and no matter how far, how hard, how desperate a man ran he could never outrun the hands of Death. Like a movie, images of Grandpa Lucas lying in his casket - I could remember his last words he said to me, 'Don't take the 'f' out of life. As soon as that is gone, existence becomes a chore.' - Dylan's massacred head swimming in blood the night I found him lying dead in his room - His last words, 'Love you,' as he hugged me for the last time - Edward, "Tell her the hardest part of all this is leaving her.' All those who had wandered into eternity before me."

Hell.
Heaven.
The afterlife.

"My stomach tightened as my mind continued streaking through the darkness. I fell to the floor and my body curled up in the fetal position as my muscles tensed and pulled me together. Tears streamed down my face as I attempted to rearrange the mess of chaotic thoughts that were burying me alive. The Devil was dancing in my mind and was pleasurably destroying what little control of self I had. Suddenly, it was like an invisible hand gripped my throat and slowly began to cut off my breathing. I rolled around on the floor trying to breath, trying to think, trying, trying, trying so hard to make sense of what was going on. I could not. The hand just tightened around my neck and I tried to pry loose the strong fingers but they clung together like a steel trap. Fear of the unknown consumed my body like the cancer. 'Oh, God! I don't know what is going on? I'm losing control…Why, God, why? I just want all to go to heaven; I want all to be saved. Why do some burn? Why do others live in glory? I don't understand! I'm scared to breathe my last. I'm scared to cross the river into the unknown and lose what I know here on earth. The earth stinks but it is all I know and I would not give it up for something I did not know. As much as I hate it, there is a certain aspect to it, which I love and cannot lose. I want to know where I am going. I want to know that all roads lead to Heaven.'

"I wanted God to send an angel and rescue me from that very moment but no angel came. 'I know you hate me, I know you're disappointed in whom I have become but God please come and rescue me!' My stomach tightened, convulsed, and vomit flew from my mouth and splattered on the floor. This made my breathing more difficult and I just rolled around trying to straighten my body out, trying to loosen the iron grip, trying to break free from whatever was holding me so tightly. My body moved in spastic motions like an old person having a seizure and I rolled about uncontrollably on the floor. The uncontrolled movements caused me to roll through my own puddle of vomit which dust and dirt then attached themselves to, like leaches. Suddenly I heard a crunching noise, which was followed by sharp pains of broken glass particles poking into my skin. I stopped and there was a single moment of clear thinking. A single moment, where I felt as though I could compose myself. I stopped rolling and just lay in the broken glass. However, my mind was like a vehicle tipping over the cliff; where I chose to go would determine whether I would spiral down or jump out of a disaster. I never knew I could have so many thoughts in just one second, even though that second felt like a couple of minutes. Looking up at God I saw His sad dejected face, which revealed His disappointment with me and I looked down to Satan and he said, 'My son, with you I am well pleased.'

"Shattered glass...vivid memories...I didn't have a choice."

--Cut--
My world was fine...
--Cut--
Everything was alright...
--Cut--
I was god...
--Cut--
Freedom....

* * * *

The world is a sugar bowl
spinning on a straw;
my mind is a spoon.
I take one taste; God,
I'm lost in a sea of faces,
which paint the land.
They all stare and swear
at who I am, the words blur my mind.
I see fog,

We Live Dying

I see black,
I'm falling,
I'm drowning in a waters of forgetfulness.
I grasp for something; God,
I can't find my way.
I'm in the belly of a monster
gasping for breath.
Between his teeth I see light.
Crawl, crawl,
keep slipping; my
breath blows out the flame.
Choking on smoke, lost in the thought of
who I was, where I came from,
who I am, where I'm going; all I see is the Devil's smile

"Blade"

"Remember: There are two types of people. Those who perceive everything just as they are and those who dig deeper and realize everything is not as it seems."

* * * *

"Oh, the high! The hallucinations! The glorious forgetfulness upon the chemical reaction! How can I forget the trips you took me on, the adventures we had, the lands we conquered. We have walked hand in hand together for I know you can bring me through anything and by you I can experience life the way I want to; the mess of my mind is swept under the carpet and forgotten. As soon as it appears again, I just take another dose and it temporarily disappears. Never does it completely vanish but I do not want the mess completely exterminated. Rather, I would like to indulge in the world of the high and the world of the low and through them I would be able to cope and control life. Oh glorious bliss! If you shall leave my side, I will have nothing left except the torture chamber I call my mind."

* * * *

"I found myself in a far off land. The landscape was barren with the occasional cactus standing tall in the desert sand. Dried skeletons of lost animals were bleached in the hot sun, which tortured the land day after day. The only living creatures I saw were vultures circling high above me in the sky. Occasionally I could hear them call out to each other probably saying, 'Only a matter of time, my friend. Only a matter of time.' Indeed, it was only a matter of time before I would collapse on the scorching sand and become like the bleached animal skeletons. I thought I could feel the vultures using their sharp beaks to devour my flesh but then I reminded myself it was only the salty beads of sweat running down my body. My tongue had become like sandpaper and hung out like an exhausted dog's does when he has chased an annoying cat. A warm gust of wind would blow through the empty land and plaster small particles of sand to my sticky body. There was no protection for my clothes had become torn and tattered from the long journey. I traveled like a robot, a mechanical being whose legs moved forward based on purely involuntary actions.

"I had seen several mirages on my journey. I remember seeing a beautiful oasis with beautiful palm trees producing cool shade and there was a spring of fresh water, which I could dip my body into and quench the burning fire. My whole body would be refreshed as the cool, fresh water coursed through my entire being. But, as soon as I got close enough to feel the cool of the shade and smell the deep purity of the water the oasis vanished. I ran to the spot where I had seen it and collapsed on the hot sand. 'No!' I screamed. I should not have used so much energy for I had to reserve every ounce I had but I could not help it. The bitter disappointment stung and I lay there crying but unable to shed any tears. I began to develop a deep hatred for mirages. It may seem pathetic, but when one is out in the desert all alone he needs something he can hate, something he can dwell on, something that can be an enemy for then he has the strength to carry on. Mirages in my mind where the dumbest things in the desert. After seeing a mirage, the rest of the journey was always more difficult. You longed for the sweet high of a mirage but the burning crash was never worth the excitement. However, my robotic legs continued to move forward as my will power and determination began to lag behind. Day turned to night and soon I began to experience the coolness of night. I couldn't decide what I liked better: Being drenched in sweat and burning like I was in Hell or shivering because of the cold when Hell froze over. My sunburnt arms wrapped around my torso as I tried to keep myself warm against the coolness of the night. Such an extreme fluctuation in temperature is hard for the body to handle and made me moody. Oh, did I mention, I hate mirages."

* * * *

"I took several trips on Blade. Blade was the new term I coined for cutting. After all, the high a person gets is as addictive as a drug, as dangerous as a whore, and as cunning as a snake. It is also the cheapest and most accessible drug on planet Earth. One could hide it in the most obvious places and parents, friends, relatives, and siblings would have no idea that the most the obvious drug, something they may have used on paper, actually concealed the deepest, darkest secrets of a person."

* * * *

"This night was the darkest night I had ever walked through on my journey. The blackness was so heavy that even the stars and the moon would not show their faces. There was absolutely no light but I continued to trudge ahead. I figured the best way to fight the cold was to keep my body moving and the blood flowing. Cactuses and dried bones were the only things I would have to worry about running into. The rest of the land was flat with no holes, no hills, no trees, no nothing except emptiness, and now, much to my dismay, pure, undefiled blackness. But then I saw a dim beam of light. Because of the darkness I could not judge its distance but I reached out my dried hand to try and grab it. I missed. Obviously the light was far away so I kept my eyes on the light and continued to move forward. I remember reading about the story of wise men and how they had followed a star to find where the Savior had been born. However, they had the benefit of a compass and multiple brains and all I had was a single beam of light. I still followed and hoped that my journey would end like the wise men's did by rejoicing and worshipping their beautiful Savior. I hoped to be able to rejoice at the end of my journey but the light was still so far away and I had many miles to cover before I would even get close. The light stayed in the same place the entire time. Not once did it move, not once did it blink, not once did it disappear. It was a light that would guide me home. Or so I thought.

"I do not know how long I walked for. It felt like I was walking forever but when I finally reached the source of the light it felt as though I had not been walking for very long at all. The source of the light was a house. I knew this for the light that illuminated an upstairs bedroom provided enough light for me see the outline of the small house. I remember very little of what the house looked like for I was not concerned with its decor. Rather, I headed straight for the door and gave it an exhausted knock."

* * * *

"Blade is a drug one takes after one has thoroughly thought through the situation and the implications of the decision. Or it is an impulsive decision and once commenced, the drug only takes a matter of seconds to work its magic. As impulsive as it is, often it is a planned event. The exact time of day, the exact circumstance, the exact emotion, the exact length, the exact depth, the exact number of red, runny lines; it becomes a subconscious habit. The tools have to be the same for it is hard to reach the same high if one does not use the same source over and over again. The familiarity makes it more stimulating and allows for one to enjoy the pleasurable experience to a greater degree. However, whatever the tool used, the high is still the same pleasurable, frightening, beautiful, horrifying experience."

* * * *

"'Greetings,' came a voice as the door swung open. The voice sounded as though I had been expected, that my visit was not a surprise. 'To whom do I owe the pleasure of the company of such a wayward stranger as yourself?'

"From the exhaustion, my voice stammered, 'Do... do... do you have... have... s-s-s-some water?' My breathing was heavy and I could barely stand. I leaned against the entrance of the door so I did not collapse on the stranger's porch floor.

"'My boy, we have plenty of water. Whoever drinks of the water that I will give him will never be thirsty again. The water that I will give him will become in him a spring of water welling up to eternal life. Come on into our humble abode and make yourself at home. I'll have you know, upstairs we have a bed prepared for your tired, aching body. Here, have a seat on the sofa as I go and fetch some cold water from the tap. You have had a long journey, Tucker. Go on now, sit.'

"'Th-th-th-ank you,' was the only words I had the strength to utter. I gently lowered my aching body onto the soft, cool sofa. My feet rejoiced at not having to carry the burden of my body as my burning lungs were able to regain a regular rhythmic breathing pattern. While my host was gone, I tried to keep my head straight and eyes alert but they kept collapsing under the weight of exhaustion. I kept twitching to keep myself awake and not be rude to my host. Out of the kitchen glided a granny who was bent over leaning on a cane made of an oak branch. She was dressed in a pink dress and had her hair done up in a cute bun. Glasses hung half way down her nose. She actually looked like a doll. The rest is a blur and I cannot accurately recount the rest of her features. All I remember was she was a petite little thing, which could not harm a house fly.

"'Here you are my boy. The coolest, crispest, most refreshing glass of water you have ever tasted. Enjoy its invigorating taste as I go and tend to some other business. I will be back in a moment.' There were the sound of words but the granny's mouth did not move. I blamed it on my exhaustion, lack of sleep, and possibly another stupid mirage. After she had said this, the granny turned on a 180-degree angle and glided out of the living room. I lifted the clear glass to my mouth and took a sip of the water. Indeed! It was the most glorious tasting water I had ever had the pleasure of indulging in. The pure taste refreshed my dried bones, rejuvenated my decaying mind, and gave me the coveted spirit of relaxation. Granny was gone for a couple of minutes (at least that is what it felt like) and soon came gliding back into the living room. "'Okay,' she said, 'I just went and started a warm bath for you. I put some natural minerals and salts in the water to soothe your muscles. I sincerely hope it in some way relieves the tension you are experiencing. Some candles are lit to give the room a relaxing atmosphere and I opened the window to allow the fresh smell of rain to enter the room. Come, follow me for I will give you rest.'

"'I shouldn't. I must continue on my way. It is rather rude of me to intrude on your household so late at night so I must be going. You have gone above and beyond what is expected and for that I thank you. But I must be going now,' I said as I peeled myself off of the couch. My head spun when I reached my feet and I reached for the couch arm to stabilize myself. I slowly walked to the door and opened it. Turning to the granny I once again said, 'Thank you so much for your hospitality.'

"Her mouth never moved but she said, 'You are most welcome my boy. I do not know where you are going or who is expecting you, but I hope you find your way back. Just know if you change your mind you are always welcome in my home. Good-bye Tucker.' She never even reached for the door and it slowly began to close. As the door was closing, I had the sudden thought, 'What do I have to get back to? Who is expecting me? Who is waiting for me? I have no idea where I am going! There will be no one waiting when I get to where ever I am going.' I decided to stay. 'Wait! Granny!' The door swung open and she was standing there with a towel.

"'That did not take you very long to change your mind but I am glad you decided to stay. Come Tucker, I just warmed up the bath water.' Granny glided up the steps like they were a flat surface and I painfully dragged my tired body over the giant steps. A bath, a warm bed, breakfast in the morning - Why would I even have thought of leaving?"

* * * *

"I discovered Blade in the top drawer of my desk, in the bathroom with my other personal hygiene, or in a public place where no one would expect to find it. Sometimes I would even let the blood stained scissors sit on my desk and no one would ever notice. If they noticed I would not be offended, in a way it was me calling out for help. The scissors worked pretty well but they had to be sharp or else they would not create the high I craved. One of the benefits of scissors is that it has a nice handle. Razor blades, I soon discovered, were the best way to get high. Ripping of the guards made for a nasty sharp edge and not much pressure had to be applied for a lovely red line to run. They are trickier though because they are so small and hard to hold. And, because they are so sharp, one has to be careful not to apply to much pressure or else a vein could be punctured very easily. Probably the most satisfying Blade was a sharp scraper I found in a public washroom. The edges were a bit rusty but sharp enough to cause blood but dull enough to have to apply pressure. This was probably my most used tool even though it was in a public place. There is something terribly satisfying about cutting with the chance of someone walking in and disturbing you (actually they would be the ones disturbed). Also, knowing that an innocent hand touched the handle as they cleaned caused a sadistic pleasure inside of me. These were three of my favorite tools."

* * * *

"The bath was indeed a grand and glorious occasion. Warm water massaged my aching muscles, the dim lighting calmed my jittery nerves, and the smell of fresh flowers shifted my mind into neutral. There was a cage full of canaries who sang their melodious songs as I tilted my head back and took a deep, relaxed breath which was the first I had taken in a very, very long time. I stayed in the bathtub for a solid thirty minutes and when I got out I looked like a raisin. My dry, muddy skin had been cleansed and had been replaced with the wonderful sight of shiny skin and wrinkles from being submersed in the water to long. I pinched my skin to see if it would keep form but it collapsed into its nature place. The bath was nice but I waited with anticipation at the thought of being able to climb into a soft bed and get a solid sleep. Sleep had been scarce on the journey because of the unknown surroundings but there was something about this house, which relaxed my spirits and I could tell I was going to have a wonderful sleep.

"I stepped out of the bathroom and was greeted with the wonderful scent of freshly baked buns. Suddenly I remembered how long it had been since the last time I had eaten. I followed the scent to the kitchen and got there just as the granny was closing the oven door. 'How was your bath Tucker?' she asked without even turning around.

"'It was absolutely wonderful! Thank you.'

"'I imagine a young man like you must be hungry after such a long day's journey. So, I made your favorite meal: fresh buns with meat and cheese. Also, there is a cup of warm milk steaming right there and I even put a teaspoon of honey in it just the way you like it. I just hope I did not forget anything.'

"'Wow! This looks wonderful!' I took as seat behind the cup of steaming milk and breathed in the wonderful aromas of the kitchen.

"'If you will excuse me for a moment, I must go downstairs and change the load of laundry. After you are done eating, I will take you to your room.'

"Granny glided off and I was left to myself. I absolutely loved fresh buns. Some of my favorite memories of home were when Mom had just finished baking a pan of fresh buns and I would take the one in the middle while they were still steaming hot. I would tear off the bottom, take my knife and spread about the butter until it melted into the fluffy white bread. I laughed at the memory. My mom was a pretty good cook but when she attempted to cook with brown flour, everything seemed to not taste as good. Her brown buns were as hard as hockey pucks, the brown bread was as flat and heavy as a brick, and the brown cinnamon buns were just plain gross. There are a few things in life a person cannot substitute and one of those things is brown flour for white flour. The meat tasted a lot different than what I was used to. It actually tasted civilized but was still very delicious. I polished off three meat sandwiches and, just as I took my last swallow of the warm milk, Granny returned.

"'How was your night snack, Tucker?'

"'It was absolutely delicious. Thank you so much!'

"'It is my pleasure. Now, let me show you where you will be spending the night.'

"We left the kitchen, went down the hallway, and my room was the last door on the right. Granny opened the door to the cutest bedroom I had ever seen. There was a queen-sized bed, an oak dresser, a full body mirror, a beautiful patio window which opened to a veranda, and a 12 inch antique television with old fashioned knobs and wooden trim. Even the remote was antique.

"'This will be your room for the night. I hope it meets your expectations. If not, just ring this bell and I will bring you whatever you desire.' With that, she turned and glided out the door, which closed softly behind her. As nice of woman as Granny was, there was something extremely odd about her but who was I to judge someone especially when they rolled out the red carpet for a complete stranger. I would enjoy the hospitality until morning when I could continue on my journey to wherever I was going to meet whoever was going to be there. Climbing into the bed I was greeted with the smell of freshly washed sheets and blankets. They must have been air dried for they smelled fresh and clean. I nestled into the mattress and buried myself in the covers. It was going to be a good night. My eyes began to close, my breathing was slowed to a rhythmic inhale/exhale and I began to fall asleep.

"Just as I was about to enter a state of unconsciousness, I heard a knock on the door and Granny entered the room. "'Tucker,' Granny said, her mouth still not moving, 'can you spare a moment and come give a poor woman a hand?'

* * * *

"Addicts use Blade for a variety of different reasons, but often it is used as a coping mechanism. There is a deep pain inside of oneself, which has no way of expressing itself. Sometimes people will first try writing as a way to express the pain but often this just makes them more confused. The pen becomes a way to vent their hatred for the world, for people, for God but mostly for themselves. Often this is the greatest reason for one to use Blade: Hating oneself. When a person hates himself, he feels as though he needs to punish himself for who he is, what he does, and for failing those around him. All this hate leads to rejection whether perceived or real. Clearly there is rejection from oneself, there may be rejection from friends and family, and one may even feel as though he has been rejected by God Himself. Because of the deep, inexpressible pain this causes, a person will start to use different coping mechanisms. It might first start with ignoring the pain. Usually this is the easiest and most comfortable form of coping. No one can see that there is pain because it is buried under five feet of fake smiles. Once this does not work, one begins to try to forget about the pain by living in an imaginary world or by pretending like he does not care. This is extremely dangerous, for the imaginary world fails to meet important emotional, physical, and spiritual needs and an "I don't care" attitude, leads to one simply deceiving himself. One obviously does care if he is trying to cover the pain so no one else can see it. These two factors usually lead to the climax, which is experimenting with Blade.

"Usually, one does not know why one chooses to use Blade. Most of the time they themselves do not know the logic behind their decision. Ultimately, they want to harm themselves as a way of expressing deep pain but also to hopefully somehow get rid of it. The use of Blade is usually done on one area of the body and the area usually feels most natural to the person. There usually is not any logic except to hide it from others or let others see. If it is hidden, then it shows the person feels a great amount of shame. Blade use can most often be found on the upper thigh (usually inside the leg), on the torso (even the breasts for girls), or on the feet. The covering is symbolic of great shame and the mentality of not wanting to deal with the pain in a vulnerable way. However, once blade is applied to the wrist or forearm a different story is beginning to be told. Both of these areas are hard to hide. Often a Blade user will not be upfront about his drug use but scabs, scars, and straight cuts clearly scream that he is need of help.

"Blade users cut for a variety of different reasons but I will name five, which I have discovered. First is because of a deep sense of pain, which usually tends to be emotional but can be fueled by a physical ailment. The feeling of rejection by those they respect or love is the second reason people choose to use Blade. Thirdly, one uses Blade because one hates oneself for who one has been created to be (personality, interests, talents, etc.). Fourth, it is used as a method of punishing oneself for making a bad decision or for simply being who one has been created to be. The fifth and final reason is because one does not feel connected to anything because everything seems to have denied one access.

* * * *

"'Tucker,' Granny said, her mouth still not moving, "can you spare a moment and come give a poor woman a hand?"

"I did not really want to but considering the amount of hospitality she had shown me I figured I owed her a helping hand. 'Sure,' I said as I climbed out of bed.

"'Thank you. Thank you so very much.' She turned and glided out the door. 'Come, follow me. Something appears to crawling around in my toolshed out back. Will you go and check what it is? There has been a stray cat running around and it has been in my shed before. It climbs through a hole in the roof and then let's itself drop right onto the cage. Thankfully, last time this happened my son was home and managed to scare it away before it got into the cage. For years, that ridiculous cat has had a peculiar habit of wanting to kill my canaries. I keep most of my canaries in a giant cage in the shed because my house is not big enough to contain them all. Tucker, I really do not want that cat killing off my canaries.'

"'Don't worry Granny. I'll go scare the cat off.' My eyes were droopy, my body ached, but I would try my best.

"'Oh, thank you Tucker! Thank you so much! See you soon dear,' she waved as I walked out the back door.

"I always hated cats so it was not a problem for me to go and scare the little rascal. Once I had a cat but it got ran over by a car and I found it on the side of the road squished like a pancake. After that cat, I got another one but it got its throat ripped open somehow and then got stuck in a grain auger and was ground to pieces. Loving cats no longer came easily. Every time I see a pathetic cat and its equally pathetic owner cuddling together I get so angry. I am reminded of all the good times I had with my cats and all the good times I could have had with them except Mother Nature, or God, would not allow it. If I had to murder the cat I would. I would feel little remorse and I would bask in watching the cat breathe its last. If my cats had to endure death then so did the rest of the wretched species. My anger was probably an issue of jealousy rather than an issue of hatred for stupid cats. However, I was also slightly upset at this minor disturbance in my relaxing night but I would never be able to sleep if I did not scare away this stupid cat.

"The path to the toolshed was completely illuminated, which made walking there relatively easy. I still had to mind the occasional shadow, which was produced by the surrounding trees, but I soon discovered I had nothing to fear. I reached the toolshed door and it swung open. 'Weird,' I thought to myself. I stepped into the shed and reached for the string, which turned on the light. Granny had said it was just to the right when I came in. My hands groped in the darkness and soon I felt the fuzzy string fall into my hands. Pulling the string, the bulb flashed on and revealed the horror of the toolshed.

"There were canaries but they were all hanging from the ceiling by thin threads of strings. Their little tongues hanging out of their silent beaks. However, there was no cage, and most importantly there was no stupid, godforsaken cat. Before me was an empty wooden table, which had chains in place for the hands, torso, and feet of a human being. The table just sat there unoccupied with a single bulb dangling above it. It sat like an electric chair waiting for its next victim. Also, like the electric chair, which would always thirst for another life, I could tell that the chains on the table were hungry for more of whatever was massacred on it. Dark stains of blood were on the table and there was the occasional splatter on the floor. As horrifying as this was, it was not the part that disturbed me the most. Through the dim light of the single bulb, I could see a mechanical creature behind the table. I could only see its backside but it soon turned around and I could see who I had intruded on. It looked like a mechanical spider with the decapitated head of a doll. The face was missing a huge black eye. The eyelid of the one remaining moved up and down like a child fascinated by the strings on a curtain. It was a menacing eye, which, even though expressionless, spoke a thousand words of hatred. Huge spots of baldness had invaded the blonde hair, which now hung in thin, wild strands. The consistent smile revealed painted teeth and created craters in the sides of the cheeks. This head was stabbed on to a piece of metal, which I assumed was the neck. The head wobbled on the neck but never fell off. It just moved in lazy, menacing motions. This neck was then attached to the core of the body, which had eight appendages like a spider. They were metal and were held together by nuts and bolts and a crappy welding job. They were robotic and had the ability to move up and down, back and forth without any hesitation. As hands, there were scissors, needles, and a spool of thread, a chainsaw, a butcher's knife, clamps, a hammer, and a skinning knife. Each of these tools were rusty and had bloodstains on them. The thing spoke, 'You know Tucker, cats are stupid animals but this has clearly revealed who the stupidest creature is of all is, has it not?' It was Granny's voice.

"I screamed and tried to rip open the shut door but it was bolted closed. The spider thing glided towards me just how I had seen Granny glide through the house. It lifted its metallic arms in the air and the clamp began to snap open and closed as if teasing me. The arms shot forward and the clamp grabbed me by the neck and lifted me up. There was not a sound except for me gasping for air and the mechanical sounds of the moving arm. The arm lifted me high up into the air and then slammed me down on the table where the chains involuntarily tightened around my arms, my torso, and my legs. As I lay there all I could see was the horrible face. What a horrible, ugly face that could not be described in a thousand pages. There were signs of abuse, there were signs of beatings; half of her face was squished in. I lay there chained to the table screaming at the top of my lungs. No one would hear me, I knew that but there was a sense of peace in such and the desperate act of screaming and cussing.

"Vroom, vroom, vroom - It was the sound of the chainsaw being revved. 'You're pathetic, Tucker Wilson, a pathetic piece of God's crap. You know what, Tucker? I love the sound of your screaming, I love the way you enunciate and pronounce your curses. They are so emphatic and dripping with emotion. You know what else I love, Tucker? I love the smell of fresh blood; I love the sound of metal cutting through bone, and most of all I like to know I have killed a boy. Boys are much easier to kill than men. Actually, I have never killed a man but I have killed plenty of boys, including my son.' It lifted the saw and was about to plow through my left arm but Granny stopped and looked at me and thoughtfully and said, 'You know that meat you ate, Tucker?' It was a rhetorical question, or at least that was how I interpreted it. 'It was your induction into the small clique of cannibals this world so angrily despises. You are a little skinny but might I say you will be good for the boys who like to watch their weight.' Vroom, vroom. Vvvrrrrrrrroom."

* * * *

"What I am talking about is not something the average person can understand. For most people Blade is something so mysterious, so morbid, and so disturbing that they wish to have no association with the drug or its addicts. They are scared because it shatters their box of what they assume to be a safe world. It takes courage for an inexperienced person to associate with the experienced. It is not something that is easily done but is crucial to the wellbeing of the addict. If everyone chooses to run then they are simply giving an addict more ammo to use Blade. Often addicts feel trapped, betrayed, locked behind bars. Every time they are just about to escape another inexperienced person comes along and makes the situation more difficult, harder, and more meaningless.

Often this is not done purposefully. Sometimes, an addict just wants to sur-render to the sound of the chainsaw for in it there is the potential for relief.

"This may not make sense and if it does not I understand. It takes an ex-perience with Blade to know exactly what I am talking about. It is something a thousand words or a thousand pages could never describe."

* * * *

"Vroom, vroom. Vvvrrrrrrrroom. Suddenly the high was wearing off and I could feel myself getting closer to rock bottom. It had been a pleasurable ex-perience but these dang hallucinations were starting to scare me. What made me think of such bizarre creatures, twisted stories, and morbid endings? Needless to say, my mind was stuck in neutral but that usually comes after I have climbed such a high ladder. I sat down and reflected on the hallucination I had just had. It made sense... kind of... but in a very twisted way. It helped me realize something, which I could not express in words. I was lost I knew that. I was pathetic but I knew that. I was God's crap and I believed that but maybe, just maybe in the morbidity of my hallucination I had indeed found a light to follow."

Even God Deserves A Second Chance

Life is a nightmare
haunted by ghosts carrying flowers in their hands
planted by liars in this barren land.
The moon, the sun in this drama,
blood red piercing the morning sky
carried by the wind whispers of love.
The calm breeds chaos;
skeletons cut off limb after limb after limb:
"I'm alright! I'm fine!" (please help!).
"You're alright you're okay:" life is a fairytale.
No one hears,
no one cares,
life is a nightmare: the ghost, the witch they come for me;
the wind, the calm never seem to be.

Suppose,
life was a child buying flowers
from the peddler on the street corner,
a penny is all it is worth.
The scream, the cry in this drama
penetrate the black night
carried by whispers of love
a ghost riding.
Smiles draw tear after tear after tear:
"I'm alright! I'm fine!" (please help!)
"You're alright you're okay:" life is a fairytale.
No one loves,
no one sees.

life is a nightmare: the smile, the hugs they come for me,
The scream, the cry they come from me,
the deaf and dumb let it be,
the blind turn and see.
My love slowly answered, "I think so"
but i think i see something else
on the horizon: a cross.
Maybe all is not for loss.

What Is Truth?

"'So,' began the good Doctor, 'tell me about your social life up to this point.'

"I felt like being difficult so I replied, 'Well Doctor, I haven't had a social life for the last while because I have been locked behind bars.'

"Don't be so smart, Tucker. Just answer the question!" For the last couple sessions I had noticed the Doctor's temper was becoming shorter and shorter, like a burning fuse on a bomb. There must have been something going on in his life too.

"Okay, well going to large social gatherings or other public events such as concerts, fundraisers, or banquets were never something I enjoyed. I never was one to enjoy large crowds of people all jammed into a confined area where there is little to no air left to breath. All I could breathe was the atrocious scent of body odor on large hairy men and the powerful smell of perfume on women who thought the world revolved around them. However, I did like to hear the laugher of people having a good time and the smiles that were produced when one was in the midst of pleasurable company. Then, of course, there were those flirty, loud, flamboyant people who try to attract attention to themselves by either commanding the conversation, being very cynical, cracking dumb jokes or wearing shirts that revealed cleavage. I always laughed at these types of people. They were always so naive and ignorant; the world to them was but a place where they could proclaim the uniqueness of their "pleasant" personalities. If they really knew what life had in store for them then they would retreat to a corner and shake like a leaf or try to run away like a scared mouse. Reality was yet to hit such people or they simply were choosing to ignore the reality by losing themselves in the dangerous game of relationships. But in the end, this was the reality they had chosen to create. I remember I always used to try and loose myself in relationships but the only way I could do so was by pretending I was somebody I was not, by pretending everything was okay and everything was as it seems. My home life had been defined by me simply behaving in ways, which would give me the approval of men. Quite frankly, I hated people. I hated them with a passion and desired to form no intimate relationship with any one of them. However, once I did go to church."

"Church! You said it yourself that you hated people so what possessed you to go to church? Isn't that the breeding ground for hypocrites? The place where masks are most prevalent? The last church I went to closed because people were not willing to put the needs of others above their own and forgive the wrong of others. I hate church." It seemed like I had hit a sore spot on Mr. Cruse's heart.

"Yes that is correct and I have the same attitude towards it as you do. I hate it immensely. That is why I was confused about why I wanted to go to church. But Doctor, I never went to church for the people, I went to church to discover a path of freedom which I was trying to make on my own but was having a terribly hard time creating."

"So you hoped God could set you free? But you are god, why would you even think that there was a God of the Bible?" Oh, that doctor was a bright fellow (I say that with sarcasm).

"Quite frankly, I had come to the end of myself. Being god was not what it was cut out to be and I needed something real, something tangible, something, which could actually give me the freedom I so desperately wanted. However, I was skeptical about going to church for a variety of different reasons. Mainly because I was afraid of being judged for whom I was as a person, where I lived, and the struggles I was in the midst of facing. Especially since my body was covered in cuts."

"Ok. So tell me of your experience," Dr. Cruse said as he grabbed his pen and notepad, ready to take notes on what I was about to say. I was beginning to view Doctor Cruse as a pathetic man who was covering up a major lie. There was something about him, which made me highly uncomfortable and I was not sure how much longer I was going to be able to tolerate him. I was already charged with two accounts of first-degree murder; why not add another charge? It was a good thing I was in the straightjacket or else he may not have survived. Actually, he didn't survive when I was through with him but I'll save that story for later. Right now, I was in the middle of telling Dr. Cruse my thoughts and opinions on church and the reasons why I wanted to go to a religious service were there are more masks than a bandit's wardrobe.

"Church had been a place where I had not been ever since I moved to the shack and, to be quite frank, I did not miss it a single bit. Actually, even the times when I was at church I really was not there but instead I was absentmindedly sitting there thinking about what was for lunch or how much longer the sermon would drag on for. Sometimes the preacher just seemed to babble on and on as if he was not trying to present a message but rather reveal the depths of intelligence he had. I hated preachers like that. Also, I did not miss all the prissy people who pranced around with the oversized Bible they packed along Sunday mornings. Actually, I saw more breast than I did Bible. It was quite a pathetic set of circumstances, which, upon looking back, was very sad. I remember the congregation would come with hair combed, clothes freshly pressed, and a beautiful smile, which told the world that they loved Jesus and had no struggles in life. They were perfect little angels whose works revealed their faith, or so they thought. Most of the time it actually revealed their lack of faith.

"Oh, and I did not miss the monotone singing, which was led by an expressionless song leader who thought she could sing but never was able to hit the right note. The song leader was probably up there simply because she had been doing it for the past forty years and it had become a tradition, which could not be over ruled no matter how frail she became. She could have her mouth stitched shut and she would insist on being up there. "Listen to me!" she would say in a high pitched squeal, "I have been up there singing for the past forty years and you ain't gonna taking me off the stage. Its tradition ya know and that must never be broken. It's bad enough we have silly young people playing the Devil's drums!" If it could not get more pathetic then that there always was the pianist, who was probably a moody wife of some board member, whose fingers stumbled over the keys and continually, played the wrong chords. I will be the first to say I am not much of a musician but I can easily tell when the wrong chord is played. It is like fingernails scraping a chalkboard. Did I mention I also hated the youth who acted one way at church and youth group but then an entirely different way during the week at school? They were disrespectful, rebellious creatures who were just doing time under their parents' roof but once the alarm rang they would be gone and they would never again enter the foyer or sanctuary of a church unless it was for a wedding or a funeral. Needless to say, I was not much different but instead of showing it, I kept it all hidden beneath the floorboards of my soul. Personally, I thought it was better to have a hypocritical heart rather than hypocritical actions. Actions others could see but the heart was concealed from sight. When I did go to church, I was like many of them but at the same time I was very much different. They seemed to not feel anything whereas I could feel everything and wanted to change but did not know how. Most of them did not want to change. But, then again, this was my reality and perhaps in theirs they saw me as a hypocritical, two-faced liar who had no right to even be a church mouse. Only God knew what their reality dictated to them.

"With all this in mind, I was greatly confused on why I was going to church, especially a small church where people would notice that I was a visitor and probably introduce themselves to me. I could just see them coming up to me, "Hi, I'm Harry.' Then I would replay with a false sense of enthusiasm (like I had done for the past fourteen years of my miserable life) and say, "Nice to meet you! I'm Tucker." I would then be quizzed on who my family was, where I lived, what I was doing, and any other question that comes when one continues to politely get to know somebody. At this point, I would continue to nod my head in agreement, ask questions like I pretended to care, lie, sound excited, and lie some more. Then once the service started Harry would go walking to the sanctuary, take a seat in the pew, feel relieved for fulfilling his godly duty, and then completely forget about me as the lousy song leader stood up to lead another off-key praise to God. I wonder if God is embarrassed when He hears such a racket. I know if these were my worshipers I would send holy fire down and burn them as sacrifices to atone for hearing loss. This was the first possible scenario. The second would be much better and quite likely the more probable. I would enter the church building and be camouflaged in the crowd. No one would even know I was there. I could sit in the back pew, suffer through the singing, then listen to the sermon and be gone before anyone even knew I was there. 'Yeah right!' I said to myself in complete doubt. If this is the kind of church I think it is then I'll be like a celebrity. Everyone will want to know who I am. If they don't, then they aren't really obeying God's commandment of love your neighbor as yourself. They will come talk to me, 99.9% sure of that. After all, they all wear their WWJD bracelets and that should remind them that Jesus hung out with tax collectors, whores, thieves, and liars. I'm a pretty bad guy but all my wretchedness is hidden deep within. They'll never see it and they will take me at my word. Unbeknownst to them, I would be Tucker Wilson, a seal of a coward.

* * * *

133

"DeMonte Community Church was what the large sign advertised. I hoped the sermon caption was not a reflection of the congregation for it said, 'A Lesson in Knitting'. I laughed. I could just see the pews being replaced with rickety old rocking chairs with a box of wool and needles resting beside. The whole congregation - both young and old - would be rocking back and forth as they went through their morning routine. Then the pastor would introduce a guest speaker which would be an aged woman from the local senior's center. In her croaky voice she would say a prayer of blessing, read the Word, and then explain the complexity of knitting and how it was a wonderful time of meditation. Then I would be surrounded by a bunch of meditating Christians who were actually thinking about lunch, how much longer the sermon would be, or who had come up with such a stupid and ridiculous sermon idea. I took a deep breath and sighed, 'It could be a long morning.' But I continued towards the entrance to the DeMonte Community Fellowship Church.

"The church was a small white building on Railroad Street East. Freshly cut grass and beautiful, colorful flowers gave the lawn an extremely civilized look. Red and yellow tulips sprouted from the dark dirt. God forbid if there be any weeds in the flower-bed! It was spotless of the little life squelching swine. God Himself probably came to earth and pulled the weeds Himself. I wonder if He even cares about the flower beds. Was He the One who gave them such a majestic beauty? In the end, I guess I should have expected it to be so well kept since the flowers were, in some way, a representation of the spirit of God's people. After all, if the flower beds were unkempt then that would reveal the lazy, uncaring heart of the congregation. Indeed it was human hands that made the lawn beautiful but they had created it with what God had provided. I wondered if the people took as good of care of their souls as they did the flower bed. Time would only tell. That time was becoming nearer and nearer as I walked the cement sidewalk to the entrance of the church building. Usually, at least in my limited experience and minute amount of knowledge, churches had a flight of concrete steps, which were covered by lousy looking carpet, that lead up to the doorway. As an offshoot, there would be wheelchair accessibility available for the elderly, the handicapped, and for the little kids to climb on. I liked how different this was. Instead of tripping up a flight of steps, one could simply walk straight into... the church."

"What am I doing here again?" I asked myself for the hundredth time. "This is no place for someone like me. I don't want this." And then I all was black and I saw the light, which was so very far away but I knew it was in my reach. "Right! It's time to give God a second chance." I took a deep, deep, deeeep breath and marched through the door.

"There was a certain part of me that hoped I would appear right on time so I could just swim into the sanctuary with the rest of the people and go unnoticed; just another fish in the pond. But there was an element of risk to trying to have perfect timing. If I was late then there would be the embarrassing moment when everyone turned to see who had the audacity to show up late for church. But when I saw the people still stewing around in the foyer I knew I was early. As soon as I entered, the smell of freshly brewed coffee filled my nostrils. It was such a foreign and delightful aroma! It had been so long since my brain had been stimulated with that smell. Dad always would make sure there was a freshly ground coffee brewing in the early morning, probably around 7 am, and he would bring a cup to my mom just as she was waking up. I never could figure out if he felt obligated to do so or genuinely desire to serve her a cup of coffee. Then there was that other odor, a rather unpleasant one, which upon taking a deeper breath, was filtered in with the coffee. I remember when I went to church there was always this smell. After everyone was gone it still lingered in the air and seemed to never leave until the next Sunday but then it would immediately be back. It was a smell that stained the skin, the nostril hairs, and the eyes. If you got close enough to the source of the smell then it would be on your clothes until the next wash. It was the smell of perfume; dead flies send forth a stinky aroma. It was the type of perfume that old, rich granny's, who still think they have style, bathe themselves in before going to a social event. Oh, how I did not miss that smell. If I needed an excuse to leave church would definitely ride the perfume until it carried me out the door to the safety of the aroma of freshly cut grass and beautiful flowers.

"'Hi! Welcome here!' it was a warm friendly voice, which full of unwavering confidence. I looked and saw some bald old man, who was probably the greeter, sticking out his trembling hand. Taking his hand, I tried to give it a confident shake. However, my attempt was in vain when I stuck my sweating palm into his aged hands. The squeeze he gave me was enough to cause me to bite my lip so I would not yelp in pain.

"'Thank you.' I replied, 'It is good to be here.' LIAR,

"'Well, I am glad you are here. Over there is some coffee if you would like some. I think there might even be a few donuts left.'

135

"'*Oh, I would love some!*'*LIAR*,

"Just then another elderly man came up to my new friend and greeted him. They gave each other a hearty handshake and I took this as my cue to exit the scene. Needless to say, I did not go into over to the coffee bar. My stomach was growling but filling it was not worth the risk of having to exchange a conversation with a complete stranger. Instead, I made my way to the sanctuary to find a seat and avoid all possibility of conversation. I attempted to give a warm handshake to the usher who handed out the bulletins but that turned out to be another failed attempt. He then gave me a pink bulletin and I entered the sanctuary to find myself a seat. I then remembered the slogan on the church sign and laughed at the thought of having to take a seat in a rocking chair. A rocker in church, which would be an experience I would never forget. But, as I expected, there were no rockers but instead there were cushioned benches lined in perfect symmetry. The backbench was still empty and I slid to the farthest, darkest corner where I hoped the shadows would somewhat conceal me so I could hang out with the church mouse. People began to file into the church and I found quite a bit of enjoyment watching them go to their seats like cows anticipating the evening milking. However, instead of giving milk, the congregation would be receiving it. I guess it depended on what the pastor decided to feed them.

"The boring, off tune singing: 'Why did I come?'

"Dang! I have to pee.

"The announcements no one paid attention to: 'Don't care.'

"Actually, if any of you care, I have to pee.

"The offering: 'All I can afford is moldy bread and sour milk. Pass on the plate and look like a cheapskate.'

"I think I felt a little dribble...

"Sharing and prayer time: 'Like I thought, no one is willing to share. All of them are thinking, 'Praise Jesus, the Lord Almighty, for He is good!' without even knowing why.'

'Pray that I don't pee my pants!'

"All I could remember from the service, besides the message, was the single fact that I had to pee.

"I hated the ritualism of church services, because it heightened the predictability. The part I had come for was the sermon and the rest of the service could go to Hell for all I cared. It seemed like forever, especially when I had to pee so badly, but finally the pastor was invited up to share the message. After a prayer of blessing on the service (I didn't pay attention because, remember, I had to pee really, really badly), the pastor began to preach. I remember very little of the details of the service other than the preacher and his sermon. He was an elderly man who stood about 6 ft. 1 in. with white hair that was combed over to cover the top of his bald head. Also, he had a white mustache, which twitched as he preached with passion, conviction and belief. I had left my Bible at home so I could not follow along but thankfully I had brought along my journal and I was able to take notes of the sermon."

"What was the sermon about? Do you remember?" asked Dr. Cruse.

* * * *

"'I hate church,' I said to myself in a bitter tone. 'Why am I even here?'

"Then the preacher opened his mouth and began to speak saying, 'Today, we will be looking at the 139th chapter of the book of Psalms. Specifically, verses thirteen and fourteen,' his voice boomed from behind the pulpit. He spoke with such a dramatic tone which was exaggerated and quickened by the exhales in the middle of the sentences and the very audible inhales. One might think this would be annoying but actually it worked as quite the opposite. He read the entire Scripture passage with the same amount of authority and vigor. Then he began, 'As we examine human life from a biblical perspective, we discover that human life has enormous significance. This chapter, Psalms 139, is my favorite passage because it displays how much God delights in His creation. The entire passage is an exhaustive poem conveying the depth of love God has for each person, the extent of God's knowledge of each individual, and His careful intention and involvement in the creation of each individual person. You have heard me read the entirety of this passage but for the purpose of this sermon, I specifically want to focus on verses 13 and 14 which say, "For you formed my inward parts; you knitted me together in my mother's womb. I praise you, for I am fearfully and wonderfully made. Wonderful are your works; my soul knows it very well."'

"I laughed. Several times I had read this specific passage but I never believed a single word of it. Actually, I told myself I never would. Maybe what the Bible is truth but it is not my truth. This is the truth for all the people in this room but as for myself, I am not included. God has taken so much from me it is obvious He does not love me. Love does not take away but rather it gives. That night when I was six years old is a perfect example. If I accepted

God's love then He would just end up hurting me because He hates who I am. 'Like God would really care about how you were created. If God really cared, why did He not take delight in who you are? Why does it feel like He was glaring down on you from His little perch in Heaven hating, despising, and hurting you?' the voices whispered in my ear.

"He continued, 'Humanism is the most prominent worldview. The humanist worldview brings a very sober, hopeless view on mankind. Mankind is now the measure of all things and his value has been reduced to a mere product of time and chance. We live in a humanist society and because of this there is no need to be interested in the individual but, instead, which the natural interests of humanism portrays, society and state. If, as according to the humanist worldview, we are indeed products of time and chance then there is nothing significant about our purpose. Our pure existence revolves around the theme of eat, drink and be merry for tomorrow we die. Mankind then becomes a mere social animal whose only purpose is to live for him and the betterment of society. The question then becomes, "If a person is not profitable to society then why should he live?" The elderly waste our tax dollars as they sit rotting away in their stalls hooked up to oxygen machines and wearing diapers. They, among the rest of the handicapped society, waste the diminishing resources of the world. Also, a baby who is handicapped either physically or mentally is also a great burden to the betterment of society and that is where abortion comes in. Abortion finishes the problem before it even starts. Handicapped people, as well as others who do not conform to society, hinder the fast-paced, busy, brainwashing aspect of a humanist society. Why not kill them? What is their purpose? Money, time, energy, and emotion are wasted on those who are not "normal" or "beneficial" to society's standards. Everything is self-existing; there is no Creator who is intrinsically involved in the process of creating life. Society ends up being the creator as it cuts and pastes people to fit, benefit, and increase the betterment of society. My friends, this is a sad painting of the modern mind towards life. We are, according to the predominant worldview, nothing more than social animals with no ultimate purpose outside of ourselves.'

"'We have lost the truth of who we are. Society attempts to define who we are and we become lost in the voices of those trying to tell us who we are. Entertainment attempts to define who we are by painting an unrealistic picture of what our lives should look like. Superficial friends try to pressure us to conform to their clique so we can be accepted and be considered cool. Our lives circulate around social networking which tell us that life is all about our-selves, that we are the center of the universe. Even our families can attempt to define who we are by telling us what they want us to do with our lives. They have a career chosen, they have a spouse chosen, they have your post-sec-ondary education paid for and now all you have to do is go along for the ride. Going along with all these voices is easy for it is exactly what we want to hear. However, does this path bring us to a place where our hearts are filled and we are confident in who we are? If our families, our friends, and all our material possessions disappeared would we still have confidence in ourselves? I would argue no because we have been defined by the things of this world which moth and rust destroy. So, the questions remains, how does a person discover the truth of who he is? We will look in the Bible for evidence of where we can dis-cover such truth. In John 15:6, Jesus Christ said, "I am the way, and the truth, and the life." In a world where truth has become relative, it is impossible for one to know what absolute truth is. However, Christ claims to be that abso-lute truth. If we look at the world through the lens of Jesus Christ and the Word of God then we can know what absolute truth is. Because of this, it is vitally important to have one's worldview based on the Scriptures. It is the only place where absolute truth can be found. In John 18:38, Pilate asks Jesus, What is truth? Though Christ does not answer Pilate, John 17:17 tells us what truth is, "Sanctify them in the truth; your word is truth." Therefore, if we want to know the truth of the value of human life and who we are we must go to God's Word, grab a shovel, and start digging.'

"I shuttered. This preacher knew what he was talking about and I felt as though he was talking directly to me.

"'Now let us look at Psalms 139:13, 14 again.' He read the passage again, carefully pronouncing and enunciating each individual word and filling his sentences with the occasional pause to let the words soak in. 'Though these verses are filled with so much truth, the single word that I want to focus on is "knit". Some of you may have laughed when you saw the catchphrase for the sermon today.' The preacher seemed to looking right at me again. Maybe this guy was God with his all-seeing eyes and thought reading abilities. 'You proba-bly imagined the sanctuary being filled with rickety rocking chairs and each chair having a basketful of yarn and needles. Then there would be an old granny up here showing you how to knit. Sorry to burst your bubble of antici-pation but rather than having a visual image let us use our imagination. Close your eyes and imagine with me a grandmother sitting on her veranda rocking back and forth in her wooden rocking chair. Beside her is an old golden retriever basking in the sun by her slippered feet. Her silver-trimmed, circular glasses hung low on the bridge of her nose as she is stooped focusing all her attention on the task at hand. In her wrinkled, feeble hands dance two long, grey needles maneuvering through the interlocking loops of wool. Every stitch is a deliberate, careful act, which produces a beautiful product. If a stitch slipped the grandmother does not continue. Rather, she stops backs up and reworks the needles so the threads run together in perfect harmony. Much time is spent carefully maneuvering the needles back and forth so something beautiful is created out of the ball of yarn. Blankets, slippers, sweaters, socks, dish clothes - These are only a few products birthed from the art of knitting.'

"'Figuratively speaking, God is like the knitting grandmother. Out of nothing He creates and forms us into something beautiful, something without any mistakes. Each one of us is a beautiful piece of God's handiwork and the person we are is to display His glory. At times, each one of us cannot help but wonder whether or not God was right in how He created us. We look at ourselves, all the horrible blemishes, personality flaws, and wonder where God went wrong. We ask God why He even bothered creating a mistake. However, the handiwork of God is so careful and deliberate that there is no mistake in His creation. Each stitch is made with careful and deliberate motions to ensure a tight weave; there are no loose strings.'

"'Do not say, "These truths may apply to some people but they do not apply to me. God just hates who He has created me to be." What I am speaking of is a universal truth which each one of needs to grab ahold of. Just imagine how one would feel if one replaced the fleeting identity of the world with the everlasting identity found in God's love! You could have confidence in every situation because of who you are in Christ and you can be joyful because you know God takes delight in who you are and loves the individual He has created."

* * * *

"The sermon had come to its completion and the pastor bowed his balding head and said a prayer of blessing on the congregation. As soon as the word amen resounded through the church, I stood up and headed for the door. During the prayer I slipped a Bible into my shirt. There was a deep desire in me to know more of what had just been preached. Now I especially did not want to be confronted by anybody else. I had already escaped one bullet and did not want to have to do it again. Much to my dismay, the pastor was already waiting at the door as the people excited by shaking his hand and telling him what a wonderful sermon he had preached. I mustered up one more smile, walked towards the exit, tried to squeeze through the crowd but then I saw a hand come out and the pastor's voice say, 'Thanks for coming.'

"'You're welcome,' I replied as I shook the pastor's warm hand. 'What a stupid way to respond,' I scolded myself as I stood there awkwardly trying my best to give a manly, confident handshake. I tried to say these words with confidence but I knew my voice sounded nervous and my eyes always averted his gaze because was afraid that if he looked into my eyes that God would give him the ability to read my soul like a barcode.

"I'll tell you one thing Doctor. The conversation with him was the most awkward time in my entire life. I tried acting calm, casual, and cool but there was just too much nervousness racing through my body that I was unable to."

"Did the preacher talk to you?" asked the Doctor.

"Oh yes. He asked, 'What's your name son?'

"'Um…' don't stall too long or he will know your lying, 'John Smith.' PANTS ON FIRE!

"'Nice to meet you John. My name is Randy Johansson but you can call me Pastor Randy. So, you just visiting in town?'

"'Yeah, sort of. Just passing through.' Not really a lie but pretty dang close. I was just passing through even though I had already been in the area for four weeks.

"'Do you have any plans for this evening?'

"I quickly went over my mental day planner. Nope, there was nothing on the agenda. 'No.'

"'Well then, tell you what, why don't you come over for supper tonight. My wife can cook a pretty mean meal,' he nudged me with his elbow and gave me a wink.

"'Um… sure, that sounds good.' I wanted to go but at the same time I did not want to go. My stomach was empty and a good home cooked meal would have the ability to reenergize my body and prepare me for the next week of starvation but I did not want to go because I would have to answer questions, a lot of personal questions.

"'Great! How does six o'clock sound?'

"'Perfect!' I masked the nervousness in my voice with enthusiasm.

"'Alright! We live in the little white house right beside the church. See you then!' He gave me another firm handshake as I turned to leave.

"'Yep!' was all I could say.

"Finally I was able to find my way to the door. I walked by a group of teens standing in a circle who were laughing hysterically at something. There was one guy who was in the center of it all and he was talking in a really loud voice for all to see and notice him. The guys laughed, the girls giggled, and one girl swatted him on the back of the shoulder in the flirtiest of fashion. Part of me wanted to go up and introduce myself to the group but then I remembered who I actually was. I was not John Smith. No, I was the little liar who is known as Tucker Wilson. What was I supposed to do? Go up to a group of seven young people and say, 'Hey guys, my name is John Smith. How are you guys today? Wanna see what I do to pass the time? Here, check out these red lines. I like to draw on my body with sharp knives. I don't even have to color for the lines are immediately filled in.' They might be polite and tolerate my presence but then when I left they would once again be left to their own peaceful world. A couple of the guys looked my way as I walked by with a look in their eye and an expression on their face that told me they wanted to come and introduce themselves to me but lacked the courage to do so. I think I saw the girl who was the clerk at the store. The glass doors were not very far away and within seconds I would be able to escape all the people. Besides, I did not have time to stand around and visit. I only had five hours to make up a really good story so the pastor would like me. I sighed. Five hours was more than enough time; it would drip by like frozen molasses. I decided that there was not much of a point returning to the shack. By the time I had made the two hour trek there I would just have to turn around and come right back. Then I would be all sweaty and gross, which would only make Pastor Randy regret he had invited me. So, for the next five hours I ventured through the streets of DeMonte, swung on the swings, and sat on a park bench as I mulled over what sort of story I was going to present to the Johansson family."

Written In Contrast

After three weeks of sleeping on the thin foam mattress on top of the metal springs, my body was beginning to complain. It was not the most comfortable bed I had ever slept in but it was better than the cold cement floor of the cell. My cell was probably 12-by-12 with a portable toilet where I pissed and a sink where I washed my hands and brushed my teeth. Other than that it was a completely naked room, not even a window to allow the warm sun to enter. Usually the lights went out at 10 pm and then I would lay there in the dark and think. Just think.

The sessions with Doctor Cruse were going well, so I thought. I always like the talks he and I have. I feel enlightened on my life every time he and I discuss what is going on in my screwed up mind. Just by being able to tell him the mess of my mind has really made my life a whole lot more understandable. Even though he knows almost everything about me, I still do not feel comfortable sharing everything with him because there was something about him which caused me to put a wall up. I think it was because Brian Cruse was everything I wanted to be. He was a clinical psychologist who probably made quite a bit of money, especially if he had to put up with crazies such as myself. I had seen a picture of his wife on his desk when I first started going for sessions. She was a beautiful woman whose eyes were full of joy and energy. However, in the last couple sessions I have noticed that the picture is no longer there. On his walls hung diplomas of different academic achievements he had won. And he had books, tons of tons of books, which made me jealous, because I absolutely love reading. He had confidence, I had none. He had a beautiful wife and the woman I loved I murdered. He was smart and my mind was a mess. Yes, sir, he was a the epitome of what I would like to accomplish, but there was also a nagging sense somewhere in the back of my mind, which told me things were falling apart in his perfect little world. I don't know what I would rather have: A world already falling apart or a world which was on the brink of destruction. Mine was already fallen apart but I would rather have an imperfect world than a perfect one. Perfection is non-existent.

* * * *

143

I now know that even when one tries to make others perceive perfection, he will fall. Brian Cruse did and he was the type of person everyone looked up to and respected. Killing Brian Cruse was the most wonderful and beautiful thing I had ever done, even though it was the hardest thing to admit who I really was.

* * * *

It had been four days since I discovered the condom package, the warm bath my wife never had, and the terrifying truth that I had failed miserably. The breath of my wife was steady and relaxed but that night I could not catch a moment of sleep. Sleep was running like a fox whose tail was caught on fire. My mind was bothered by the actions of my wife but that was not what was ultimately keeping me awake that night. My mind was on Tucker Wilson. It may seem hard to believe but I was jealous of him. There was something about the pure ugliness, the wretched, obvious sin and the horrifying truth of who he was. He was not afraid to show who he was. Tucker wore his heart on his sleeve and was willing to admit the mistakes he had made. But I, Brian Cruse, was ashamed to show, even my wife, who I really was. I knew if I did she would reject me. Now, as I look at my secure world, which is now falling away, I do not have anything to lose. My reputation would be lost; I would lose my job, go to trial, and ultimately be sentenced to life behind bars. Was such a loss worth showing who I truly was?

I then thought about the camping trip Adelaide and I were going to go on. For obvious reasons, I did not want to go anymore. It would be awkward cuddling in our two person tent, talking late into the night, and kissing her lips. For some time I laid there trying to think of what would be the best course of action. We would be alone in the woods, just her and me and Mother Nature. There would be a lot of time spent together and there would be the potential to confront her about what she had done. I would tell her the evidence and see if my assumptions were wrong. Looking back, I never even gave myself the chance to repent but as I lay on top of her naked body I told her what I knew and did what the voice told me to do. It had to be done I did not have a choice.

I now know that it was worth losing it all in order to gain the freedom I have found. Killing Brian Cruse was the wonderful and beautiful thing I had ever done even though it was the hardest thing to admit who I really was.

* * * *

Confused,

I

am

so

terribly

confused.

A Little More Of This, A Little More of That

"So Tucker, tell me about the Johansson's." I once again found myself in Doctor Cruse's office. The picture of his wife was still gone and there was a mound of paperwork to be done on his desk. His eyes had huge bags underneath them and he seemed distracted and lacked the patience he had first had when we had started.

"Doctor, is everything ok?" I asked.

He did not reply. Mr. Curse just lowered his head and stared at the floor. I could not tell if he was seething in anger or about to cry. Regardless, his shoulders hung defeated by the burden he bore.

Looking up at me with so distant, so lost, so confused eyes he replied, "Yes. Everything is fine. Now tell me about the Johansson's." Even the tone of his voice sounded defeated and lost. Usually he would get mad at me if I asked such personal questions but that day he answered and told me a lie. As I sat there I remember thinking, "The floorboards are coming undone."

"Ok. Well, six o'clock had come and I found myself standing outside of Pastor Randy's house. A white picket fence protected the cute little house from any unwelcome visitors. In front of the fence was a very well taken care of flower-bed. It was neat and orderly with a wide range of vibrant colors. The yard was not very big either, which was practical for an elderly couple like the Johansson's. I rang the doorbell and waited. A chipper elderly woman came to the door and greeted me, 'Welcome! You must be John Smith. I am Florence. Come on in! Randy,' she yelled over her shoulder, 'Our company is here.'

"Then came the balding pastor who stuck out his hand giving me another firm handshake and a warm smile, 'John! Hey, good to see you again! Come on into the living room and make yourself at home. The women should be done cooking the food within a matter of minutes.'

"I never really heard what Pastor Randy said for my attention was completely focused on a couple of guitars hanging from the wall. 'You play?' I asked.

"'Not as much as I would like to but I used to play quite a bit. I led a worship band in church but then arthritis settled into my fingers and now it hurts too much to play. There were some good times playing with all my buddies. I certainly do miss them. Do you play at all?'

"'Yeah, I love playing but I haven't played for a while.' I rubbed the neck of an electric guitar.

"Pastor Randy reached up and took one of the acoustic guitars off the wall and held it out to me. 'Here, why don't you play us a tune?'

"I blushed and stammered, 'Well... um... I'm actually not that good. I just like to mess around and make my own stuff up.' I took the guitar from his hands a strummed a couple chords. 'Wow! This has a very nice sound.'

"'Yes, it's my favorite guitar. Actually, my wife bought it for me as a fortieth wedding anniversary present. Hand crafted in California.' He laughed, 'I named her Victoria. So what kind of stuff do you write?'

"'I try writing songs but I've actually never finished one. I always come up with random riffs, which I can never form into an actual song. I cannot keep a steady beat worth my life but it doesn't matter that much. I'm much more of a lyricist than musician anyways.'

"'You write lyrics?' the preacher perked up with interest.

"'Yeah. I try to anyways. I'm not very good at it either but I enjoy playing with words, ideas, and themes by putting them into a poem or story.' My stale fingers stumbled over the strings as I tried to recollect the songs I had written in the past. They were slowly beginning to come back to me but I did not have the same dexterity and strength as I did before.

"Mrs. Johansson popped her head into the living room and announced, 'Suppertime!'

"We left the living room and made our way to the kitchen. It was down a short hall which, when turning to the right, led into the cozy kitchen and dining room. The walls were painted a light yellow and the cupboards were a brilliant white. This set a very cheery mood in the room. The oak table was garnished in a white tablecloth. On the center of the table was a huge platter of turkey. Around that platter was a bowl of mashed potatoes, stuffing, Jell-O and cooked corn. It seemed like a regular Thanksgiving meal.

"'Wow!' I exclaimed, 'This looks excellent.'

"'Like I said, my wife is the greatest cook on the planet,' and he gave his wife a peck on her wrinkled cheek.

"'Mari just went down to grab some napkins. She should be back in a moment. But until then have a seat and make yourselves comfortable.'

"'Mari is our granddaughter,' informed Pastor Randy. 'She has been living with us for several years now.'

"We had just taken our seats when Mari entered the kitchen with the napkins. 'Here you are Grandma!'

"'Mari, this is the young man who visited our church today. John meet Mari, Mari meet John.'

"I gave a slight nod of the head and replied, 'Nice to meet you.'

"'Nice to meet you too.' Mari nodded with a cute, knowing smile. Indeed, Mari was the clerk at the grocery store and the girl in the crowd of young people at church. Dang!

"I awkwardly smiled back and looked down at my plate. She knew too much about me already. Not many people would forget a young man who went to a grocery store and bought all the outdated products. When I first saw her, I would have never guessed she lived with to elderly people who had spent the last thirty years in ministry. She did not seem like the stereotypical pastor's granddaughter. She had a hoop in her nose and I could tell by the movements of her mouth, though very subtle, there was a piercing on her tongue. Tight pants and a blank white V-neck shirt seemed a little of place for a girl who, at least when I saw her at church, would have conformed to all the accessories and latest fashionable things her friends were wearing. Mari took the seat across from me and we bowed our heads to pray. Pastor Randy thanked God for all His provisions, for the time we could have together, and for the food. He even thanked God that I had come to visit. When he said my name I kind of looked up to see because I was taken by surprise. I had never heard anyone thank God for my company. Wherever I went I always felt like a burden on the shoulders of my host. No one else opened their eyes but I saw the mouth of Mrs. Johansson say, 'Yes, Father,' and she nodded her head in approval. Soon the preacher said 'amen,' and the food was passed around. A peaceful silence lasted for no more than a minute when Mrs. Johansson opened up the conversation which led to a barrage of questions which all opened up with the phrase, 'So John, tell us about yourself.'

"It was a good thing I had five hours earlier that afternoon to rehearse what I was going to say. Some of my answers came out in little white lies, which were sugar-coated just enough so no follow-up questions could be asked. However, the questions about my parents, my brothers, and my friends were mostly true except I made them all sound a little better than what they actually were. Soon the conversation switched to topics, which made me quite a bit more comfortable and I was able to be honest about how I felt about them. We talked about writing, music, and politics, which Pastor Randy was quite educated in. They told me stories about their camping trips and how much fun they were. This reminded me of the times I had gone camping with my Mom's side of the family. The Johansson family sat around the table and shared story after story with me about all the good times they had had together. My immediate and extended family used to camp together all the time but they were not the most memorable moments. Actually, the memories hurt and confuse me even to this day. I never understood the yelling matches my Mom's sister and her brother had as the family lounged on the beach. The sandcastle I was building was coming along quite nicely when my mom suddenly commanded me, in the sternest and threatening voice, to go back to the campsite with my dad and aunt. I asked why and she told me it was none of my business but I could tell it was something serious for tears were running down my mom's face and she was behaving in a way she never had before. She never raises her voice especially when she in a public place. She is not the type who wants to draw attention to herself. I left with my dad and aunt and as I looked over my shoulder I saw my mom's sister standing in front of her brother flailing her arms wildly and talking in the nastiest of tone. I never understood, for the rest of the week, why there was a tension hanging over the campground. I never understood why conversations between the two different camps always seemed to be forced. Looking back, I know the only reason why we stayed out there for the rest of the week was so we kids would not start asking questions the parents would have to answer. Even though I was just a young boy I saw it all and felt its heavy presence: They all pretended everything was okay; everything was as it seemed. However, camping with my immediate family was always a fun and enjoyable time.

"I genuinely enjoyed hearing the laughter around the table and the smiles the three of them portrayed. They truly were a happy family who truly loved each other and did not simply put up with each other. I just sat there and laughed along with them and showed interest in what they were talking about. It was a way I could keep the conversation off of myself and on a light topic, which brought joy to the room rather then the bunch of lies I was producing. Most of all I loved to hear Mari's laugh. It came right from her belly, through her esophagus and flew out of her mouth in the cutest of fashion. I always hated romance novels and the cheesy factor each one had but now I know why so many of the lines sounded so cheesy: There was no other way to describe the sound, the sight, or the feeling. Her laugh was like a robin singing through the open window as the sun casts its life-giving beams into the room. It gives you the energy and the strength to get out of bed and enjoy the simple things of life. I knew for sure she had a tongue piercing for I saw it when she stuck her tongue out when I accidentally spilled my glass of juice. I was quite embarrassed but she laughed and so did her grandparents. I was slightly taken back by their response but it lightened the atmosphere and I was able to laugh at myself. This was the first time in a long time I had been able to do so.

"Time flies when you're having fun and soon I realized it was time for me to go. I still wanted it to be somewhat light out when I walked back home. Preacher Randy, being the kind Christian fellow he was, offered to drive me home. But I made up some lies about having parked my non-existent car by the park because I wanted to walk around the town and enjoy the fresh summer air. I really enjoyed my time at the Johansson's. This was the first time I knew I loved Mari. There was something about her mannerisms, her attitude, and her laughter, which spawned a new feeling inside of my heart. This feeling was new and foreign to me and made me feel uncomfortable: Around her I felt that everything was okay, everything was as it seems, and there is no pain in the world.

"I may as well tell you this right now, Doctor. Even though I enjoyed every moment I had with Mari it all ended two days before I killed her. One day she told me there was no pain in the world. When I talked about questions and struggles I had (I never told her I was addicted to Blade. I never told anybody unless they asked) she told me I had to have a little more faith, read a little more Scripture, and pray another long prayer then the pain would go away. I would tell her it was not that easy but she said it was. Tell me Doctor, how can she say something like that when there is so much obvious pain? That praying will fix everything? I look around and the pain I see in this world burdens me. Doctor, it keeps me up at night and gives me horrifying nightmares. It is not the pain that bothers me so much but it is how people choose to mask it. Mari lived in this little box, which she called her world. Anything that did not fit inside her box she either attempted to fix or, when proven to be beyond repair, would throw out. She tried to fix me many times but I wouldn't let her. I was not going to transform into a naive, ignorant angel whose life was perfect. No

Doctor, I would rather live a life of pain than a life of perfection. In the pain, a person actually feels alive. Pain causes a person to wrestle, to struggle, to question, and to form strong convictions and philosophies. Tell me Doctor, would you rather live a life of pain or of perfection?"

He took a deep breath and replied, "I don't know anymore."

The Mere Existence of God

"I was walking along through the woods but the weight of what Pastor Randy had said at the service burdened my shoulders so much that I could barely keep going. My legs were quivering under the burden and it was not to long until I found myself collapsed on the forest ground with tears pooling in my eyes and running down my cheeks. Something around the Johansson's dinner table had triggered a long neglected thought and emotion, which was buried deep within my heart. It was something about the genuine pleasure and joy they found in each other. Not a single smile was fake, not a single word was forced, and they seemed to accept each other for who they were instead of expecting each other to be something they were not. Then the words of the pastor's sermon whispered in my mind and I could not stop the Voice. It was whispering, 'Come unto me all who are weary and I will give you rest.' And, 'Die to yourself and find the fullness of life inside of Me.' Even during my time living in the shack I still considered myself to be a person who believed God existed, otherwise I would have killed myself. But then I was reminded that even the demons believe in the existence of God. Did I actually believe in God rather than the mere existence of God? There is huge difference.

"Even growing up I always felt as though I was missing something. There was always a deep darkness inside of myself that even when I felt closest to God something made it feels so different, so distant, and so impossible. As I lay there amongst the thick trees and the tall grass, my thin body drenched with the sweat of fear and quivering because of my bad nerves, I wanted it all to end. I needed this peace which was whispering in my ear, I needed to have the joy the Johansson's had. I needed to feel loved, significant, and worth something to somebody. I laid there crying, not wanting to move but just have all the torment of my heart and mind gone. I was tired of the voices that whispered to me in the night, telling me I was nothing more than a programed robot that was simply controlled by a giant computer in the sky. The voices and the hallucinations were actually the things I feared the most. The voices were audible and came in whispers, shouts, or in an emotion. They disguised themselves in a beautiful rose, but as soon as I stopped to take a whiff, a hidden bee would sting me. And little did I know that the hallucinations I experienced and the voices I heard would eventually place me where I am today. I should have known for the mind of man is pregnant with action.

"'God!' I began to scream into the darkness of the night. 'There has got to be more to You than this. Why do I still feel empty? What am I missing? Perhaps, I'm not missing anything, maybe you are the missing. God! My heart is breaking; I only want You to mend it. It still doesn't feel right. What am I doing wrong? Is it me? Is it who I am? God! Show me what is wrong! I can't do this on my own. What do You want from me? What kind of surrender do You want? Have my dreams, have my ambitions, have my life, have my goals, take every part of me! I just want to be set free from how I feel because I feel like moldy skin peeling off rotten bones. I JUST WANT TO BE FREE! I have nowhere else to turn to but You. God, I just need Your help. Set me free from the chains that are wrapped around my heart. I don't know what to do so I'll just throw everything at Your feet and trust that You will deal with it accordingly. God, I don't care if You kill me. Just... set... me... free!' I continued screaming as I pulled at the grass and tore it out of the dry ground. I grabbed sticks and threw them into the trees. My fist pounded the ground as I got to my hands and knees but then fell again under the burden of my grief. I just lay there and wept bitterly. I let my tears water the thirsty grass. And Doctor, it was after this I actually believed in God.

"Then there were the voices. The too real, the too close, the too tempting voices of the demons in my head. There was a voice which said, 'Feel anything, Tucker?' I felt someone touch my back and I looked up, through blurry, swollen eyes, to see the physical manifestation of the voices in my head. Dorothy was standing beside me and was still dressed in complete black but still had the eyes of an angel, the smile of a pleased mother, and the body of an experienced whore.

"'No,' I said in a defeated tone. 'All I feel is the numbness of not feeling anything.'

"'See, God left you all alone again. He doesn't really care about you. He just wants to make sure He has the most souls captured so my father cannot claim victory. But, we are winning Tucker. God hates you and has left you alone. You really want to obey an untrustworthy source such as God? It seems to me like pretty big risk.'

"'That is not right! I thought... He wouldn't leave... but... is it that... This cannot be the truth!'

"'What is truth Tucker? You have claimed to be god and have declared yourself worthless. Therefore, the truth, according to your own belief system, is that you are worthless. I remember once that Jesus said, "The truth will set you free." Even Jesus Himself knows you just need to accept the truth. Accept the truth Tucker and set yourself free.'

"'But what about what Pastor Randy talked about...,' I started but then I was cut off by Dorothy as she bent down and nibbled on my ear whispering, 'Remember, Tucker, that is Pastor Randy's reality. That is how he created it. You are well aware that your reality is completely different. Therefore, truth is relative and Pastor Randy's truth is not your truth. Do you understand what I am saying?'

"I nodded my head but did not say anything as she disappeared into the woods. "

* * * *

I have learned that the steps to freedom are much more painful than the slavery but in the end the freedom is much more rewarding. In my experience, it seems like as soon as one decides one wants to be free from slavery, the real battle begins. I could feel the demons were right on the doorstep after I said that prayer and they absolutely paralyzed my mind. I will never forget that night. The horror was something I cannot explain. How is someone to explain something he does not even understand? It is only by experience one can somewhat relate to the mysterious and bizarre. Without experience, such circumstances become something one tries to imagine. I laugh when people say they understand. What a lie! They do not understand, nobody understands! I do not even understand. All I have is the knowledge of my own dreadful experiences. Often an experience is enough to give one a complete subconscious understanding of something unexplainable. One night I had one of those experiences, which I do not understand but somehow I understand it completely. Or at least pretend to. Even now, after looking back on my past, I still don't understand it but for some bizarre reason it all makes perfect sense.

* * * *

I was so confused. My mind was a tangled ball of yarn, and soon I lost all control. When I lose control I go into a state of delusion where I do not know what is going on. It is like being a robot and whatever voice whispers in my ear I listen to it and do as it says. Because I am a Blade user, I take out my anger on myself even if I don't have Blade on me. Actually, anything can become Blade as long as it does the trick. My teeth were clenched to my lower lip and I could soon start to taste the blood that slowly leaked out of teeth marks. From the screaming, my throat was dry and throbbing, feeling like it was swollen to the size of an elephant's trunk. But I could still feel the warm blood trickling down my throat and landing on the knot in my anxious stomach. My eyes were dyed red from crying and they were swollen like a well-cooked marshmallow. Knots tied my stomach together and I had a terribly difficult breathing. It felt as though a noose was tied around his neck and it was slowly beginning to tighten for me to hang from the Tree of Death. Soon my breathing was reduced to something that was almost non-existent. They came in gasps of cries and each one took the entire strength of my weak body. My shivering fingers grabbed the grass on which I sat and he tore it out of the ground, throwing it into the air. Dirt crawled on my hands as I continued to dig deeper and deeper. I bent my head down and let out the most blood curdling of screams. The grass cringed underneath my breath and the curses were so poisonous that the weeds surrendered their lives to them. All my senses were on high alert and my ears picked up the sound of a cracking twig. He looked and through his blood shot, blurry eyes he saw a silhouette of woman coming out from behind the trees. She was clothed in a wedding gown, which was torn in several places. The dress wrapped around her chest and stomach showing the ribs that caused ribbons in her body. She held out her hand as if to rescue him. I stared into her bright blue eyes as she slowly walked across the lawn towards me. The hand that protruded from her body was holding Blade, a bright, shinning, shimmering piece of Blade. It was alive and vibrant and spoke the language of love. Inside, my heart told me to run but there was something about her eyes that made me immobile. They were something so familiar yet so mysterious. I began to shake all over as she got closer and closer.

"'Who are you?' I asked in a quivering voice.

"'I am the butcher's only daughter and I have come to set you free. I was just on my way back to the butcher shop from making a delivery and I heard you screaming in the woods. My heart stopped and I wanted to help whoever was in such a dire state of distress. You see, I don't like hearing a person in pain. It makes me feel all gross inside and causes me to become nauseous.'

"'That is very thoughtful of you but how can you help,' I said in a bitter tone. Several people had told me they could help but I never believed a single one of them.

155

"'The only thing I have is this,' she said as she pulled out Blade from her purse. 'This is what I use all the time and it always does the trick. Here try it.'

"I looked at Blade and then slowly moved my eyes back towards her face. As my eyes met her's, I felt as though I had seen them before. I never forget the eyes for they are something that never changes. The deep brown reminded me of someone but I could not quite remember. I decided it did not really matter. If she too used Blade then there was nothing to be ashamed of. With that, I slowly extended my right hand and began to raise it towards the shaft of Blade. My hands were shaking like a person who had drank too much coffee or an addict who was going through withdrawal. My fingertips felt the palm of the woman's hand and wrapped around the handle. My mind went into a trance (this always happens when one knows he is going to use Blade). Nothing was registering in my brain. All the alert systems were down, the panic button was but a dull ring in my ear and I was now free in the lost thought of complete nothingness.

--Cut--

My world was fine…

--Cut--

Everything was alright…

--Cut--

I was god…

--Cut--

Freedom….

"The smell of blood began to linger in my nostrils and I squinted my eyes and saw that blood was beginning to pour from the middle of my forearm. I looked up to find the eyes of the woman but he was instead greeted with the stars frowning down upon him. The pain from the open wounds all of a sudden entered the nervous system and once again tears began to well up in my eyes. I did not know whether I was crying because it physically hurt or because I had once again failed."

Repeat.
Repeat.
Repeat.

                                                                  Repent.

Repeat.

                      God, a never ending cycle that I can't kill.

          And I still don't feel forgive.

"God, I hate these voices.

It was after this when I began questioning who I was."

* * * *

"Now, as I sit here telling you about my experiences which made me use Blade, I see that faith is not an emotion but rather a decision. Reflecting on this time of my life I know I was looking for the feeling that God had forgiven me, that God looked at me with pleasure, that God actually cared about me. However, because I was looking for an emotion, I was unable to be set free. I was captivated by the belief that in order for something to exist I needed to be able to feel it so I could therefore somehow be able to describe and understand it. But then again, I always had to ask myself whether or not it was even worth striving for. Was the emotion of being forgiven actually worth all the pain I would have to endure to come to realize this? That night I decided freedom was worth fighting for and I engaged in battle but, much to my dismay, I could not handle all that life was throwing at me. The voices and hallucination - I did not know what was actually part of my reality or if they were merely a dream. Eventually, I decided to believe they were all simply reality, which I could no longer control."

Frienemies

"Mari was the first girl I had ever loved. Actually, she was only one of two women who I ever loved. The funny thing is that they are both now dead. One is physically dead as the other will forever remain dead to me. Even though Mari had a couple rebellious years, when I got to know her, she had her life in perfect order. So it seemed. Underneath the pain was still eating away at her and eventually it got the best of her. Her shack was one decorated with a beautiful, attractive exterior but a completely chaotic interior. She could never deal with the chaos and continually chose to sweep it all under the rug. This only makes things worse at least that is what the voices told me so.

"Before I asked her out, we would spend much of our time hanging out in group settings.

These were always the times when I would be confused about life. I have already admitted I am a very confused person but when Mari and I would go hang out with her group of friends the voices would grow louder and I could never think straight. Her friends were nice individuals who were mostly of the church-going breed. You know the ones with the nicely combed hair, the golf shirts, and the freshly pressed pair of jeans. All they did was smile and talk about preachers, sermons, and ridiculous, nonsensical stuff like that. I always laughed when they would answer a question by saying, 'Well Preacher X said, blah blah blah blah blah blah, and that is what I believe. I stand by that you know because Preacher X is a very godly man.' This in and of itself proved to me that in the perfection of life a person never really believes anything but what others tell them. Their narrow-mindedness made me sick to my stomach and made me want to throw up and then return to my vomit and lap it up like a sick dog. I thought it was ridiculous to believe something just because some well-dressed preacher man decided it was truth. I guess they don't understand that we all have our own realities and though Truth is applicable to each reality it must be presented in a way, which each individual person can understand and relate to. It took me a long time to understand this and I pray to God that one day they will understand this too before it is too late. To me, they seemed to create their realities based on what others said. How pathetic! For this reason, I never enjoyed hanging out with her while she was with her friends.

"There was one day when she invited me to one of her friend's birthday parties. I hesitated going but it was a chance I could spend time with her so I went. To this day, I still don't know why she invited me. But, then again, I don't even know why I went considering the circumstances I now face. I remember that time like a horrible nightmare and I still do not understand all the complications of my thoughts, feelings, and emotions. It was late at night, probably eleven or shortly after and we were all sitting around a fire visiting, laughing, cracking jokes, and singing campfire songs. Oh, they were visiting laughing, cracking jokes, and singing campfire songs. I was sitting in the circle but I did not feel like I belonged. I felt like that one crack in the line, which breaks the bond of a complete circle. I remember looking around at all the smiling faces, which were so full of joy and satisfaction. None of them seemed to have a care in the world, every face had the story that life was perfect and everything was fine.

"Through the past couple months, I had come to know most them, at least the guys and Mari, fairly well and knew that many of them were gifted with many different talents and abilities. Everything seemed to come with ease whether it was sports, music, or being a goof. Each of them seemed to be brewing with confidence, ready to take on the entire world in one night. They knew with certainty that each one of them had a mother and father who loved their children deeply and the children returned that love. I would quietly laugh when I heard some of the boys talk about what they had done with their dads earlier in the week. 'Yeah, my dad did that stuff with me to but it was only because he was obligated to not because he actually wanted to,' was what I wanted to say. All I was a goof that knew nothing, did nothing, and when trying something new, felt like an idiot and a hindrance to the progress of the other guys. I felt like a loser who was getting nearer and nearer to the gates of Hell.

"These people didn't seem to know what it was like to experience pain. Unless there was pain but they just kept it buried under the mask of 'Jesus loves me this I know for the Bible tells me so.' Somehow someone, or in this case something, told me this and accepting it was completely different than someone telling me and me actually believing it. Remember, I had heard these words since I was a little guy and not once did I actually believe them but instead I just knew them. There is a huge difference. To them, life was an adventure, which would go in their favor every turn of the way. Each one of them was an optimist to the core and I deeply hated their viewpoint. It was not reality. Reality of each one of our lives is that there is pain and if we do not deal with the pain it will eat us alive. But to me life had no meaning. It was a bore. The entire world seemed to be against me and at every corner there was another valley to trudge through. The only excitement was to survive another day in the midst of all the voices. That night I felt nauseating feeling which I had neglected for so long. However, instead of burying it and pretending everything was okay, I accepted the voice and let it seep into my brain.

"'There is nothing special about you,' came its seductive tone.

Then there was another Voice, which I had not heard for a long time. 'Yes, you are not special in the eyes of the world. However, there is One who takes great delight in you and considers you the work of His very hands.' I thought.

"'Don't think Tucker. What do you feel? How do you feel? Feelings are the key to life and by them you will know right from wrong, truth from lies.'

"I looked around. They all had so much confidence. All the guys could make the girls smile and laugh while I just stand on the side silently, aware of what's going on but not participating. It hurts. It really hurts to not feel like a man and be good at things like all the other guys are. But this is who I am! Did God create me to feel like a loser? Did God create me to feel the way I do? Is this all there is? I am afraid the answer is yes. This is who God created me to be. We all have our gifts but there is something dreadfully wrong with the picture that I am painting with my life. It's like a child just grabbed a bucket of paint and threw it against the wall. I guess even then, some people can see the beauty in such randomness. They say that everything is found in Jesus but why can I not feel it. I know I have given my life to Him and I don't know if I'm really any different than my old self. Everything is in Jesus but how can everything be found in Him when I feel as though I have found nothing other than a line in which I don't know which way to go. On one side, God's side, I see His loving arms, His saving grace, and all the joy and peace a man could ever want. On the other side I see Hell; a pit of fire which smells like flesh burning. I see the flames and the smoke and I see a little girl rolling in the flames, her hair was on fire and she was screaming her head off. Hell is torture but Heaven is perfect happiness. Then why does Hell look so attractive? Oh, wait, I forgot, God doesn't exist. Forgiveness doesn't exist. Salvation doesn't exist. My skills and talents don't exist. And most of all, Heaven and Hell don't exist. In fact, I don't even exist. It's all a dream, a figment of the imagination.

I HATE PEOPLE.

* * * *

Journal Entry #8

Oh how I want to cut to the sound of your voice!! The very vibrations of your vocal cords make my stomach turn to knots and I can feel it slipping. God my hands are shaking again!! The voices! The voices! The voices! - Oh how beautiful it sounds to the one deceived but how wretched to the man that listens to it on rewind. Nothing makes sense except for the confusion waging war in my mind. I feel out of control. Like the floor is slowly disappearing and underneath it is the darkness of despair and the oh, so familiar dark clouds. What is the reality? In my mind? No, for reality can't be conjured up in a biased mind clouded by personal experiences and brainwashing. We all have our own reality. My world is one of a momentary blue sky and then the long lasting black and grey clouds. It rains Hell. Hell rains on me. How I wish I could grab an eraser and blot out the blackness. My eraser only leads to blood, wounds, and scars. I want everything, absolutely everything, to disappear like a ghost creeping across the waters. One minute you can see it's silhouette against the dark tree line and then in a twinkle of an eye it is gone and low and behold all that is left is the idea that you saw something. But this is not reality. It is my reality. But you never saw the ghost therefore it wasn't reality. But it has to be!! For I saw it with my own eyes!! I feel the hairs on the back of my neck stand on edge, beckoning the emotion to come over me like a flood. The sweat began to mount on my forehead and under my arm pits it ran like a dripping faucet. Tell me this isn't reality!!!! Tell me this is a lie!!! Tell me I don't know what I know I know!!! I know I don't know what you know but what I know is better than what you know for what I know is the reality of knowing the truth of life. What I know is my reality; what you know is yours. Nothing makes sense and nothing ever will! My insides rot like a bucket of tomatoes left out in the heat of the sun. Confusion blocks the synapses of my brain and all I know is what I don't know. You say, "I hope this brightens up your day like you do for me. Wherever I see you, you are having a good time or in a deep conversation. You are greatly loved."This is your reality not mine.

Call me self-centered!! Drown me in self-pity! It's not what I want but it's all I have. But that is my reality.

* * * *

I sat around the fire trying to eat hotdogs and marshmallows but my stomach was not able to handle the feeling of self-centered gratification. My eyes scan the people around the fire and I saw smile after smile, laugh after laugh. They all seem to be having a great time talking to each other about stupid things like movies, celebrities, and anything else that has to do with the Internet, television, or whatever. I hate it. My mind instead wonders to the reality of where we live and what we experience. In my mind there is one world and in this one world we each create our own world. This world that we create is made from our choices, our experiences, our personal thoughts and philosophies, as well as fate. Everyone has their own little world and as we humans interact with people and get to know them we try to fuse our two worlds together into one world but even in a fused world there is two entirely separate worlds. Why else would there be fighting? Divorce? Suicide? One world divided into billions realities.

* * * *

Then the voices
    came haunting,
        "Maybe you
            were meant
                to be cut
                    out as a loner."

We are the invisible people.

* * * *

Standing over my grave, don't cry.　　　　　　*In the shallow puddles*

I killed myself drowning　　　　　　*of pointless*
people,
　　　useless words;　　　　　　*a deep puddle could save my*
life.

* * * *

--Cut--
My world was fine...
--Cut--
Everything was alright...
--Cut--
I was god...
--Cut--
Freedom....

...I will **cut**, I will
cut out the **pain**.

"I want to
cut to the
sound of
your
voice."

I am nothing special...

"I want to
cut to the
sound of
my own
voice."

You Write The Part, I'll Play The Role

"Most of those kids were idiots and hated each one of them. Maybe it is just the memories I have of them for they are not the most pleasant. They never meant any harm by what they did and I understand that their intentions were not to offend or upset me. Even though their intentions and motives were just to have fun, I still consider them to be idiots. The more I think back on the situation the angrier I feel. Despite all that has happened, I still need to work forgiveness in my heart towards them. I'm just not sure if I will get the chance any more. I know the police are on my trail and it will not be much longer until they have me arrested and behind bars. My present thought is, 'If I'm going to jail I wish I would have killed all those actors too. They thought they were so funny.'

The stage was a campfire in the backyard of the Johansson family. The cast consisted of four jerks who thought it would be funny to put on an improvised sketch of humorous situations which had a satirical bend to them. I enjoy satire but only when it forces a person to reconsider a situation. Satire only goes so far before it turns to mockery and when the mockery is personal it cuts deep, literally. Even though the rest of the group of ten was sitting there, I once again felt as though I was the only one in the audience. I felt like they were speaking to me, mocking me, and showing the world what a shame I am. What a shame so many people like me are. I am ashamed sure but there is more shame in pretending everything is all right, that everything is as it seems.

"As the flames danced and cast shadows over the group, the five idiots stood up and began to improv a situation. They used utensils, plates, lawn chairs, and even food as props to make their scene funnier. Actually, it was pretty funny. They were good, really good until they took it too far. I'll never forget what happened as long as I live.

"Johnny asked, 'Dennis, what do you have in your hand?'

"'Oh, just a knife,' replied Dennis as he examined it, not knowing what he was going to use it for.

"'What are you going to do with it?' Johnny asked as he too began examining the shiny blade.

"'I don't know,' came Dennis' response.

"Suddenly Darryl butted in, 'Guys! Guys! My heart is breaking! The pain is too much to bear. I must! I can't! I have to!' He had the dull back end of the knife against his forearm pacing back and forth. 'Everyone hates me; I cannot feel the love.'

"At first Dennis and Johnny did not know how to respond but soon assumed the role of bullies and started laughing at Darryl.

"'Hey emo kid! What you gonna do? Cut yourself?,' yelled Dennis.

"Johnny began laughing, 'You idiot! Normal people don't do that!' Then to Dennis turned and yelled, 'Loser!'

"'I can't take it anymore!' screamed Darryl and he began moving the dull side of the knife back and forth against his forearm. 'Oh, it hurts. Oh no! I think I hit an artery but this feels so good!' He said these words in the most sarcastic, mocking tone I had ever heard. Perhaps it was just accelerated by the fact that my left forearm was itching and I was beginning to hear the voices whispering again. The guys continued on this way for quite some time.

"Finally I had enough and stood up. 'Guys, this isn't that funny!'

"There was a sudden pause in the action but then the silence was broken by someone asking, 'Why? No one is getting hurt.'

"'Doesn't matter,' I replied with rising anger. 'Do something else.' They did not listen to me, but instead resumed in their mockery. I decided I was not going to tolerate their stupidity and I marched off into the darkness. Mari called after me but I just kept going; I let her words bounce off my eardrums.

"That night as I walked back to the shack, I felt a great amount of shame. I felt as though all the ground I had gained disappeared and now I was only left with one conclusion. The scars on my forearm felt twice as big, twice as deep, and twice as noticeable. I knew I was being overly sensitive but the memories were to warm, the feelings too real, and the damage too deep. They did not know what I was struggling with and neither did I expect them to. What hurt the most was how they disrespected me by not stopping when I asked. This simple decision of theirs was enough to knock me into a whole new cycle of hell. It happened later that night.

"Oh, by the way, this was the last time I saw any of them, except Mari."

Tyler J. Klumpenhower

Friends are like shallow puddles
which I constantly dip my face into,
slurping up the parasites.
Like sandpaper
being rubbed furiously on my tongue,
dances the slimy worm;
it bleeds out the black, bloody letters.
I feel it chew.
Then devour.
Then defecate
under my tongue.
I grind it up into tiny particles
as my mouth begins to taste the blood;
bone chips swim in the saliva.
I swallow.
I regurgitate.

Oh God!

Journal Entry #9

It's back again! Oh God!! The frantic feeling where the world seems to be closing over top of you and nothing makes sense. Everything, even the good, becomes a frightful mess of lies and confusion. I wish I could describe the way it feels. The stomach tightens up like a cloth being wrung out after soaking up spilled milk. It's draining out all the truth and soaking up the lies.

Tonight I lay on the bed for a half hour. My eyes burned from the salt of my tears and the only way I could breathe was out of my mouth for my nose was plugged with snot. With each gasp of breath I would choke on strings of mucus and be thrown into a coughing spree. My body would not straighten out for the muscles of my stomach were pulling my legs closer and closer to my torso. I wish I could describe the feeling. Actually I don't. It's like Hell minus the flames. Nothing but lies penetrating the crevices of the mind. The Truth tries to fight back but the lies are so much easier to believe. After all, it's what I've believed for the majority of my life. Breaking a habit is never easy but breaking a certain thought pattern is even harder.

"You're a failure," the voices scream. "No one likes you. You shouldn't even like yourself. THERE IS NOTHING SPECIAL ABOUT YOU!!!"

Oh but the lies!! I then hear the Voice of Truth combat the lies. "You're loved, forgiven, accepted, and worthy." Such words, so hard to hear. I verbalize the truth in incoherent speech as I continue to gasp for breath. "It's true", I think to myself, "but how can something that doesn't feel true be true?"

The lies feel so much better. The lies are my home. The lies are MINE!!! They are part of who I am! The clouds become darker and I can hear Dorothy whispering in my ear, "Freedom. Freedom." My mind is a mass confusion of truth and lies, reality and dreams which are all dampened by the simple fact that such a mess of string is not worth sorting out and it is easier to cut the strings and loosen the knot. The cold metallic feel of my jacket zipper triggers an idea as I dry the tears out of my eyes by rubbing my face with the sweater. It's sharp enough. "God!! No!! Please! Not this again! This isn't what I want. This isn't what I need!" My heart races and my mind crashes and I know not what to do. It's so easy to do what is wrong; to fall into the cycle: Repeat, repeat, repent, and repeat. God, no! Through my blurred vision I see my Bible lying beside me. I had forgotten about."

"What do you have for me God?" I ask. My tone is biting and sarcastic, full of pessimism, skepticism, with the desire to burn every page of that book. "If what I believe are indeed lies show me something in Your Word that combats the brutality of the reality I am living in." With shaking hands, I turn the thin pages and scan the pages for anything that grabs my attention. Bold headings followed by meaningless words are the only things I can find. My heart drops but then my eyes land on a verse in Psalms 63. I read the words:

"But those who seek to destroy my life shall go down into the depths of the earth;
    they shall be given over to the power of the sword;
    they shall be a portion for jackals."

Immediately my mind wanted to reason up an argument against the words. Why does the destroyer always seem to succeed? Why do I always feel as though I am the one who is given over to the power of the sword? I scream out to God but I can't feel Him, all I feel is the teeth of the jackals ripping into my chest and devouring my wretched body. A still small voice whispered in the chaos, "Faith is not an emotion; it is a decision to believe." My soul trembles at the Truth on the page. It resonates and fulfills something, somewhere, deep within. It is beyond explanation. My heart knows not what to do with such Truth. It wants to cling to the words, hold them dear the heart and fasten them on like a button on a winter jacket. It's so new, something beyond words. Such a promise!

* * * *

"With tears streaming down my face, I look to the ceiling and say, 'God help my unbelief.' But then, as soon as I uttered that heartfelt prayer, I saw Dorothy on the horizon. She was coming closer, closer, closer. A shiny blade in her right hand. I grabbed the scissors. I don't know what is wrong and neither do I really care. The tension inside is much too great! I don't understand what is going on! Nothing makes sense. Everything hurts! I can't even concentrate on the smallest activity. One small cut! One small cut reminding me that God hates me. One small cut to remind myself I hate myself. One small cut to remind me that others hate me. One small cut to remind others to hate me. But what about the Voice? What about the promise?

R-A-Z-O-R-S
| (God hates me,
C
| I hate me,
U
| They hate me,
T
| I hate everything!)

L-I-K-E

| (Failure,
A
| Rejection,
D
| Disappointment,
R
| Anger,
U
| Unbelief - For I do not understand my own
|actions. I do not do what I want, but
| I do the very thing I hate.)
G
\ (Ouch! That one slipped).

* * * *

--Cut--
My world was fine...
--Cut--
Everything was alright...
--Cut--
I was god...
--Cut--
Freedom....

* * * *

"I dabbed the cut with some toilet paper and rolled down my sleeve to press the wound. The blood would eventually stop flowing and healing would set in. My forearm was a mess from nine two-inch long cuts that have finally scabbed over. I never washed the blood off; for some reason I like the sight of dried, cracking blood spread along my arm. Shame is ever present and for a while I wore long sleeves wherever I went to makes sure nobody saw what I did to myself. I only talked about it if somebody caught me being negligent and had the courage to ask about the cuts. I didn't like explaining, I didn't like lying, and I didn't like telling the truth so I choose to hide my pain from the rest of the world. The cuts came like a blood bath soaked into my sweater gluing the two together. I liked to look at the scars. For some reason there was a great peace in seeing self-inflicted wounds. It was like the outside of the cottage beside the lake. Actually, when the situation regarded itself as so the truth was that the smile on my face was actually a reflection of my heart. A single cut and I was able to smile from the depths of my heart and I actually felt free. It was such a horrifying, frightening, captivating, and exciting adventure.

But it was not worth it. We must choose to forgive and forget."

* * * *

"This may seem like a strange turn of events, but the struggle towards belief is much more difficult than simply accepting something as knowledge. As soon as I took steps towards actually believing, my life became hell. I thought it would be easier but the truth is that life became a lot more unpleasant and meaningless but, on the contrary, it seemed to be blooming with meaning. Just meaning found beyond myself. In hindsight I realize now how much more I have gained because I stopped listening to the voices and began listening to the Voice. The voices don't like to be shut out and turned off. It makes them mad and causes them to attack the heart, soul and mind with a barrage of seductive lies, which are very easy to buy into. I bought the lies all the time until I realized that there were voices and then the Voice. When I started listening to the Voice life became worse but the reward is much, much greater than the loss."

* * * *

"Most people, especially those who are stricken with narrow-minded thinking would expect cutting to be horrifying and cause a great amount of pain. But, the exact opposite was true. It brought me much joy and pleasure; an experience, which I would not soon forget and an experience, which I would love to experience again but wished to never experience again. Like everything, there are consequences to decisions made. And now, due to the impulsive decisions I have made, I bear the scars of my past. They will forever be remainders of who I am and what hopelessness is found in searching for truth within the world, within one's self. Am I ashamed? Of course I am. How could I not be? Everyone can see the decision I have made and the disgusting morbidity of who I am and what I have struggled with. It's like a permanent tattoo, which will always tell a story of some kind. Many different people will take a different story from the scars. No one should be horrified, even the narrow-minded, for we all bare scars. We all have a story because we all live dying."

* * * *

"Like I said, I chose to wear long sleeves for an extended period of time, but then decided I would screw that and bare the truth of whom I was. As expected, people responded in different ways. Some did not know how to react to the scars and chose to withdraw from me. They saw me as a depressed individual with a dark mind that enjoys and takes delight in seeing pain. The truth is that I hate pain but the greater truth is that in the pain Truth is discovered."

Truth vs. Lie

"Then, like a dark cloud blotting out the sun, I could hear the voices encroaching on my rejoicing."

"You don't deserve this!"

"I know…"

"This is meaningless"

"Everything is meaningless…"

"The joy is nothing but the foreshadowing of disappointment and more pain that is not even worth getting excited about. Are you excited for pain?"

"No! I just want to FEEL happy…"

"You're a worthless jerk with nothing to offer to no one!"

"I am worth something…"

"You are not worth loving!"

"I am loved…"

"Nothing makes sense!"

"No, nothing does but somehow God makes sense of the senseless…"

* * * *

"The truth of who I was, immediately confronted by the lies of who I was in my own mind. I could feel her again. My hands started to shake. I collapsed to the floor and started gasping for breath as tears began to pour from my eyes. Nothing made sense! I don't deserve this! Everything I am is a lie and every-thing that is possible is a lie!!!! I live in a lie!!! I stood up and began pacing through the room. This did not last long and collapsed on the chair as the tears began to roll down faster, saltier and more desperate. The glass still lay on the floor beckoning me to take hold if its mercy. I carefully grabbed the edge of the broken glass and held the sharp blade against my forearm. A strong itch came to my forearm and I knew the only way to wash it away would be through the running of blood. My hands continued to shake as the battle in my mind progressed and became more and more intense.

"'No!!!' I screamed under my breath. 'Can't! Won't! Should! God, it hurts!!! Shut up Dorothy!!!' I threw the glass against the wall where it shat-tered into fragments and collapsed to the floor and rolled around on it in great emotional turmoil.

"'God it hurts! God no!!! Please God! Make it stop! Make it stop make it stop!!!!' All this I screamed under my breath.

"Nothing made sense. My mind was like a corn maze with a child lost in it. The sky was beginning to darken and the parents had gone on without him. Over the heads of the corn, the sky burned like fire as the boy continued to walk down the path. On either side of him were rows of corn stalks. They seemed to be smiling at him. Suddenly faces morphed into the stalks and the plants began to whisper, "Burn. Burn. Burn,' like a steady whisper that floated like a feather in a gentle spring breeze. They began to move and soon the boy was surrounded by talking corn stalks whose eyes darted back and forth like a scared rabbit. The boy not knowing what to do stood there and screamed. He cried for his mother, his father, someone, anyone to come and rescue him from the talking corn stalks. No one. Nothing. Knowing God might exist, the boy screamed out His name but again there was no answer. He either had to fight for his life or just give it up to the pain. This was my head.

"The pen talks like a mechanical robot. Ink acts as a tongue, which com-municates the innermost feelings of the soul. I grabbed a pen and started to scratch random words onto the paper. Anything to make everything make a little bit of sense:

Joy-want to cut-not disappointed-a little-knows God answers prayer-negative thoughts-why can't I be happy for once!!! Cut! Cut! Cut! I don't deserve this!!! Oh God....

"I continued and scratched three more pages of random thoughts and threw down the journal. This wasn't helping. It wasn't making sense. I had to get out of the house. I had to go somewhere to someone! I didn't care who I just needed to leave before I hurt myself. Climbing to my feet I slowly made my way over to the door. I was bent over and tears continued to drip to the floor. I didn't have the strength to make it and I collapsed on the floor as another wave of emotion overcame my weakening body. I just laid there and cried. Minutes passed and I crawled to the door and slowly opened it. I managed to get to my feet and I stumbled through the rest of the house and barged out the front door where I then collapsed on the lawn.

But I <u>DID NOT</u> cut myself...."

Present, Past, Present, Past....

I can't sleep. How can a person sleep when the mind is a bed of unrestful thoughts and confusion? "Tell me you can sleep! Tell me you had a great night! With your warm covers snuggled around your fresh face. The warmth of the room crawling up your nose and lulling your mind to sleep. Your snore sneaks through the cracks of the wall. Oh, you sleep like a child but little do you know of the reality of that sleep." I thought these things as I lay by Adelaide. What she had done was literally eating away at me. I had lost several pounds and ate almost nothing. Each day I was haunted by the voices telling me of how I should carry out my revenge. At the penitentiary we had the motto, "God have mercy on your soul." He would probably have mercy on her soul too. More than likely I would be the one who would be given over to the power of the sword and devoured by the hungry jackals. In my reality, God has a way of punishing those who didn't deserve it.

* * * *

"I now pronounce you Mr. And Mrs. Cruse. Brian, you may kiss the bride." At the preacher's command, I wrapped my arms around Adelaide and tucked her lips into my mouth. It was the first time I had ever kissed a girl and boy did it ever feel good. She was everything I had ever wanted. A true soul mate who put the needs of others above her own. A person who lived a genuine life and truly cared about those around even when it cost her something. She was gorgeous too! Rosy cheeks, brilliant eyes, a dazzling smile - My heart pounded in my throat as she marched up the aisle and stood at the altar. She was mine and would be so, until death do us part.

* * * *

Tell me you can feel! Tell me I'm not the only one who sees the things I see and feel the things I do. No one else seems to care! Don't give me a reason to hate you. Don't make hating easy. But you make it all too easy; all too easy for me to hate you.

    I.
    Hate.
    You.

* * * *

I actually had loved another girl but she could not love me in return.

* * * *

Then I see you walk. Walk through the house in your confident, arrogant strut! You don't know reality. You don't know truth! The truth is what I see and feel but too often it is clouded by the lies of the Devil. On my shoulder the voices whisper what to believe. I know it's not true but it is so easy to fall back into the trap. It feels like home. It's been home for too many years and now I have to give it up, all for the sake of you. Dorothy, oh glorious, mysterious Dorothy, come and take this pain away.

It hurts, it burns, and it sucks. Why has God not heard my prayers? I think it's time to throw in the towel and come to a conclusion of some sort. It's not worth smiling when the devil clutches your stomach. Or maybe it's God causing all the pain. It's not worth living when a person feels like he has been used and abused, cheated and swindled. This is the second time a girl has left me high and dry. I began to think it was not me who had to suffer but those who had hurt me. After all, God was not going to punish them so I had to.

* * * *

Journal Entry #10

Like a whore, I'll wonder the crevices of this tottering mind and become lost in the maze of confusion. Dancing on the streets, I'll sell myself to my own feelings. I live with them until the day I die to myself, however far that day may be. Sometimes it feels as though it is like the sun peaking over the horizon in the morning. The yellow, pink, and red hues warm the soul and a glimmer of hope is found in the valley. But soon such warmth is cloaked by the coldness of the black clouds of reality. My reality. Not his reality, not her reality, my reality. It's like a curtain at a theater. The actors inside anticipate the spotlight when the curtains are drawn back but nothing or no one can pull the rope. It's too heavy. Reality doesn't exist.

* * * *

I believe we all live in a dream. Somehow, in this dream, we interact with each other on an emotional, physical, and spiritual level. When we die we snap out of our dream and are confronted with reality. The only reality that exists is what one does with God for that will dictate the reality of which we are and what we are about. Death is the only train to reality. The train chugs through the valleys and over the mountains of this dream called life. We know our destination and that is the only reality we are aware: Heaven or Hell. Life leads to the reality of death, which, upon being cloaked in blackness, we reach the only true reality we will ever know. This, the only reality that will ever exist, is found in Heaven or Hell.

It took me awhile to learn this.

If we all have our own reality then there is no absolute and therefore there is no God. Each individual can make up their own god because they all perceive God differently. If the reality of God is created by the minds of man then one God does not exist. "God, I'm drowning in my own pain. I have my eyes focused on myself and that doesn't seem to be changing. It hurts, it sucks, I'm about to die."

* * * *

It has been several weeks since I have last seen the Doctor. Now the police are looking for me because I am charged with three accounts of first-degree murder. However, to the public they will only know of two because the third was a person that everyone knew but no one really knew. I'll confess right now that

177

I killed him and I loved every second of clutching my hands around his throat and squeezing. I enjoyed seeing his eyes bulge in his sockets and then pop like squished grapes. Tearing the skin off his face delighted me for then I could see what was underneath. Blood, flesh, cells - the pure truth of what a human is made of. The voices didn't tell me to do it but instead it was the Voice. He told me to kill Brian Cruse because Brian Cruse was not the truth of who I was.

Forlorn Lover, Am I Not By My Own Doing

"Hey there George! Is Mari working today?" George was the owner of the grocery store. He was a real generous man with a soft heart but when it came to business he was extremely cunning. Mari had nothing but praise for the man. Not once did I ever hear her complain about him as a boss or as a person.

"Yeah but she is in the back putting some stock away. She saw you coming but said she did not have time to talk. However, she wanted me to give you this note."

"Oh. Thanks."

Mari was not the type of girl who would have the courage to ask me something if it was not something she was really nervous about. Mind you, most of the stuff we had talked about had been shallow but I thought I had given her ample opportunity to know who I actually was. Mind you, I did hold back several details for I was afraid that if they got out then I would lose my friendship with her. Sure, I liked her. She was cool, smart, and funny. Every moment I had with her were treasures in my heart and I considered those times a great privilege. The nitty-gritty details were only ones I shared in relationships where I felt secure and right now everything was on such fragile ground that under no circumstances could I allow the secret of the shack out. Those secrets would hurt those who I had invested so much time into me and ultimately I feared I would lose these relationships. Remember, the fear of rejection was one thing that made me stay in the shack for the feeling of not being wanted only made the voices, the hallucinations, and the desire for Blade even stronger. With sweaty hands I opened the note and read its contents. It was short and to the point but it was enough to make my stomach turn for between the lines I knew that she knew something about me that I had not been willing to share.

Tucker,
Can we talk sometime? The sooner the better.
Mari.

Yep, that was all it was. I still have the note tucked away in my journal and I even pulled it out so I could get the message word for word. I did not know how to take this but I knew I had to talk to her sooner or later, no matter what the topic of conversation was going to be about. I wrote a quick response and gave it to the boss to give to Mari. He told me I could just go to the back and tell her myself so I did exactly that. Mari was hard at work putting away groceries, from which I concluded because of the amount, they must have just gotten on the freight truck today.

"Mari!" She turned and looked at me, a bit surprised to be interrupted by me. Some loose strands of hair were sticking to her sweaty brow and she brushed them aside as I continued, "I got your note. How does right after work sound?"

She was brief and to the point. "Sure. Meet you at the park at 6:30?"

"Sure."

That was our conversation. I knew something was wrong, I just knew it from her expressionless voice, her distant eyes, and her cold welcoming. It was not typical of her. I am a profiler and I can tell when someone breaks their normal habits and routine and that, the expression, the voice, the distance, was definitely out of character for her. Obviously Mari was contemplating something deep in the back of her brain. Oh well, within the next couple hours I would know what it was about if I didn't already. I decided to be an optimist and hope the topic of conversation was levied towards her and something she was dealing with rather than what seemed to be the obvious assumed topic of conversation: My use of Blade. It was already four o'clock so I decided to meander to the park where I would loiter until Mari showed up. And, without a doubt, stew over what our conversation would be about and imagine the best-case scenarios and all the worst-case scenarios.

I did not have a watch but I knew it must be shortly past six o'clock for I could see her walking down the road coming towards the park. As she came nearer I could see she was as pale as a ghost. Under her eyes I could see the stress building up and in her eyes I could see fear. A strange sense of fear for a girl who I had always seen as brave and confident. Mari was everything but that on this night. Her hair was unkempt as if she had ran her hands through her hair as a result of the stress she was experiencing and her eyes were red and were full of thin bloodlines. When she came up to me she sat on the park bench right beside me and gave me a quick smile and said a polite hello. I wanted to see how her day was but she cut the small talk and got right to the point.

"See, the reason why I wanted to talk to you was to ask a couple of questions. And I want honest answers okay?" Her voice was soft, timid, and caring.

"Ok. Go for it." I tried to sound enthused and tried to bluff my way into the conversation but I had a feeling she saw right through what I was trying to do.

"First, let me ask you, are we friends?" She was nervously fiddling with her hands.

"Of course we are." This I always doubted.

"Then you won't get mad at me for asking this?" There was a slight quiver in her voice.

I knew with certainty what she was going to ask about, so I said, "No. That is not being a friend."

She took a deep breath. "The other day when we were hanging out I noticed a several cuts on your arm. Is everything okay?"

Oh boy! I took a deep breath and started, "Actually, no, everything is not okay. I was scared to tell you this but I... uh... I struggle with cutting myself."

"Why didn't you tell me?" she asked in an angry, compassionate voice.

In a shamed voice I replied, "Because, I was scared how you would respond",

"How I would respond! Tucker, do you know what this means? This changes everything. I was beginning to have feelings for you, but I can't let myself like a guy who does that to himself. It scares me." And she began to cry.

"I know. And I am trying to stop but... It's getting better. I've been clean for two weeks."

"Two weeks isn't that much Tucker."

"I know, but at least that's progress right? I'm working through it, honest." My voice was desperate, trying to reel her in as she slowly sank into the murky water. I knew I was losing her.

"What else are you not telling me?"

I sighed. The situation was already bad but now it had just gotten worse. How was I supposed to tell her about where I lived when she was already crying about the cuts on my arms? "You don't want to know."

"Yes I do," Mari said in a demanding tone, which was mixed with a hint of sympathy. "You're not from here are you?"

"No. I... I ran away from home five months ago and have been... um... living in a shack in the woods just east of town."

"Why?" she gasped at looked at me in unbelief as she shook her head.

"I don't know. I guess it was the only place that really felt like home."

"What about your family?"

Now she was just starting to get under my nerves. "You know Mari, not everyone has the perfect little life you have. Actually, I would venture to guess that your life isn't as perfect as you make it out to be. You walk around with this 'my life is perfect because God loves me' attitude but guess what, life isn't all smiles and laughter. If anything it is the exact opposite. I know God loves me too and as much as I struggle with that and with as much unbelief as I have, I am confident of that. My life doesn't have to be wrapped up in a pretty little box with a bow tie on it for God to love. He loves me when my box is falling to pieces and even when I am no longer contained inside of it. It is during these times where a person actually experiences God's love because he knows darn well that there is absolutely nothing inside of him that is making him deserve such love. I would wager to bet that your life is not perfect but rather you choose to ignore the hell inside your own soul. Mari that pain is going to eat you alive if you do not deal with it."

"And cutting yourself is dealing with the pain?" she asked in complete horror and disgust.

"Yes, it is the way my pain is coming out but I am dealing with it, honest. We all deal with pain differently and this is how I deal with it."

Her confused voice whispered, "I don't understand."

"I don't even understand yet it is getting better, I know it is! It's been two weeks!" A huge smile came across my face. Sure two weeks wasn't a long time but every day was a victory.

"Tucker, I can't believe this." Mari was crying uncontrollably and I knew it was over. Her voice trembled as she spoke. "You scare me Tucker. I… I don't know if… I don't know… I just can't develop feelings for a guy like you who… I don't know… does that to himself. It scares me and I don't want anything to do with it. You frighten me."

"Sometimes the truth hurts."

"I know but… I just don't understand it and… I am scared."

"Let me ask you this, Mari. How do you deal with pain?" My voice was soft as I reached out and touched her shoulder.

Tears were now streaming down her face and her words came out in between gasps of air and sniffles. Clouds were beginning to role in and the rain was beginning to fall. "Goodbye Tucker." With those last two words she ran up the road towards her grandparent's house.

"I… I thought we were friends," I said, my voice trailing off as she disappeared.

To say I was hurt would be an understatement. The words she said pounded between my ears and sank deep into my heart. Life would no longer be the same, I knew that for certain, but now that it has all happened I see how that moment changed every aspect of my life and the lives of those around me. When one reveals that he is dwelling in the shack it makes people examine their own houses to see what they are living in. Usually all the dirt is swept underneath the rug and the toys stuffed under the bed forgotten until someone reminds them that it is there. Little did I know that Dorothy would now settle among those I had once socialized with and begin to haunt their lives.

W(h)en Tw(o) Become (w)One

I was sick and tired of being Brian Cruse, a psychologist in the psychiatric ward in Bermingham Penitentiary. My job was a bore and I knew that who I was was not actually who I was. The whole pursuit into the field of psychology had been a way of proving to me that I was smarter than those around me. If I could get a degree in university then I was worth something, then people would look up to me, my parents would be proud of me, and then God would finally love me. Seeing the diplomas and looking through my report cards brings me no satisfaction like it once used to. It leaves me feeling angry. All is meaningless and in vain, a simple chasing after the wind, like a wise man once said.

Finally, I had finished with Tucker Wilson. Well, I actually wasn't finished with him; I would never be until the day he died. Even then his ghost would haunt the woods. But, as I had promised Adelaide a couple weeks ago, we prepared to go on our camping trip. I could see through Adelaide's disguise and knew she really didn't want to go but was simply going because if she did not I would question her reasoning. Remember, there are two types of people: Those who simply perceive and those who actually perceive. There is a huge difference and I hope you, the reader, will discover so. I wanted to go. Honestly. I was looking forward to confronting Adelaide on her little escapade with that mysterious man who remained unknown to me. However, before I went camping I was murdered by Tucker Wilson.

* * * *

It happened two days after I had discovered the evidence of Adelaide having an affair with a male customer at the restaurant where she worked. One day while Adelaide was gone I decided to violate her privacy and scan her journal in order to find out exactly what had happened. I knew she would be the type of woman who would document the experience whether it was pleasurable or not. Scanning the pages, I soon came to the right date and began to scan the paragraphs she had written that day. She must have been bored for there were three pages full of thoughts. The first page she vented on how frustrating I had been because I had neglected to spend time with her. I would agree to this but reading her thoughts should me that I had indeed failed my wife. She complained how she did not feel loved or significant. Then it got interesting. . . .

My relationship with Tomas Newsome has finally had a breaking point. It all started the other day he came into the restaurant and asked me if I wanted to go for coffee after work. I was done at three so I decided I had enough time before Brian got home. He's home late all the time and hardly ever has any time for me anymore. He changed sooo much. I don't know what it is and I am scared to ask what is bothering him. I think it has something to do with Tucker Wilson. Anyways, we talked for a couple hours. A week later we went out for coffee again but this time he asked if he could drive me home because I had walked. I said he could know what his intention, and my intention, was. It was silent for the whole trip.

We came to the house and I invited him in. One step in the door way and our lips were locked. Slowly we moved to the couch but then thought better of it just in case Brian surprised me by coming home early. The bedroom was the safest place in the whole house to have sex so that is where we went. Our time in bed was a wonderful time. I've never felt so loved... or used. Either way it was a very enjoyable time. I just can't let Brian find out or he'll be really mad. Then he might flip and I'd hate to see what would happen. He's too nice of man to hurt me though. He loves me too much.

As I was sitting there reading through her journal entry, I heard someone enter through the front door. This person, whoever he or she was, did not even bother to knock. It may have been Adelaide but right now I did not care if she saw me going through her journal. I didn't really care about anything anymore. I then heard the footsteps climb the stairs, stop for a brief moment and then move down the hall towards our bedroom. Then I heard the creak of the bedroom door and I turned my head full expecting to see Adelaide and be bombarded by her screaming at me for reading her personal journal. The damage was done already, what more could be accomplished.

"Hi Brian, how are you today?" asked Tucker Wilson.

"Pretty crappy." My voice was tired and defeated.

185

"Are things in your world not fulfilling your expectations?"

"Tucker, my world is crumbling and I don't know what to do. I hate who I have created myself to be. I lost myself a long time ago when I first thought I had to be somebody in order to feel loved. But now that I am somebody the very person I loved has gone and cheated on me. I wish I hadn't become what I am today. I wish I could have shaped my reality differently but I'll lose everything if I become what I truly am."

"It sounds to me you don't have much to lose," Tucker responded.

He was right. Tucker Wilson was always right. "How do I become free?"

"You need to die to yourself. Do you have a rope?"

"Not in the bedroom. Besides, what good will those do?"

"I'll show you," he replied as he scanned the room. "Here. Your wife's bathrobe string should work fine."

"Wait! What are you doing with that?"

"I'm going to kill you," Tucker said, very straight faced and blunt.

"You can't! You'll be charged for murder! You'll never escape!" my heart was pounding in my chest as I began to scream for help at the top of my lungs.

"I don't care. I'm already wanted for three murders so what is one more going to do? Put me in jail for an additional five years? Besides, no one will even know you are gone. You're just a figment of the imagination, a created facade to mask who you truly are. I am who you really are and I am tired of Brian Cruse just as much as Brian Cruse is tired of life. Now come here, I want to get this over with before Adelaide gets home."

"You can't do this to me! This is who I am! I am Brian Cruse a successful psychologist at the Bermingham Penitentiary."

"I believe that like I believe that your wife actually loves you." With this final statement he lunged towards me and wrapped his arms around my neck. Tucker was not a big guy but there was enough force to knock me to the floor. It did not take him long to beat me into submission and I just sat there as he grabbed the bathrobe rope and tied it around my neck. Tucker ordered me to climb on top of the bed as he pulled on the fan to make sure it was strong enough to hold me. Then he tied me to it and slowly began raising me. I could feel my lungs start to burn as I gasped for air. My heart pounded as I panicked for I knew there was nothing I could do anymore. I, Brian Cruse, was going to reach the shores of eternity within a matter of minutes. My eyes began to bulge out of my skull and I could feel the tendons in the back of my head loosening. Just as it felt my brain was going to explode the bed slipped out from underneath me.

The next thing I saw was the lifeless body of Brian Cruse hanging from the ceiling fan. It was a beautiful and glorious sight to behold!

* * * *

An old-fashioned camping trailer hooked up, matches, a hatchet, food, water, and a first-aid kit - Our car was packed with the necessary gear for our exciting wilderness adventure. It was silent for most of the trip up. A little small talk here and there but only when it was necessary. There was a tension hanging in the air, which I could not explain but was continually broken by the annoying twang of country music. To this day I wonder if she felt the tension I was experiencing. I wonder if she knew what was going on in my mind as I continued to accelerate her to her demise. Adelaide slept the most of the way so I do not think she had a single clue of what my intentions really were. On and on we continued to drive into towards the campground, which was hidden deep in the woods.

When we reached our destination we began to set up immediately for our week stay. It soon felt like old times again. We were laughing at each other, cracking corny jokes and talking like we had not done for a very long time. The tension had dissipated and I felt as though I could be myself. Actually, I completely forgot about what Adelaide did to me. Our camping site was soon set up, complete with a crackling fire and the country tunes continuing to twang. As annoying as the music was it reminded me of the first couple dates Adelaide and I went on. Back then she was hardcore into country and would only listen to songs about sexy tractors, farmer tans, and broken hearts. But it was all a game and I was about to make the first move.

"Babe, you look so beautiful today. Let's make love! We haven't done that in such a long time. It's so peaceful and quiet out here, who's going to disturb us," I whispered in her ear as I stood behind her and began caressing her neck with my lips and allowing my hand to crawl underneath the front her shirt. She didn't refuse. When I first started to kiss her, I never even thought of how Tomas had defiled my wife's body. But as the clothes began to fall to the ground, I was reminded of the pain, reminded of the hatred, reminded of my intention of the whole camping trip. Indeed, it was going to be a short trip but I hoped her trip across the Jordan River took forever. She deserved to feel such pain.

Eventually I had her right where I wanted her. We were on the ground, lost in the tall grass of the woods and I knew it was now my time to strike. I unlocked our lips, nibbled on the lobe of her ear as, "You dirty whore," gently slipped out of my mouth.

Immediately she stopped rubbing my back and there was a still silence in the air. A stiff, strong, disturbing silence, which made me feel nauseous. "What do you mean?" she asked in false innocence and a sense of ignorance.

"You know what I mean." I continued kissing the side of her neck and ear but took the occasional break to tell her what I knew. "The dry bathtub and towels, the nightgown, the open condom package on the floor. Don't tell me you are not a slut," I whispered. She tried to get out from under me but I had her pinned between the earth and my body. She was not moving.

"What are you going to do?" she asked in a distant voice as our eyes met. They were so full of fear and brought much fulfillment to my deprived mind. I liked to see her eyes full of pain for I felt as though she finally understood what kind of world I actually lived in.

"Babe, I'm going give you what you deserve. Something happened to me long ago that showed me that love and happiness are all merely perceptions and vary according to the reality one chooses to create." I rolled off her and went to the chopping block where I withdrew the hatchet. I turned and there I saw her eyes, so much terror, so much fear, and so much regret. "What? You're scared? Don't you worry, it will only hurt for a few pleasurable seconds." Her body was shuffling backwards, her eyes darting from side to side looking for an escape but knowing there was absolutely none. "You thought you would get away with this but now you know that your assumption was wrong. Darling, as you created your reality it inevitably led to where you are today. My, my, don't you regret playing God. You'll regret it even more when you taste the flames of Hell." I had a clump of her hair in my hands and the axe towering above my head ready to strike.

"What happened to you, Brian?" she asked, knowing her life was about to slip away.

"Oh, I forgot to tell you, sweetheart. My name isn't Brian Cruse. It is actually Tucker Wilson. Brian Cruse is dead and actually never even existed."

"What! You mean all along you were him?" She was screaming at the top of her lungs.

"Yes. I was. Didn't I have you fooled? Didn't I have this whole stupid country fooled?" I sneered.

Newspaper Headlines

TWO LOCALS FOUND DEAD
(October 14, 2001)

Local authorities have confirmed the death of two citizens of DeMonte. Randy Johansson and Mari Johansson were discovered in the afternoon of October 13th, 2001. The bodies of Randy and Mari were discovered in their residence and their deaths are considered a homicide. Mari is the granddaughter of Randy and Anita Johansson, who served at DeMonte Community Church and has been there for the past ten years. Anita Johansson went unharmed and did not hear the murderer embark on his quest. Police are still investigating the crimes but do believe the deaths are connected. Both bodies are being sent to autopsy as the police continue their investigation. Police say they have no evidence to help the case progress at a rapid pace. Meanwhile, police asks the public to keep their eyes and ears open for any leads. Authorities do not believe the rest of the public is in danger for each victim is relationally connected.

* * * *

Police Report: Eyewitness Account of Johansson Murders

On the morning of October 13th, 2001 at 12:04 a.m., (name censored) reported seeing Mr. Tucker Wilson at the Johansson's house, the scene of the crime. According to (name censored), Mr. Tucker Wilson seemed to have an accomplice but (name censored) said (gender censored) had not seen the other individual before. The written statement claimed he spent no more than ten minutes in the Johansson residents. No scream, no gun-fire, no slammed doors - (name censored) never heard a single sound. Also, not a single light in the house was turned on nor was there any flashlight beam shining through the dark windows. (Name censored) watched for a few minutes just to be sure everything was okay and then went to the washroom, which was the reason she awoke. At 12:15 am, Tucker Wilson was seen leaving the Johansson's residence alone.

* * * *

MURDERER CAUGHT AND BEHIND BARS
(October 15, 2001)

The man accused of murdering Randy, and Mari Johansson is now behind bars. After following leads by an eyewitness, police tracked Tucker Wilson and arrested him without incident. Wilson will be staying in Bermingham Penitentiary where he will be kept in the psychiatric ward under maximum security. Mental insanity is strongly believed to have played in role in Wilson's decision to commit murder. His court appearance is pending but is predicted to be within the next month.

* * * *

MURDERER ESCAPES MAXIMUM SECURITY PRISON
(November 1, 2001)

Two days before his court appearance, Tucker Wilson has escaped out of the Bermingham Penitentiary. Authorities are not giving many details however Chief Newsome will be holding a press conference on November 2. Wilson was the only prisoner to escape the penitentiary, which causes much speculation to circulate about the escape. For the time being, the general public is not believed to be at risk. However, if any one has any tips on the whereabouts of Wilson, be sure to call Crime Busters.

* * * *

ESCAPED MURDERER'S CASE CLOSED
(October 14, 2011)

After ten years of being unable to track the whereabouts of Tucker Wilson, authorities have called the case to a close. Wilson escaped from Bermingham Penitentiary on November 1, 2001 and has not been seen sense. Many experts, ranging from the country's top psychologists to the most decorated detective, have been unable to explain the sudden disappearance of the convicted criminal. "It is not unusual for a schizophrenic to suddenly disappear and leave not a hint of his whereabouts. Usually such characters as Tucker Wilson believe they are being guided by voices," says psychologist Brian Cruse. "Who knows, he could have assumed an alter ego and is now living among us."

Author's Note

If freedom can be found, then the darkness must be removed. For the longest time, Blade cut the darkness out and it would seep through my flesh and evaporate into the air. It was freedom. Freedom found in the blood of myself. However, such a freedom was not enduring but rather it would lead to the tightening of chains and a heavier ball. I thought it would bring me to freedom for the momentary pain was an eraser, which blanked me from the reality of life. Over and over again I was trapped in the cycle of "freedom," and then greater and greater captivity. In the darkness there is nothing but despair and hopelessness. It was home. A beautiful cottage surrounded by the forest and nestled along a beautiful placid lake. As dark and frightening as it was, there was a certain sense of beauty within the darkness. There is beauty within the darkness for from the darkness one begins to see the light. The sooner we see, understand, and embrace the darkness within our own hearts the sooner the light can invade and begin to set us free. This is what I have come to understand in the cottage of my own soul. Such revelation is not pretty but it is necessary. In order to discover the light, one must crawl through the valleys, climb the mountains, and surrender one's self to the mystery of faith.

CPSIA information can be obtained at www.ICGtesting.com
Printed in the USA
LVOW08s0455261113

362775LV00001B/71/P